ELSIE'S WOMANHOOD

ELSIE'S WOMANHOOD

Martha Finley

An Imprint of
Holly Hall Publications, Inc.

Elsie's Womanhood
Book 4 of The Elsie Books
by Martha Finley

© 1997 Holly Hall Publications
ISBN 1-888306-34-3

Published by Holly Hall Publications
255 South Bridge Street
P.O. Box 254
Elkton, MD 21922-0254
Tel. (888)-669-4693

Send requests for information to the above address.

Cover & book design by Mark Dinsmore
Arkworks@aol.com

Printed in the United States of America.

PREFACE

A perfect woman, nobly plann'd
To warn, to comfort, and command;
And yet a spirit still, and bright,
With something of an angel light.

—WORDSWORTH

THE CALL FOR A SEQUEL to "Elsie's Girlhood" having become too loud and importunate to be resisted, the pleasant task of writing it was undertaken.

Dates compelled the bringing in of the late war, and it has been the earnest desire and effort of the author to so treat the subject as to wound the feelings of none; to be as impartial as if writing history; and, by drawing a true, though alas, but faint picture, of the great losses and sufferings on both sides, to make the very thought of a renewal of the awful strife utterly abhorrent to every lover of humanity, and especially of this, our own dear native land.

Are we not one people, speaking the same language; worshipping the one true and living God; having a common history, a common ancestry; and being united by the tenderest ties of blood? And is not this great grand, glorious old Union—known and respected all over the world—our common country, our joy and pride? O! Let us forget all bitterness, and live henceforth in love, harmony, and mutual helpfulness.

For all I know of the Teche country I am indebted to

Mr. Edward King's Old and New Louisiana; for facts and dates in regard to the war, and in large measure for Mr. Dinsmore's views as to its cause, etc., principally to Headley's History of the Great Rebellion.

The description of Andersonville, and the life led by the prisoners there, was supplied by one who shared it for six months. An effort was made to obtain a sketch of a Northern prison also, but without success.

Yet what need to balance accounts in respect to these matters? The unnatural strife is over, and we are again one united people.

—M.F.

CHAPTER FIRST

Oh! there is one affection which no stain
Of earth can ever darken;—when two find,
The softer and the manlier, that a chain
Of kindred taste has fastened mind to mind.

—Percival's Poems

IN ONE OF THE COOL green alleys at the Oaks, Rose and Adelaide Dinsmore were pacing slowly to and fro, each with an arm about the other's waist, in girlish fashion, while they conversed together in low, confidential tones.

At a little distance to one side, the young son and heir had thrown himself prone upon the grass in the shade of a magnificent oak, story-book in hand. Much interested he seemed in his book, yet occasionally his eye would wander from its fascinating pages to watch, with pride and delight, the tiny Rosebud steady herself against the tree, then run with eager, tottering steps and a crow of delight into her nurse's outstretched arms, to be hugged, kissed, praised, and coaxed to try it over again.

As Rose and Adelaide turned at one end of the alley, Mr. Horace Dinsmore entered it at the other. Hurriedly approaching the little toddler, he stooped and held out his hands, saying, in tender, half-tremulous tones, "Come, darling, come to papa."

She ran into his arms, crying, "Papa," in her sweet baby voice, and catching her up, he covered her face with kisses; then, holding her clasped fondly to his breast, walked on towards his wife and sister.

"What is it, Horace?" asked Rose anxiously, as they neared each other, for she saw that his face was pale and troubled.

"I bring you strange tidings, my Rose," he answered low and sadly, as she laid her hand upon his arm with an affectionate look up into his face.

Hers grew pale. "Bad news from home?" she almost gasped.

"No, no; I've had no word from our absent relatives or friends, and I'm not sure I ought to call it bad news either, though I cannot yet think of it with equanimity, it has come upon me so suddenly."

"What?" asked both ladies in a breath; "don't keep us in suspense."

"It has been going on for years—on his part—I can see it now—but, blind fool that I was, I never suspected it till today, when it came upon me like a thunderbolt."

"What? Who?"

"Travilla. After years of patient waiting he has won her at last—our darling—and—and I've given her to him."

Both ladies stood dumb with astonishment, while young Horace, who had come running up in time to catch the last words, cried out with vehemence, "Papa! What! Give our Elsie away? How could you? How can we ever do without her? But she shan't go, for she belongs to me too, and I'll never give consent!"

Mr. Dinsmore and the ladies smiled faintly.

"They seemed to think mine quite sufficient, Horace," replied his father, "and I'm afraid will hardly consider it necessary to ask yours."

"But, papa, we can't spare her—you know we can't—and why should you go and give her away to Mr. Travilla or anybody?"

"My son, had I refused, it would have caused her great unhappiness."

"Then she ought to be ashamed to go and love Mr. Travilla better than you and all of us."

"I was never more astonished in my life!" cried Adelaide.

"Nor I," said Rose. "And he's a great deal too old for her."

"That is an objection," replied her husband, "but if not insuperable to her, need not be to us."

"Think of your intimate friend addressing you as father!" laughed Adelaide. "It's really too ridiculous."

"That need not be—is not an inevitable consequence of the match," smiled Mr. Dinsmore, softly caressing the little one clinging about his neck.

Still conversing on the same subject, the minds of all being full of it to the exclusion of every other, they moved on as if by common consent towards the house.

"Do you think it can be possible that she is really and truly in love with him?" queried Rose. "A man so much older than herself, and so intimate in the family since her early childhood."

"Judge for yourself, my dear," said Mr. Dinsmore, as a turn in the path brought them within a few yards of the lovers, who were moving slowly in their direction so that two parties must meet in another moment.

One glance at the beaming faces, the rich color coming and going in Elsie's cheek, the soft, glad light in her sweet brown eyes, was a sufficient reply to Rose's question. She looked at her husband with a satisfied smile, which he returned.

But little Horace, leaving her father's side, rushed up to Elsie, and catching her hand in his, cried, "I'll never give my consent! And you belong to me. Mr. Travilla, you can't have her."

To the child's surprise Elsie only blushed and smiled, while Mr. Travilla, without the slightest appearance of alarm or vexation, said, "Ah, my dear boy, you may just as well; for she is willing to be mine and your papa has given her to me."

But the others had come up, and inquiring looks, smiles and kindly greetings were exchanged.

"Mr. Travilla," said Rose, half playfully but with a

tear trembling in her eye, "you have stolen a march upon us, and I can hardly forgive you just yet."

"I regret that exceedingly, my dear madam," he answered, with a smile that belied his words. "But Miss Adelaide, you will still stand my friend?"

"I don't know," she answered demurely. "There's only one serious objection in my mind, if Elsie is satisfied: that I don't quite fancy having a nephew some years older than myself."

"Ah, well! I shall be quite willing to be considered a brother-in-law."

"Company to dinner!" shouted Horace. "I see a carriage; don't you, papa?"

"It is your Uncle Edward's," said Mr. Travilla.

"Yes," said Adelaide, "Lora and her tribe are in it, no doubt; and probably Mrs. Bowles too—Carry Howard you know, Elsie. They have been late in calling."

"Some good reason for it, and they are none the less welcome," remarked Rose, quickening her pace.

The one party reached the house just as the other two had fairly alighted, and a scene of joyous greeting ensued.

"You dear child! How good of you to come back to us again, and single too," exclaimed Mrs. Bowles, clasping Elsie in a warm embrace. "I'd almost given it up, and expected by every mail to hear you had become Lady or Countess this, or Duchess that."

Elsie smiled and blushed, and meeting the eye of her betrothed fixed for an instant upon her with an expression of unutterable content, thankfulness, love and pride, smiled and blushed again.

Carry caught the look and its effect upon her friend, and almost breathless with astonishment, took the first opportunity, after all were seated in the drawing-room, to prefer a whispered request to be taken to Elsie's own private apartment for a moment, to see that her hair and dress were in proper order.

They had come to spend the day, and bonnets and shawls had already been carried away by the servant in attendance.

"Now girls, don't run off for an interminable chat by yourselves," said Mrs. Howard, as the two rose and crossed the room together.

"No, Aunt Lora, we'll not stay long," said Elsie; "for I want to improve every moment of your visit, in renewing my acquaintance with you and my young cousins."

"Your family has grown, Lora," remarked her brother.

"Yes, rather faster than yours," she said, looking round with pride upon her little group of four boys, and a girl yet in her nurse's arms. "Go and speak to your uncle, Ned, Walter, Horace, and Arthur. You see I have given you a namesake, and this little pet we call Rose Louise, for her two aunties. Yours is Rose, too! And what a darling! And how little Horace has grown!"

"Elsie, it can't be possible!" cried Carry, the instant they found themselves alone.

"What can't?" and Elsie's blush and smile were charming.

"That you and Mr. Travilla are lovers! I saw it in your faces; but, 'tis too absurd! Why, he's your father's friend, and nearly as old."

"All the wiser and better for that, Carry, dear. But he is young in heart, and far from looking old, I think. I have grown so sick of your silly, brainless fops, who expect women neither to talk sense nor understand it."

"Ah, I dare say! And Mr. Travilla is the most sensible and polished of men—always excepting my own spouse, of course. And you won't be taken away from us; so I give my consent."

Elsie's only answer was a mirthful, amused look.

"Oh, but I am glad to see you back!" Carry ran on. "It seems an age you went away."

"Thank you. And your husband? What is he like?"

"I was never good at description, but he is a fine specimen of a Kentucky planter, and very fond of his wife. By the way, you must blame me that Edward and Lora were so late in welcoming you home. I arrived only yesterday morning, quite fatigued with my journey, and begged them to wait till today, and bring me with them."

"That was right. We have not seen Enna yet, or Arthur. Grandpa and Mrs. Dinsmore and Walter called yesterday. But there is the dinner-bell. Let me conduct you to the dining-room."

They were just in time to sit down with the others.

Elsie quickly perceived by her Aunt Lora's look and manner, that she, too, had heard the news, but no remark was make on the subject till the ladies had retired to the drawing-room, leaving the gentlemen to the enjoyment of their after-dinner cigars.

Then Mrs. Howard, facing round upon her niece as they entered the room, exclaimed, "Elsie, you naughty child! Are you not ashamed of yourself?"

"On account of what, auntie?"

"Such unconscious innocence!" cried Lora, throwing up the white and jeweled hands she had rested lightly for an instant upon the young girl's shoulder, while gazing steadily into the smiling, blushing, sparkling face. "You haven't been planning and promising to give Adelaide and me a nephew older than ourselves? I tell you, miss, I refuse my consent. Why, it's absurd! The very idea! I used to think him almost an elderly gentleman when you were a chit of eight or nine."

"I remember having had some such idea myself, but he must have been growing young since then," returned Elsie, demurely.

"He seems to have been standing still—waiting for you, I suppose—but I never was more astonished in my life!" said Lora, dropping into a chair.

"It has been a genuine surprise to us all," remarked Rose.

"To me as much as any one, mamma," said Elsie. "I—had thought he was engaged to you, Aunt Adie."

"To me, child!"

"Why, my dear, I surely told you about her engagement to my brother Edward?" exclaimed Adelaide and Rose simultaneously.

"You tried, mamma, and it was all my own fault that

I did not hear the whole truth. And, Aunt Adie, I cannot understand how he could ever fancy me, while he might have hoped there was a possibility of winning you."

"'Twould have been a much more suitable match," said Lora. "Though I'd have preferred the one in contemplation, except that in the other case, she would not be carried quite away from us. But suppose we proceed to business. We should have a double wedding, I think."

"Oh, don't talk of it yet," said Rose, with a slight tremble in her voice, and looking at Elsie's flushed, conscious face with eyes full of unshed tears. "Adelaide's is to be within the next two months, and—we cannot give up Elsie so suddenly."

"Of course not," said Adelaide; "and I should have serious objections to being used as a foil to Elsie's youth and beauty."

The Howards and Mr. Travilla stayed to tea, and shortly before that meal the party was increased by the arrival of Walter Dinsmore and Mrs. Dick Percival.

Enna had lost flesh and color, and long indulgence of a fretful, peevish temper had drawn down the corners of her mouth, lined her forehead, and left its ugly penciling here and there over the once pretty face, so that it already began to look old and care-worn. She was very gaily dressed, in the height of the fashion, and rather overloaded with jewelry, but powder and rouge could not altogether conceal the ravages of discontent and passion. She was conscious of the fact, and inwardly dwelt with mortification and chagrin upon the contrast presented by her own faded face to that of Elsie, so fair and blooming, so almost childish in its sweet purity and innocence of expression.

"So you are single yet," Enna said, with a covert sneer, "and not likely to marry either, so far as I've been able to learn. They'll soon begin to call you an old maid."

"Will they?" said Mr. Dinsmore, with a laugh in which all present joined, Enna herself excepted. "Well, if she is a fair specimen of that much-abused class, they are more attractive than is generally supposed."

"You needn't laugh," said Enna. "I was four years younger than she is now, when I married. I wasn't going to wait till they began to call me an old maid."

"To bear that reproach is not the worst calamity that can befall a woman," replied Mr. Dinsmore gravely; then changed the subject by a kind inquiry in regard to Arthur.

"Slowly and steadily improving," answered Walter. "The doctors are now satisfied that he is not permanently crippled, though he still uses a crutch."

CHAPTER SECOND

Mutual love, the crown of all our bliss.

—MILTON'S PARADISE LOST

AFTER A HALF HOUR of waiting for her son's return, Mrs. Travilla sat down to her lonely cup of tea. There was no lack of delicacies on the table, and in all Edward's taste had been consulted. To make him comfortable and happy was, next to serving her God, the great aim and object of his mother's life; and, in a less degree, of that of every servant in the house. They had all been born and brought up at Ion, and had all these years known him as the kindest, most reasonable and considerate of masters.

"Wish Massa Edward come. Dese waffles jes' prime tonight, an' he so fond ob dem," remarked a pretty mulatto girl, handing a plate of them to her mistress.

"Yes, Prilla, he expected to be at home, but is probably taking tea at the Oaks or Roselands." And the old lady supped her tea and ate her waffles with a serene, happy face, now and then lighted up by a pleased smile which her attendant handmaiden was at a loss to interpret.

Having finished her meal, Mrs. Travilla threw a shawl about her shoulders and stepped out upon the veranda; then, tempted by the beauty of the night, walked down the avenue to meet her son or see if there were any signs of his approach.

She had not gone half the distance ere the sound of horses' hoofs reached her ear—distant at first but coming rapidly nearer, till a lady and gentleman drew rein at the gate, while the servant who had been riding in the rear dismounted and threw it open.

They came dashing up, but paused and drew rein again at sight of the old lady standing there under the trees.

"Mother," cried her son, springing from the saddle, "you were not alarmed? Anxious, surely?"

"No, no, Edward, but glad to see you—and Elsie! My dear child, this is very kind."

"Not at all, dear Mrs. Travilla; it is so lovely an evening for a ride—or walk either," she added, giving her hand to her escort and springing lightly to the ground.

Mr. Travilla put the hand into that of his mother.

"Take her to your heart, mother; she is mine—ours!" he said, in low tones tremulous with joy.

The old lady folded the slight girlish form to her breast for a moment, with a silence more eloquent than words.

"Thank God! Thank God!" she murmured at length. "He has given me my heart's desire;" and mingled caresses and tears fell upon Elsie's face. "For many years I have loved you as my own child, and now I am to have you. How bright our home will be, Edward. But we are darkening another. Her father; can he—has he—"

"He has given her to me," answered the son quickly, "and she has—we have given ourselves to each other. Let me give an arm to each of you and we will go into the house."

The veranda at the Oaks was deserted, and the house very quiet, though lights still shone here and there, as Mr. Travilla and Elsie rode up and dismounted on their return from Ion.

A servant rose from the grass, where he had been lying at his ease, came forward and led away his young mistress's pony, while the lover bade her a tender good-night, sprang into the saddle again, and presently disappeared, lost to view amid the trees and the windings of the road, though the sound of horse's hoofs still came faintly to Elsie's ear as she stood intently listening, a sweet smile irradiating every feature.

Absorbed in her own thoughts, and in the effort to catch those fast-retreating sounds, she did not hear a step approaching from behind; but an arm encircled her waist, and a low-breathed "My darling" woke her from her reverie.

She looked up, her eyes beaming with affection. "Papa; I am rather late, am I not?"

"Not very. Hark! The clock is but just striking ten. Come, let us sit down here for a little. We have hardly had a chat together today." He sighed slightly as he drew her closer to him.

"No, papa dear, there has been so much company," she answered, laying her head on his shoulder. "And—"

"And what?" as she paused. "Your father used to know all that concerned you one way or the other. Is he to be shut out from your confidence now? Ah, I think he must have been for some time past."

"I could not tell you that, papa," she murmured, blushing visibly in the moonlight. "Indeed, I hardly knew it myself till—"

"Till when?"

"The night of Sophie's wedding.'

"Ah!" he said, musingly. "But I cannot get over my surprise. He is your senior by so many years, and you have known him from childhood and looked upon him a sort of uncle. I wonder at your choice."

"But you don't object, papa?"

"No, if I must give you away—and I've always known that would come some time—I would rather it should be to him than any one else, for I can never doubt that he will be tender and true to my precious one, when she leaves her father's home for his."

"Papa, papa, don't speak of it," she cried, winding her arms about his neck. "I can't bear to think of it, that our home will no longer be the same, that I can't come to you every night and be folded to your heart as I have been ever since I was a little girl."

"Well, dearest," he said, after a moment, in which he held her very close and caressed her with exceeding tenderness, "we shall not be far apart or miss passing some time together many days of the year. And you are not in haste to leave me?"

"Oh, no, no! Why should I be? Please keep me a little while yet."

"I intend to. It will take at least a year to get used to the thought of doing without you, and so long Travilla must be content to wait. Nor can we give you up wholly even then; your suite of rooms shall still be yours, and you must come now and occupy them for days or weeks at a time.

"Now, daughter, good-night. Come to me tomorrow morning in my study, soon after breakfast. I have something more of importance to say to you."

"I shall obey, and without fear," she answered gaily, "though I remember once being quite frightened at a similar order; but that was when I was silly little girl and didn't know how dearly my own papa loved me."

"And when he was strangely stern to his own little child," he answered, with another tender caress.

CHAPTER THIRD

So fair that had you beauty's picture took,
It must like her, or not like beauty look.

—ALLEYN'S HENRY VII

ELSIE PAUSED at the half-open door of her father's private room.

Mr. Dinsmore, like most men, was fond of light and air. Through the wide open windows the morning breeze stole softly in, laden with sweets from garden and lawn, and the rich carpet of oak and green was flecked with gold where the sunbeams came shimmering down between the fluttering leaves of a beautiful vine that had festooned itself about the one looking to the east.

Mr. Dinsmore was seated at his desk with a pile of papers before him—legal documents in appearance. He would open one, glance over its contents, lay it aside, and take up another only to treat it in like manner.

Elsie stood but a moment watching him with loving, admiring eyes, then, gliding noiselessly across the floor, dropped gracefully at his feet and, laying her folded hands upon his knee, looked up into his face with an arch, sweet smile.

"Mon père, I have come for my lecture, or whatever you have laid up in store for me," she announced with mock gravity and a slight tremble of pretended fear in her voice.

Dropping the paper he held, and passing one hand caressingly over her shining hair, "My darling, how very,

very lovely you are!" he said, the words bursting spontaneously from his lips. "There is no flaw in your beauty, and your face beams with happiness."

"Papa turned flatterer!" she cried, springing up and allowing him to draw her to his knee.

"I'm waiting for the lecture," she said presently, "you know I always like to have disagreeable things over as soon as possible."

"Who told you there was a lecture?"

"Nobody, sir."

"What have you been doing that you feel entitles you to one?"

"I don't remember."

"Nor I either. So let us to business. Here, take this chair beside me. Do you know how much you are worth?"

"Not precisely, sir," she answered demurely, taking the chair and folding her hands pensively in her lap; "but very little, I presume, since you have given me away for nothing."

"By no means," he said, with a slight smile of amusement at her unwonted mood. "It was for your own happiness, which is no trifle in my esteem. But you belong to me still."

She looked at him with glistening eyes. "Thank you, dearest papa; yes, I do belong to you and always shall. Please excuse my willful misunderstanding of your query. I do not know how much money and other property I own, but have an idea it is a million more or less."

"My dear child! It is fully three times that."

"Papa! Is it indeed?"

"Yes, it was about a million at the time of your Grandfather Grayson's death, and has increased very much during your mamma's minority and yours; which you know has been a very long one. You own several stores and a dwelling house in New Orleans, a fine plantation with between two and three hundred negroes, and I have invested largely for you in stocks of various kinds—both in your own country and in England. I wish you to examine all the papers, certificates of stock, bonds, deeds, mortgages, and so forth."

"Oh, papa!" she cried, lifting her hands in dismay. "What a task. Please excuse me. You know all about it, and is not that sufficient?"

"No, the property is yours. I have been only your steward, and must now render up an account to you for the way in which I have handled your property."

"You render an account to me, my own dear father," she said low and tremulously, while her face flushed crimson. "I cannot bear to hear you speak so, I am fully satisfied, and very, very thankful for all your kind care of it and of me."

He regarded her with a smile of mingled tenderness and amusement, while softly patting and stroking the small white hand laid lovingly upon his.

"Could I—could any father—do less for his own beloved child?" he asked.

"Not you, I know, papa. But may I ask you a question?"

"As many as you like."

"How much are you worth? Ah, you needn't look so quizzical. I mean how much do you own in money, land, etc.?"

"Something less than a million. I cannot tell you the exact number of dollars and cents."

"Hardly a third as much as I! It doesn't seem right. Papa, take half of mine."

"That wouldn't balance the scales either," he said laughingly; "and besides, Mr. Travilla has now some right to be consulted."

"Papa, I could never love him again, if he should object to my giving you all but a few hundred thousands."

"He would not. He says he will never touch a cent of your property; it must be settled entirely upon yourself, and subject to your control. And that is quite right, for he, too, is wealthy."

"Papa, I don't think I deserve so much. I don't want the care of so much. I do wish you would be so good as to take half for your own, and continue to manage the other half for me as you think best."

"What you deserve is not the question just now. This is one of the talents which God has given you, and I think you ought, at least for the present, to keep the principal and decide for yourself what shall be done with interest. You are old enough now to do so, and I hope do not wish to shirk the responsibility, since God, in his good providence, has laid it upon you."

He spoke very gravely and Elsie's face reflected the expression of his.

"No, I do not wish it now, papa," she said, in a low, sweet voice. "I will undertake it, asking him for wisdom and grace to do it aright."

They were busy for the next hour or two over the papers.

"There!" cried Elsie, at length. "We have examined the last one, and I think I understand it all pretty thoroughly."

"I think you do. And now another thing. Ought you not to go and see for yourself your property in Louisiana?"

Elsie assented, on condition that he would take her.

"Certainly, my dear child, can you suppose I would ever think of permitting you to go alone?"

"Thank you, papa. And if poor mammy objects this time, she may take her choice of going or staying, but go I must, and see how my poor people are faring at Viamede. I have dim, dreamy recollections of it as a kind of earthly paradise. Papa, do you know why mammy has always been so distressed whenever I talked of going there?"

"Painful associations, no doubt. Poor creature! It was there her husband—an unruly negro belonging to a neighboring planter—was sold away from her, and there she lost her children, one by accidental drowning, the others by some epidemic disease. Your own mother, too, died there, and Chloe I think never loved one of her own children better."

"No, I'm sure not. But she never told me of her husband and children, and I thought she had never had any.

And now, papa, that we are done with business for the present, I have a request to make."

"Well, daughter, what is it?"

"That you will permit me to renew my old intimacy with Lucy Carrington, or at least to call on her. You remember she was not well enough to be at the wedding. She is here at Ashlands with her baby. Mr. and Mrs. Carrington called yesterday while you were out, and both urged me not to be ceremonious with Lucy, as she is hardly well enough to make calls and is longing to see me."

"And what answer did you give them?" he asked with some curiosity.

"That I should do so if possible. That meant if I could obtain your permission, papa."

"You have it. Lucy is in some sort taken into the family now, and you are safely engaged—to say nothing of your mature years," he added laughingly, as she seated herself on his knee again and thanked him with a hug and kiss.

"You dear good papa!"

"Some girls of your age, heiresses in their own right, would merely have said, 'I'm going,' never asking permission."

"Ah, but I like to be ruled by you. So please don't give it up. Now about Enna?"

"If I had any authority in the matter, I should say, you shall not give her a cent. She doesn't deserve it from you or any one."

"Then I shall wait till you change you mind."

Mr. Dinsmore shook his head. "Ah, my little girl, you don't realize how much someone else's opinion will soon weigh with you," he answered, putting an arm about her and looking with fatherly delight into the sweet face.

"Ah, papa!" she cried, laying her cheek to his. "Please don't talk so; it hurts me."

"Then, dearest, I shall not say it again, though indeed I was not reproaching you. It is right, very right, that husband and wife should be more than all the world beside to each other."

Elsie's cheek crimsoned. "It has not come to that yet, father dear," she murmured, half averting her blushing face; "and—I don't know which of you I love best—or how I could ever do without either; the love differs in kind rather than in degree."

He drew her closer. "Thank you, my darling. What more could I ask or desire?"

A slight tap on the door and Mrs. Dinsmore looked in. "Any admittance?" she asked playfully.

"Always to my wife," answered her husband, releasing Elsie and rising to hand Rose a chair.

"Thanks, my dear, but I haven't time to sit down," she said. "Here is a note of invitation for us all to spend the day at Roselands. Shall we go?"

"Certainly, if it suits you, Rose," replied Mr. Dinsmore; "and Elsie;" he added, "will you go, daughter?"

"If you wish it, papa," she answered cheerfully; yet there was a slight reluctance in her tone.

He gave her a kind, fond look. "You are your own mistress, and can accept or decline as your judgment and wishes dictate."

"But you would rather have me go, papa?"

"I would, because it would seem more kind and courteous. But what is the objection in your mind? Perhaps it could be removed."

"I wanted so much to see Lucy this morning," Elsie answered with a blush; "but tomorrow will do."

"But both might be accomplished if mamma and Adelaide like to have Caesar drive them and the little ones over to Roselands. Then you and I will mount our horses and away to Ashlands for a call, leaving there in good time to join the dinner party at Roselands. How will that do?"

"Oh, bravely, you dear darling papa! Always contriving for my enjoyment."

Mr. Dinsmore followed his wife from the room. "'Twill be an early return of Carrington's call," he said, "but I have a little business with him."

"Yes, I'm very glad. It is a good plan; but don't hurry Elsie away. She and Lucy will want a long talk."

"I promise to be careful to obey orders," he answered, sportively. "Is that all?"

"Yes, only see that you don't stay too long, and keep the dinner waiting at Roselands."

"Mamma," asked Elsie, bringing up the rear as they entered the sitting-room, "can't you go, too—you and Aunt Adelaide? Four make as nice a party as two, and the babies can be driven over quite safely, with their mammies to take care of them."

"No," said Rose. "I never accept such late invitations; I shall—"

"My dear," said her husband, "we would be very glad."

"No, no; the first arrangement is decidedly the best," putting on an air of pretended pique.

"Babies! Do you call me a baby?" cried young Horace, who had sprung to his feet with a flash of indignation in his great black eyes. "I'm nine years old, Elsie. Rosie there's the only baby belonging to this house. Do you think papa would let a baby have a pony like Gip? And a pistol of his own, too?"

Elsie put her arms round his neck, and gave him a kiss. "I beg ten thousand pardons."

"Elsie, my daughter, don't allow yourself to speak so extravagantly," interrupted her father.

"I will try not, papa," she answered. "I beg your pardon, Horace dear, and assure you I think you are quite a manly young man. Now I must prepare for my ride, papa. I shall be ready by the time the horse can be brought to the door."

"Papa," said Horace, as the door closed upon his sister, "may I ride Gip today?"

"If you promise me to keep close beside the carriage."

"Oh, papa, can't I ride on ahead a little, now and then, or fall a few paces behind if I wish?"

"No; you may do just what I have given permission for, and nothing else."

CHAPTER FOURTH

Grace was in all her steps, heaven in her eye,
In ev'ry gesture, dignity and love.

—MILTON'S PARADISE LOST

"BUT, ELSIE, what of Mr. Travilla?" asked her father, as he handed her into the saddle.

"He will not be here till evening, sir," she answered, the rose on her cheek deepening slightly.

"Then I can have undisturbed possession for today at least," replied Mr. Dinsmore, mounting. "We couldn't have a lovelier day for a ride."

"Nor better company," added Elsie, archly, keeping her horse's head on a line with that of her father's larger steed, as they followed the winding carriage road at a brisk canter.

"Why, you conceited little puss!" returned Mr. Dinsmore, laughing.

Elsie blushed more deeply this time. "Why, papa, you are the company today, are you not? I wished to go, and you kindly arranged to accompany me."

"Ah! And that is how you look at it? Well, I recall my rebuke, and thank you for your—what shall I say—pretty compliment, or appreciation of my society?"

"Both, if you like. Oh, how nice it is to be at home again in our own dear native land."

"And what do you call your own dear native land?"

"What a strange question, papa! The great, grand old union to be sure—North and South, East and West—is it not all mine? Have you not taught me so yourself?"

"Yes," he said musingly.

They rode on in silence for some minutes, and when he spoke again, it was upon a subject entirely foreign to the last.

"The place looks natural," he remarked, as they turned into the avenue leading to the fine old dwelling of the Carringtons.

"How kind, how very kind, to come so soon!" was Mrs. Carrington's cordial, joyful salutation. "Mr. Dinsmore, I owe you a thousand thanks for not only permitting your daughter to come, but bringing her yourself."

"You are very welcome, my dear madam," he answered courteously; "and, indeed, I should like to see Mrs. Rose myself, when she is well enough and feels that it will be agreeable to her."

A few moments' chat in the drawing-room, and Mr. Dinsmore drew out his watch. "How long a talk do you want with your old friend today, Elsie?" he asked.

"Oh, just as long as I can be allowed, papa!" she cried, with much of the old childish eagerness.

"Then the sooner you begin, the better, I think, for we ought to be on our way to Roselands in an hour, or an hour and a quarter at the farthest."

Upon that the gentlemen retired to the library to talk over business matters, and Mrs. Carrington led the way for Elsie to Lucy's room. But pausing in the upper hall, she took the young girl in her arms, folding her in a close, loving embrace, and heaping upon her tearful, tender, silent caresses.

"My poor boy! My poor dear Herbert," she murmured at length, as she released her hold. "Darling, I can never forget that you might have been my daughter. But there—I will leave you. Lucy occupies her old rooms, and yonder is her door. You know the way."

"But come in with me, dear Mrs. Carrington," urged Elsie, the tears shining in her eyes.

"No, dear, not just yet. Lucy would prefer to see you quite alone at first, I know." And she glided away in the opposite direction.

A soft, cooing sound came to Elsie's ear, mingled with fondling words, in a negro voice, as she stood an instant waiting admittance. Lucy, a good deal paler and thinner than the Lucy of old, lay back in an easy chair, languidly turning the leaves of a new magazine.

"Open the door, mammy," she said, "I thought I heard a rap." Then at sight of Elsie, the magazine was hastily tossed aside, and with a cry of joy, "Oh, you darling! I thought I'd never see you again," she sprang forward, caught her friend in a close embrace, and wept upon her neck.

Elsie soothed her with caresses and words of endearment, and presently she calmed down, made her friend take a seat, and sinking back into her own, wiped away the tears still welling up in her eyes, and with a little hysterical laugh, said, "Please don't look so concerned, or think I'm unhappy with my dear old Phil, or going to die, or any such nonsense. It's just my nerves—hateful, torturing things! I wish I'd never found out I had any."

"You poor dear, I'm so sorry for your lost health," said Elsie, exchanging her chair for a low ottoman at Lucy's feet, and taking the small thin hands in hers, stroking and patting them caressingly. "I know nerves won't be reasoned with, and that tears are often a great relief."

"And I've everything to make me happy," sobbed Lucy—"the best husband in the world, and the darlingest babies, to say nothing of mamma and papa, and the rest, and really almost everything one could desire."

"Oh, the baby, yes!" cried Elsie, turning towards it with eager interest. "The sweet, pretty darling. May I take him a moment, Lucy?"

"Certainly, if he's not too heavy—bring him here, mammy. I remember your father would not allow you to lift or carry little Horace."

"Ah, but that was years ago! Ah, how lovely he is!" as the babe accepted her mute invitation to come to her. "You are rich indeed, with this treasure added to all your others. And you and your Phil don't quarrel yet?"

"No indeed! Not the first cross word yet. Mamma calls us her turtle-doves: says we're always billing and cooing. Ah, Elsie, how beautiful you are! I've always thought you just as lovely as possible, yet there's an added something—I can't divine what—that increases even your peerless attractions."

"O Lucy, Lucy, still a flatterer!" laughed her friend.

"Yet you've come back to us single," Lucy went on, ignoring the interruption, "though we all know you had ever so many good offers. Pray, do you intend to remain single all your days?"

At that, Elsie's face dimpled all over with blushes and smiles.

Lucy signed to the nurse to take the babe, and as the woman walked away with it in her arms, turned eagerly to her friend.

"Now do tell me, for I'm sure you are not going to live single. Shall we have the pleasure of hailing you as duchess yet?"

"No, Lucy. I intend to marry, am actually engaged, but not to a foreigner."

"Dear me! I don't believe I could have resisted the title. That is," she added, hastily, "if I'd been heart-whole like you: but after seeing my Phil, of course, I wouldn't give him up for all the nobles in Europe, Asia, and Africa. But do tell me who is the fortunate man?"

"Suppose you try your skill at guessing."

"Perfectly useless, never had any. It must be somebody I don't know."

"My good little woman, you know him well."

"Either of Harry's brothers-in-law? Richard? Harold?"

"No, no, no; you are wide of the mark! Could you suppose papa would ever consent to such a mixture of relationships? Why, it would make papa my brother and mamma's brother her son-in-law."

"So it would. Well, I give up and beg you to put a speedy end to my suspense."

Lucy bent her head to listen, and Elsie murmured the name low and softly, the rose deepening on her cheek as she spoke. For a moment Lucy seemed struck dumb with astonishment. Then, "Elsie!" she exclaimed. "I can't believe it; you are only jesting."

Elsie shook her head with a low, musical, happy laugh.

"He's splendid, I don't deny that; but then—only think—your father's most intimate friend from boyhood up, and almost as old."

"Some people seem like wine—to improve with age. But Mr. Travilla is not old to me now. He has been standing still, I believe, while I have grown up to him."

"And you really are in love with him?"

"He has all my heart, all the love I could give to any-one, and I respect, honor, and trust him as I do no one else but my father."

"And that reminds me; I was so afraid your father would not let you come to see me. But—you are your own mistress now, of course."

"Papa tells me so sometimes," laughed Elsie, "and yet I know he would be greatly surprised should I take the liberty of doing anything he would not approve. I asked his permission to come, and he not only gave consent but brought me himself."

"That was good in him; but I hope he won't hurry you away. I want to hear about your European conquests, and have ever so much to say besides."

"No, he has kindly promised me the time for a long talk. Besides, I can ride over any day and supplement it with another."

Mr. Dinsmore was as good as his word; their chat had lasted more than an hour when his summons came, yet Lucy declared it had not been half long enough, and would not be satisfied to let Elsie go without a promise to come again very soon.

"Roselands, too, looks very natural, and very home-like," remarked Mr. Dinsmore, as they rode up its avenue.

"Yes, papa; and yet, do you know, it seems to me it has grown smaller and less grand since I lived here as a child."

"Ah! Did you think it very grand then, daughter?" he asked, turning to her with a smile.

"I believe so, papa; but it is beautiful yet, even after all the fine places we have seen in our own country and Europe."

Adelaide met them at the door. "Just in time," she said, "for there is the dressing-bell. Your own old room, Elsie dear. You know the way and will find Aunt Chloe in waiting. Horace, you will make yourself at home, of course."

It was strictly a family party, sociable and informal. Elsie had not met Arthur since their return, and at the first moment scarcely recognized him in the moustached and bewhiskered young man who rose and came forward, with a slight limp, to meet her as she entered the drawing-room.

"How do you do?" he said, holding out his right hand, while steadying himself with a cane held in the left. "I hope you're glad to get back to America?"

"Arthur, is it? Yes; thank you; and I'm very glad your injuries have proved less serious than was at first feared," she said, kindly meeting his advances halfway.

"Oh yes," he replied, with attempted nonchalance. "I shall be all right by and by."

Then retreating to the seat from which he had just risen, the corner of a sofa by the side of his sister Adelaide, his eye following Elsie as she crossed the room to pay her respects to her grandfather and others. "What on earth you call that girl little for, I can't imagine," he remarked in an undertone. "Why, she's quite above the average height, graceful as a young fawn, too; splendid figure, and actually the most beautiful face I ever saw. I don't wonder she turned the heads of lords and dukes on the other side of the water. But what do you call her little for?"

"I hardly know, Art. With me it's a term of endearment more than anything else, I believe," replied his sister; "but there is something in the expression of her face—something that has always been there, a sweet simplicity and innocence—that moves one to a sort of protecting love as to a little one who has not yet attained sufficient worldly wisdom to take care of herself."

Old Mr. Dinsmore greeted his lovely granddaughter almost affectionately, holding her hand in his for a moment, and looking from her to her father. "Really, she's a girl to be proud of, Horace," he said with a paternal smile. "But I've no need to tell you that."

"No, she is not bad looking," observed his wife with a slight sneer; "few girls would be in such elegant attire; but it surprises me to see that, with all her advantages and opportunities for improvement, she has not yet lost that baby expression she always had. She'll never be half the woman Enna is."

The days were past in which the lady mother had gloried in the fact that anywhere Enna would have been taken for the elder of the two; and now the contrast between her faded, fretful face and Elsie's fresh bloom was a sore trial to madam's love, and pride in her household pet.

But no one deemed it necessary to reply to the unpleasant remark. Elsie only smiled up into her father's face as he came forward and stood at her side, and meeting his look of loving content and pride in her, just as she was, and calling to mind how fully satisfied with her was another, whose loving approbation was no less precious, turned away with a half-breathed sigh of heartfelt happiness, and finished her greetings, and, the dinner-bell ringing at that moment, accepted Walter's offered arm to the dining-room.

Arthur was more and more charmed with his niece as he noted the modest ease and grace of her manners, both at the table, and afterwards in the drawing-room; listened to her music—greatly improved under the instructions of some of the first masters of Europe—and her conversation with his father and others, in which she almost unconsciously revealed rich stores of varied information gathered from books, the discourse of the wise and learned met in her travels, and her own keen yet kindly observations of men and things. These, with the elegance of her diction, and the ready play of wit and fancy, made her a fascinating talker.

Contrary to Elsie's expectations, it was decided by the elders of the party that all should remain to tea.

As the others returned to the drawing-room on leaving the table, she stole out upon the moonlighted veranda. Gazing wistfully down the avenue, was she thinking of one probably even then on his way to the Oaks—thinking of him and his disappointment at not finding her there?

"It's a nice night, this," remarked Arthur's voice at her side. "I say, Elsie, suppose we bury the hatchet, you and I."

"I never had any enmity towards you, Arthur," she answered, still gazing straight before her.

"Well, its odd if you hadn't. I gave you cause enough, as you did me by your niggardly refusal to lend me a small sum, on occasions when I was hard up. But I'm willing to let by-gones be by-gones, if you are."

"Certainly. I should be glad to forget all that has been unpleasant in the past."

"You have improved wonderfully since I saw you last. You were a pretty girl then, but now you are without exception the most superbly beautiful, graceful, accomplished, and intelligent woman I ever saw."

"I do not like flattery, Arthur," she answered, turning coldly away.

"Pooh! The truth's never flattery. I declare if we were not so nearly related, I'd marry you myself."

"You forget," she said, half scornfully, "that it takes two to make a bargain—three in this case; and two of us would not consent."

"Nonsense! I'd soon manage it by clever courting. A man can always get the woman he wants if he's only sufficiently determined."

"In that you are sadly mistaken. But why broach so disagreeable a subject, since we are so nearly related the very thought seems almost a sin and a crime?"

"And so you're going to throw yourself away on old Travilla?"

Elsie faced him with flashing eyes. "No, it will be no throwing away of myself, nor will I allow him to be spoken of in such disrespectful terms, in my presence."

"Humph!" laughed Arthur. "Well, I've found out how to make you angry, at all events. And I'm free to confess I don't like Travilla, or forgive him all old scores."

Elsie scarcely seemed to hear. A horse was coming at a quiet canter up the avenue. Both the steed and his rider wore a familiar aspect, and the young girl's heart gave a joyous bound as the latter dismounted, throwing the reins to a servant, and came up the steps into the veranda.

She glided toward him; there was an earnest, tender clasping of hands, a word or two of cordial greeting, and they passed into the house and entered the drawing-room.

"Humph! Not much sentiment there; act towards each other pretty much as they always have," said Arthur to himself, taking a cigar from his pocket and lighting it with a match. "I wonder now what's the attraction to her for an old codger like that," he added, watching the smoke as it curled lazily up from the end of his Havana.

There was indeed nothing sentimental in the conduct of Mr. Travilla or Elsie: deep, true, heartfelt happiness there was on both sides, but calm and quiet, indulging in little demonstration, except when they were quite alone with each other. There was no secret made of the engagement, and it was soon known to all their friends and acquaintance. Mr. Travilla had always been in the habit of visiting the Oaks daily, and finding himself very much at home there; and he continued to come and go as formerly, all welcoming him with great cordiality, making him, if possible, more one of themselves than ever, while there was little change in Elsie's manner, except that all her late reserve had fled, and given place to the old ease and freedom, the sweet, affectionate confidences of earlier days.

Mr. Dinsmore's determination to delay the marriage for a year was decidedly a keen disappointment to the middle-aged lover, who had already endured so long and patient a waiting for his prize; yet so thankful and joyous was he that he had at last won her for his own, that, finding remonstrance and entreaties alike unavailing, he presently accepted the conditions with a very good grace, comforting himself with the certainty of the permanence of her love. Elsie had no coquettish arts, was simple-hearted, straightforward, and true, as in her childhood, and their confidence in each other was unbounded.

CHAPTER FIFTH

*Joy never feasts so high
As when the first course is of misery.*

—SUCKLING

ADELAIDE'S MARRIAGE was fixed for Christmas eve, and Mr. Dinsmore and Elsie decided to take their trip to Louisiana at once, that they might be able to return in season for the wedding, at which Elsie was to be first bridesmaid.

It was Elsie herself who broke the news of her intended journey to her faithful old nurse, explaining why she felt it her duty to go, and kindly leaving to Chloe's own decision whether she would accompany her or not.

The dusky face grew very sad for a moment, tears springing to the dark eyes, but the voice was almost cheerful as she answered, "Yes, you's right, honey darlin', you's all right to go and see 'bout dem poor souls and let em see dere beau'ful young missus, and your ole mammy'll go 'long too, for she neber could stay and let her chile run all dem risks on de boats an' cars an' she no dar to take ob her."

"That's right, my own dear old mammy. I shall be glad to have you along, and hope you will find it pleasanter than you expect; but we must trust the Lord to take care of us all; for he only can prevent the accidents you fear."

"Yes, yes, honey, dat's de truff; an' we'll trust him an' not be 'fraid, 'cause don't he say, 'not a hair ob your head shall perish.'"

"'What time I am afraid I will trust in Thee,'" murmured Elsie, softly. "Ah, the joy, the peace, of knowing that his presence and his love will ever go with us everywhere; and that he has all power in heaven and in earth."

A week later, Mr. Dinsmore was showing his daughter the beauties of New Orleans, where they had arrived without accident or loss. They remained in the city long enough to attend thoroughly to the business which had called them there, and to see everything worth looking at.

Elsie's plantation was in the Teche country, the very loveliest part of grand old Louisiana. In order that suitable preparations might be made for their reception, word had been sent that they might be expected on a certain day.

"We have allowed more time than necessary for this place," said Mr. Dinsmore to his daughter one evening on returning to their hotel, after seeing the last of the lions of the Crescent City. "We have two days to spare. What shall be done in them?"

"Let us go on to Viamede at once then, papa," replied Elsie, promptly. "I have been regretting that we sent notice of our coming. I doubt if it would not have been wiser to take them by surprise."

"There would not be the same preparations for your comfort," replied her father, taking a seat by her on the sofa, for they were in their own private parlor. "You may find unaired bed-linen and an empty larder, which, beside inconveniencing yourself, would sorely mortify and trouble Aunt Phillis and her right-hand woman, Sarah, the cook."

"I should be sorry you should have an inhospitable reception, papa, but fires are soon kindled and linen aired, and is not the pantry kept supplied with canned and preserved fruits? And are there not fresh fruits, vegetables, chickens, and eggs at hand for immediate use?"

"Yes, certainly; and we are not likely to suffer. We will, then, leave here tomorrow, if you wish, taking the steamer for Berwick Bay. But why prefer to come upon them unexpectedly?"

Elsie smiled, and blushed slightly. "You know I never have any concealments from you, papa, and I will be frank about this," she said. "I don't think I am apt to be suspicious, and yet the thought has come to me several times within the last few days, that the overseer has had every opportunity to abuse my poor people if he happens to be of a cruel disposition. And if he is ill-treating them I should like to catch him at it," she added, her eyes kindling, and the color deepening on her cheek.

"And what would you do in that case?" her father asked, with a slight smile, drawing her close to him and touching his lips to the blooming cheek.

"Dismiss him, I suppose, papa. I don't know what else I could do to punish him or prevent further cruelties. I should not like to shoot him down," she added, laughingly, "and I doubt if I should have strength to flog him."

"Doubt?" laughed her father. "Certainly you could not, single-handed—unless his politeness should lead him to refrain from any effort to defend himself. And I, it would seem, am not expected to have anything to do with the matter."

A deeper blush than before now suffused Elsie's fair cheek. "Forgive me, dear papa," she said, laying her head on his shoulder, and fondly stroking his face with her pretty white hand. "Please consider yourself master there as truly as at the Oaks, and as you have been for years; and understand that your daughter means to take no important step without your entire approval."

"No, I do not go there as master, but as your guest," he answered, half playfully, half tenderly.

"My guest? That seems pleasant indeed, papa; and yet I want you to be master too. But you will at least advise me?"

"To the best of my ability, my little girl."

"Thank you, my dear kind father. I have another reason for wishing to start tomorrow. I'm growing anxious and impatient to see my birthplace again, and," she added low and tenderly, "mamma's grave."

"Yes, we will visit it together for the first time; though I have stood there alone again and again, and her baby daughter used to be taken there frequently to scatter flowers over it and play beside it. Do you remember that?"

"Yes, sir, as an almost forgotten dream, as I do the house and grounds and some of the old servants who petted and humored me."

While father and daughter conversed thus together in the parlor, a dusky figure sat at a window in the adjoining bedroom, gazing out upon the moonlighted streets and watching the passer-by. But her thoughts, too, were straying to Viamede; fast-coming memories of earlier days, some all bright and joyous, others filled with the gloom and thick darkness of a terrible anguish, made her by turns long for and dread the arrival at her journey's end.

A light touch on her shoulder, and she turned to find her young mistress at her side.

"My poor old mammy, I bring you news you will be sorry to hear," said Elsie, setting herself upon the ample lap, and laying her arms across the broad shoulders.

"What dat, honey?"

"We start tomorrow for Viamede. Papa has sent John to engage our passage on the steamer."

"Dat all, darlin'?" queried Chloe, with a sigh of relief. "If we's got to go, might's well go quick an' hab it ober."

"Well, I'm glad you take so sensible a view of it," remarked Elsie, relieved in her turn; "and I hope you will find much less pain and more pleasure than you expect in going back to the old home."

The next morning, as Mr. Dinsmore and his daughter sat upon the deck of the steamer, enjoying the sunlight, the breeze, and the dancing of the water, having cleared their port and gotten fairly out into the gulf, a startling incident occurred.

Chloe stood at a respectful distance, leaning over the side of the vessel, watching the play of the wheel and the rainbow in that spray that fell in showers at its every revolution. An old negro busied about the deck; drew near and addressed her:

"Well, auntie, you watchin' dat ole wheel dar? Fust time you trable on dis boat, eh?"

Chloe started at the sound of the voice, turned suddenly round and faced the speaker, her features working with emotion: one moment of earnest scrutiny on the part of both, and with a wild cry, "Aunt Chloe! My ole woman," "Uncle Joe! It can't be you," they rushed into each other's arms, and hung about each other's neck, weeping and sobbing like two children.

"Papa! What is it?" exclaimed Elsie, greatly surprised at the little scene.

"Her husband, no doubt. He's too old to be a son."

"Oh, how glad, how glad I am!" and Elsie started to her feet, her eyes full of tears, and her sweet face sparkling all over with sympathetic joy. "Papa, I shall buy him! They must never be parted again until death comes between."

A little crowd had already gathered about the excited couple, everyone on deck hurrying to the spot, eager to learn the cause of the tumult of joy and grief into which the two seemed to have been so suddenly thrown.

Mr. Dinsmore rose, and giving his arm to Elsie, led her toward the throng, saying in answer to her last remark, "Better act through me, then, daughter, or you will probably be asked two or three prices."

"O papa, yes; please attend to it for me—only—only I must have him; for dear old mammy's sake, at whatever cost."

The crowd opened to the lady and gentleman as they drew near.

"My poor old mammy, what is it? Whom have you found?" asked Elsie.

But Chloe was speechless with a joy so deep that it wore the aspect of an almost heart-breaking sorrow. She could only cling with choking sobs to her husband's arm.

"What's all this fuss, Uncle Joe?" queried the captain. "Let go the old darkie. What's she to you?"

"My wife, sah, dat I ain't seed for twenty years, sah," replied the old man, trying to steady his trembling tones, obeying the order, but making no effort to shake off Chloe's clinging hold.

"Leave him for a little now, mammy dear. You shall never be parted again," whispered Elsie in her nurse's ear. "Come with me, and let papa talk to the captain."

Chloe obeyed, silently following her young mistress to the other side of the deck, but ever and anon turning her head to look back with wet eyes at the old wrinkled black face and white beard that to her were so dear, so charming. His eyes were following her with a look of longing, yearning affection, and involuntarily he stretched out his arms towards her.

"Off to your work, sir," ordered the captain, "and let's have no more of this nonsense."

Old Joe moved away with a patient sigh.

"The woman is your property, I presume, sir?" the captain remarked in a respectful tone, addressing Mr. Dinsmore.

"Yes, my daughter's, which amounts to the same thing," that gentleman replied in a tone of indifference; then changing the subject, made some inquiries about the speed and safety of the boat, the length of her trips, etc.

The captain answered pleasantly, showing pride in his vessel. Then they spoke of other things: the country, the crops, the weather.

"Sit down, mammy," said Elsie pityingly, as they reached the settee where she and her father had been sitting. "You are trembling so you can scarcely stand."

"O darlin', dat's true 'nuff, I'se mos' ready to drop," she said tremulously, coming down heavily upon a trunk that stood close at hand. "Oh, de good Lord hab bring me face to face wid my ole Uncle Joe; oh, I neber 'spected to see him no more in dis wicked world. But dey'll take 'im off again an' dis ole heart'll break," she added, with a bursting sob.

"No, no, mammy, you shall have him, if money can accomplish it."

"You buy 'im, darlin'? Oh, your ole mammy can neber t'ank you 'nuff!" and a low, happy laugh mingled with the choking sobs. "But dey'll ask heaps ob money."

"You shall have him, let the price be what it will," was Elsie's assurance. "See, papa is bargaining with the captain now, for they look at Uncle Joe as they talk."

Chloe regarded them with eager interest. Yes, they were looking at Uncle Joe, and evidently speaking of him.

"By the way," Mr. Dinsmore remarked carelessly, "does Uncle Joe belong to you? Or is he merely a hired hand?"

"He's my property, sir."

"Would you like to sell?"

"I am not anxious; he's a good hand, faithful and honest: quite a religious character in fact," he concluded with a sneer; "overshoots the mark in prayin' and psalm-singing. But do you want to buy?"

"Well, yes; my daughter is fond of her ole mammy, and for her sake would be willing to give a reasonable sum. What do you ask?"

"Make me an offer."

"Five hundred dollars."

"Five hundred? Ridiculous! He's worth twice that."

"I think not, he is old—not far from seventy and will soon be past work and only a burden and expense. My offer is a good one."

"Make it seven hundred and I'll take it."

Mr. Dinsmore considered a moment. "That is too high," he said at length, "but for the sake of making two poor creatures happy, I will give it."

"Cash down?"

"Yes, a check on a New Orleans bank."

"Please walk down into the cabin then, sir, and we'll conclude the business at once."

In a few moments Mr. Dinsmore returned to his daughter's side, and placing the receipted bill of sale in her hands, asked, "Have I given too much?"

"Oh, no, papa, no indeed! I should have given a thousand without a moment's hesitation, if asked it—five, ten thousand, if need be, rather then have them parted again," she exclaimed, the bright tears shining in her eyes. Mammy, my poor old mammy, Uncle Joe belongs to me now, and you can have him always with you as long as the Lord spares your lives."

"Now bress de Lord!" cried the old woman devoutly, raising her streaming eyes and clasped hands to heaven; "de good Lord dat hears de prayers ob his chillen's cryin' to him when dere hearts is oberwhelmed!"

"Go break the news to Uncle Joe, mammy," said Elsie. "See, yonder he stands looking so eager and wistful."

Chloe hurried to his side, spoke a few rapid words; there was another long, clinging, tearful embrace, and they hastened to their master and mistress to pour out their thanks and blessings upon them, mingled with praises and fervent thanksgivings to the Giver of all good.

The joy and gratitude of the poor old couple were very sweet, very delightful to Elsie, and scarcely less so to her father.

"Mammy dear, I never saw you wear so happy a face," Elsie said, as Chloe returned to her after an hour or two spent in close conversation with her newly recovered spouse.

"Ah, honey, your ole mammy tinks she neber so glad in all her life!" cried the poor old creature, clasping her hands together in an ecstasy of joy and gratitude while the big tears shone in her eyes. "I'se got ole Uncle Joe back again, an' he not the same, he bettah man, Christian man. He say, 'Aunt Chloe we uns trabble de same road now, honey: young Joe proud, angry, swearin', drinkin' boy, your Ole Joe he lub de Lord an' try to serve him wid all he might. And de Lord good Massa. De debbil berry bad one.'"

"Dear mammy, I am very glad for you. I think nothing else could have made you so happy."

Chloe, weeping again for joy, went on to tell her young mistress that Uncle Joe had discovered a grandchild in New Orleans, Dinah by name, waiting-maid in a wealthy family.

"But how is that, mammy? Papa and I thought all your children died young."

"No, darlin', when Massa Grayson buy me in New Orleans, an' de odder gentleman buy Uncle Joe, we hab little girl four years ole, an' de ole missus keep her," sobbed Chloe, living over again the agony of the parting, "an' Dinah her chile."

"Mammy, if money will buy her, you shall have her, too," said Elsie earnestly.

The remainder of the short voyage was a happy time to the whole of the little party—Chloe, with her restored husband by her side, now looking forward to the visit to Viamede with almost unmingled pleasure.

As they passed up the bay, entered Teche Bayou and pressed on, threading their way through lake and lakelet, past plain and forest, plantation and swamp, Elsie exclaimed again and again at the beauty of the scenery. Cool shady dells carpeted with a rich growth of flowers, miles upon miles of lawns as smoothly shaven, as velvety green and as nobly shaded by magnificent oaks and magnolias, as any king's demesne; lordly villas peering through groves of orange trees, tall white sugar-houses and the long rows of cabins of the laborers; united to form a panorama of surpassing loveliness.

"Is Viamede as lovely as that, papa?" Elsie would ask, as they steamed past one fine residence after another.

"Quite," he would reply with a smile, at length adding, "There is not a more beautiful or valuable estate in the country; as you may judge for yourself, for this is it."

"This, papa? Oh, it is lovely, lovely! And everything in such perfect order," she cried delightedly, as they swept on past a large sugar-house and an immense orange orchard, whose golden fruit and glossy leaves shone brightly in the slanting rays of the nearly setting sun, to the lawn as large, as thickly carpeted with smoothly shaven grass and many-hued flowers, and as finely shaded with giant oaks, graceful magnolias, and groves of orange trees, as any they had passed. The house—a grand old mansion with spacious rooms, wide cool halls and corridors—was now in full view, now half concealed by the trees and shrubbery.

The boat rounded to at a little pier opposite the dwelling, and in another moment our friends had landed and, leaving the servants to attend to the baggage, were walking on towards the house.

CHAPTER SIXTH

Wilt thou draw near the nature of the gods?
Draw near them then in being merciful,
Sweet mercy is nobility's true badge.

—SHAKESPEARE

"PAPA, IT SEEMS an earthly paradise," said Elsie, "and like a dream that I have seen all before."

"A dream that was a reality. And it is all your own, my darling," he answered with a proud, fond look into the bright animated face, keenly enjoying her pleasure.

"But what, what is going on there?" she asked, gazing intently in the direction of the negro quarter, where a large crowd of them, probably all belonging to the plantation, were assembled.

At that instant something rose in the air and descended again, and a wild shriek, a woman's wail of agony, rent the air.

Elsie flew over the ground as though she had been a winged creature, her father having to exert himself to keep pace with her. But the whip had descended again and again, another and another of those wild shrieks testifying to the sharpness of it sting, ere they were near enough to interfere.

So taken up with the excitement of the revolting scene were all present, that the landing and the approach of our friends had not been observed until Elsie, nearing the edge of the crowd, called out in a voice of authority, and indignation, "Stop! Not another blow!"

The crowd parted, showing a middle-aged negress stripped to the waist and tied to a whipping post, writhing and sobbing with pain and terror, while a white man stood over her with a horse-whip in his uplifted hand, stayed in mid-air by the sudden appearance of those in authority over him.

"How dare you! How dare you!" cried Elsie, stamping her foot, and drawing a long, sobbing breath. "Take her down this instant."

"Mr. Spriggs, what is the meaning of this?" asked Mr. Dinsmore, in tones of calm displeasure. "Did I not forbid all cruel punishment on this estate?"

"I've got to make 'em work; I'm bound they shall, and nothing but the whip'll do it with this lazy wretch," muttered Spriggs, dropping his whip and stepping back a little, while two stalwart fellows obeyed Elsie's order to take the woman down, a murmur at the same time running from lip to lip, "It's Marse Dinsmore, and our young missus."

Elsie shuddered and wept at sight of the bleeding back and shoulders. "Cover her up quickly, and take her away where she can lie down and rest," she said to the women who were crowding round to greet and welcome herself. "I will speak to you all afterward. I'm glad to be here among you." Then leaning over the sufferer for an instant, with fast-dropping tears, "Be comforted," she said, in tones of gentle compassion, "you shall never have this to endure again."

"Come, daughter, speak to these eager people, and let us go into the house," said Mr. Dinsmore.

"Yes, papa, in one moment."

Drawing herself up to her full height, and flashing one look of scorn and indignation out of her dark eyes upon the crestfallen Spriggs, she addressed him with the air of a queen. "You, sir, will meet me in the library at eight o'clock this evening."

Turning to the men, "Dig up the post, and split it into kindling wood for the kitchen fire."

Her father, while shaking hands with the blacks, speaking a kindly word to each, regarded her with mingled curiosity and admiration; thoroughly acquainted with his child as he had believed himself to be, he now saw her in a new character.

She took his arm, and he felt that she was trembling very much. He supported her tenderly, while the women flocked about them, eagerly welcoming her to Viamede; kissing her hand, and declaring with tears in their eyes, that it was just their "dear dead young missus come back to them, like a beautiful white angel."

The first who claimed her attention, introduced herself as "Aunt Phillis de housekeepah. An' I'se got eberything ready for you, honey; de beds is aired, de fires laid in de drawin'-room, an' library, an' sleepin' rooms, an' de pantry full ob the nicest tings dis chile an' ole Aunt Sally know how to cook; an' I sent Jack right to de house to start de fires de fust minute dese ole eyes catch sight ob massa an' young missus, an' knows dey heyah."

"My dear child, all this is quite too much for you," said Mr. Dinsmore, attempting to draw his daughter away.

"Just a moment, papa, please," she answered in a slightly unsteady voice; "let me speak to them all." He yielded, but cut short the garrulity of some who would have liked to mingle reminiscences of her babyhood with their rejoicing over her return, telling them they must reserve such communication for a more suitable time, as their young mistress was faint and weary, and must have rest.

The appearance of Chloe and her recovered husband upon the scene now created a diversion in their favor, and he presently succeeded in leading Elsie to the house.

A young mulatto girl followed them into the drawing-room, where a bright wood fire was blazing on the hearth, asking if she should take Miss Elsie's things.

"Yes," Mr. Dinsmore said, removing his daughter's hat and shawl, and handing them to her.

She left the room; and taking Elsie in his arms, and

gently laying her head upon his breast, "Let the tears have their way, darling," he said, "it will do you good."

For several minutes the tears came in floods. "Oh, papa," she sobbed, "to think that my people, my poor people, should be so served. It must never, never be again!"

"No," he said, "we will find means to prevent it. There, you feel better now, do you not?"

"Yes, sir. Papa dear, welcome, welcome to my house; the dearest guest that could come to it." And wiping away her tears, she lifted her loving eyes to his, a tender smile playing about the sweet lips.

"Save one," he answered half-playfully, passing his hand caressingly over her hair, and bending down to press his lips on brow, and cheeks, and mouth. "Is not that so?"

"No, my own dear father, save none," with a charming blush, but eyes looking steadily into his. "When he comes, it shall be as master, not guest. But now tell me, please, what can I do with this Spriggs? I should like to pay him a month's wages in advance, and start him off early tomorrow morning."

Mr. Dinsmore shook his head gravely. "It would not do, my child. The sugar-making season will shortly begin. He understands the business thoroughly; we could not supply his place at a moment's notice, or probably in a number of months, and the whole crop would be lost. We must not be hasty or rash, but remember the Bible command, 'Let your moderation be known unto all men.' Nor should we allow ourselves to judge the man too hardly."

"Too hardly, papa! Too hardly, when he has shown himself so cruel! But I beg pardon for interrupting you."

"Yes, too hardly, daughter. He is a New Englander, used to see everyone about him working with steady, preserving industry, and the indolent, dawdling ways of the blacks, which we take as a matter of course, are exceedingly trying to him. I think he has been very faithful to your interests, and that probably his desire and determination to see them advanced to the utmost, led, more than anything else, to the act which seems to us so cruel."

"And could he suppose that I have blood wrung from my poor people that a few more dollars might find their way into my purse?" she cried in indignant sorrow and anger. "Oh, papa, I am not so cruel, you know I am not."

"Yes, my darling, I know you have a very tender, loving heart."

"But what shall I do with Spriggs?"

"For tonight, express your sentiments and feelings on the subject as calmly and moderately as you can, and enjoin it upon him to act in accordance with them. Then we may consider at our leisure what further measures can be taken."

"Papa, you are so much wiser and better than I," she said, with loving admiration. "I'm afraid if you had not been here to advise me, I should have sent him away at once, with never a thought of crops or anything except securing my people from his cruelties."

"You should never allow yourself to act from mere impulse, except it be unquestionably a right one, and the case admitting of no time for deliberation. As to my superior wisdom," he added with a smile, "I have lived some years longer than you, and had more experience in the management of business matters.

"I am very sorry, my darling, that the pleasure of your return to the home of your infancy should be so marred. But you have scarcely taken a look yet at even this room. What do you think of it?"

She glanced about her with freshly aroused curiosity and interest. "Papa, it is just to my taste!"

The firelight gleamed upon rare old cabinets, gems of art in painting and statuary, and rich, massive, well-preserved, though old-fashioned sofas, chairs, tables, etc. But it was already growing dark; deep shadows were gathering in the more distant parts of the spacious apartment, and only near the fire could objects be distinctly seen. Elsie was about to ring for lights, when

Sarah, the mulatto girl, appeared, bringing them, Chloe following close in the rear.

"Have you fires and lights in the library, the dining-room, and your master's rooms and mine?" inquired Elsie.

"De fires is lit, Miss Elsie."

"Then add the lights at once, and put them all in the principal rooms of the house. We will have an illumination in honor our arrival, papa," she said, in a sprightly tone, turning to him with one of her sweetest smiles, "and besides, I want to see the whole house now."

"Are you not too much fatigued, daughter? And would it be better to defer it till tomorrow?"

"I don't think I'm too tired, papa, but if you forbid me—"

"No, I don't forbid or even advise, if you are sure you feel equal to the exertion."

"Thank you, sir, I think I'll be better able to sleep if I've seen at least the most of it. Old memories are troubling me, and I want to see how far they are correct. You will go with me?"

"Certainly," he said, giving her his arm. "But while the servants are obeying your order in regard to the lights, let us examine these paintings more attentively. They will repay close scrutiny, for some of them are by the first masters. Your Grandfather Grayson seems to have been a man of cultivated taste, as well as great business talent."

"Yes, papa. What is it mammy?"

"Does you want me, darlin'?"

"No, not now. Go and enjoy yourself with your husband and old friends."

Chloe expressed her grateful thanks, and withdrew.

Elsie found the paintings and statuary a study, and had scarcely finished her survey of the drawing-room and its treasures of art, when Aunt Phillis came to ask if they would have tea served up immediately.

Elsie looked at her father.

"Yes," he said; "you will feel stronger after eating,

and it is about our usual time."

"Then let us have it, Aunt Phillis. How is that poor creature now?" asked her young mistress.

"Suse, honey? Oh, she'll do well 'nuff; don't do her no harm to take some ob de lazy blood out. Massa Spriggs not so terrible cross, Miss Elsie; but he bound de work git done, an' Suse she mighty powerful lazy, jes' set in de sun an' do nuffin' from mornin' to night, ef nobody roun' to make her work."

"Ah, that is very bad. We must try to reform her in some way. But perhaps she's not well."

"Dunno, missus. She's always 'plaining ob de misery in her back, an' misery in her head; but don't ebery one hab a misery, some kind, most days? An' go on workin' all de same. No, missus, Suse she powerful lazy ole nigga."

With that Phillis retired, and shortly after, tea was announced as ready.

Elsie played the part of hostess to perfection, presiding over the tea-urn with ease and grace, and pressing upon her father the numerous dainties with which the table was loaded. She seemed to have recovered her spirits, and as she sat there gaily chatting—of the room, which pleased her as entirely as the other, and of her plans for usefulness and pleasure during her stay—he thought he had never seen her look happier or more beautiful.

"What room have you prepared for your mistress, Aunt Phillis?" asked Mr. Dinsmore, as they rose from the table.

"The same whar she was born, massa, an' whar her dear bressed ma stay when she livin' heyah."

A slight shadow stole over Elsie's bright face. "That was right," she said, low and softly. "I should prefer them to any others. But where are papa's rooms?"

"Jes' across de hall, Miss Elsie."

"That is a good arrangement," said Mr. Dinsmore. "Now, daughter, I think we should repair to the library. It is near the hour you appointed for Mr. Spriggs."

"Just as handsome, as tastefully, appropriately, and luxuriously furnished as the others," was Elsie's comment on the library. "I seem to see the same hand everywhere."

"Yes, and it is the same all over the house," replied her father. "The books here will delight you; for a private library it is a very fine one, containing many hundred volumes, as you may see at a glance; standard works on history, and the arts and sciences, biographies, travels, works of reference, the works of the best poets, novelists, etc."

"Ah, how will we enjoy them while here! But it seems a sad pity they should have lain on those shelves unused for so many years."

"Not entirely, my child. I have enjoyed them in my brief visits to the plantation, and have always allowed the overseer free access to them, on the single condition that they should be handled with care, and each returned promptly to its proper place when done with. But come, take this easy chair by this table; here are some fine engravings I want you to look at."

Elsie obeyed, but had scarcely seated herself when the door was thrown open and a servant's voice announced, "Massa Spriggs, Massa Dinsmore, and Miss Elsie.'

Spriggs, a tall, broad-shouldered, powerfully-built man, with dark hair and beard and a small, keen black eye, came forward with a bold free air and a "Goodeven', miss, goodeven', sir;" adding, as he helped himself to a seat without waiting for an invitation, "Well, here I am, and I s'pose you've somethin' to say or you wouldn't have appointed the meetin'."

"Yes, Mr., Spriggs," said Elsie, folding her pretty hands in her lap and looking steadily and coldly into his brazen face. "I have this to say; that I entirely disapprove of flogging, and will have none of it on the estate. I hope you understand me."

"That's plain English and easy understood, Miss Dinsmore, and of course you have a right to dictate in the matter. But I tell you what, these darkies o' yours are a dreadful lazy set, specially that Suse, and its mighty hard for folks that's been used to seein' things done up spick and span and smart to put up with it."

"But some amount of patience with the natural slowness of the negro is a necessary trait in the character of an overseer who wishes to remain in my employ."

"Well, miss, I always calculate to do the very best I can by my employers, and when you come to look round the estate, I guess you'll find things in prime order; but I couldn't ha' done it without lettin' the darkies know they'd got to toe the mark right straight."

"They must attend to the work, of course, and if they won't do so willingly, must under compulsion; but there are milder measures than this brutal flogging."

"What do you prescribe, Miss Dinsmore?"

"Deprive them of some privilege, or lock them up on bread and water for a few days," Elsie answered; then turned an appealing look upon her father, who had as yet played the part as a mere listener.

"I have never allowed any flogging on my estate," he observed, addressing Spriggs, "and I cannot think it at all necessary."

There was a moment of silence, Spriggs sitting looking into the fire, a half-smile playing about his lips. Then turning to Elsie, "I thought, miss, you'd a mind this evening to dismiss me on the spot," he remarked inquiringly.

She flushed slightly, but replied with dignity, "If you will comply with my directions, sir, pledging yourself never again to be so cruel, I have no desire to dismiss you from my service."

"All right then, miss. I promise, and shall still do the best I can for your interests; but if they suffer because I'm forbidden to use the lash, please remember it's not my fault."

"I am willing to take the risk," she answered, intimating with a motion of her hand that she considered the interview at an end; whereupon he rose and bowed himself out.

"Now, papa, for our tour of inspection," she cried

gaily, rising as she spoke, and ringing for a servant to carry the light. "But first please tell me if I was sufficiently moderate."

"You did very well," he answered, smiling. "You take to the role of mistress much more naturally than I expected."

"Yet it does seem very odd to me to be giving orders while you sit by a mere looker-on. But, dear papa, please remember I am still your own child, and ready to submit to your authority, whenever you see fit to exert it."

"I know it, my darling," he said, passing an arm about her waist, as they stood together in front of the fire, and gazing fondly down into the sweet fair face.

Aunt Chloe answered the bell, bringing a lamp in her hand.

"That is right, mammy," Elsie said. "Now lead the way over the house."

As they passed from room to room, and from one spacious hall or corridor to another, Elsie expressed her entire satisfaction with them and their appointments, and accorded to Aunt Phillis the meed of praise due her careful housekeeping.

"And here, my darling," Mr. Dinsmore said at length, leading the way through a beautiful boudoir and dressing-room into an equally elegant and attractive bedroom beyond, "they tell me you were born, and your beloved mother passed from the earth to heaven."

"An' eberything in de room stands jes' as dey did den, honey," said Aunt Chloe. And approaching the bed, her eyes swimming in tears, and laying her hand upon the pillow, "jes' here my precious young missus lie, wid cheeks 'mos' as white as de linen, an' eyes so big an' bright, an' de lubly curls streamin' all roun', an' she say, weak an' low, 'Mammy, bring me my baby.' Den I put you in her arms, darlin', an' she kiss you all ober your tiny face, an' de tears an' sobs come fast while she say, 'Poor little baby; no fader, no mudder to lub her! Nobody but you, mammy. Take her an' bring her up to lub de dear Lord Jesus.'"

Silent tears rolled down Elsie's cheeks as she looked and listened; but her father drew her to his breast and kissed them away, his own eyes brimming, his heart too full for speech.

Presently he led her back to the boudoir, and showed her the portraits of her maternal grandparents, and one of her mother, taken at ten or twelve years of age.

"What a lovely little girl she was," murmured Elsie, gazing lovingly upon it.

"Very much like what her daughter was at the same age," he answered. "But come, this, too, will interest you." And lifting the lid of a dainty work-basket, he pointed to a bit of embroidery, in which the needle was still sticking, as though it had been laid down by the deft fingers but a few moments ago.

Elsie caught it up and kissed it, thinking of the touch of those dear dead fingers, that seemed to linger over it yet.

CHAPTER SEVENTH

*She was the pride
Of her familiar sphere, the daily joy
Of all who on her gracefulness might gaze,
And in the light and music of her way
Have a companion's portrait.*

—WILLIS' POEMS

ELSIE HAD FALLEN asleep thinking of the dear mother whose wealth she inherited, and whose place she was now filling; thinking of her as supremely blest, in that glorious, happy land, where sin and sorrow are unknown. Thinking, too, of him, through whose shed blood she had found admittance there.

The same sweet thoughts were still in the loving daughter's mind, as she woke to find the morning sun shining brightly, a fire blazing cheerily on the hearth, and Aunt Chloe coming in with a silver waiter filled with oranges prepared for eating in the manner usual in the topics.

She had gathered them the night before, taken off the peel, leaving the thick white skin underneath except on the top of each, where she cut it away from a spot about the size of a silver quarter of a dollar. She then placed them on the waiter, with the cut part uttermost, and set them where the dew would fall on them all night. Morning found them with the skin hard and leathery, but filled with delicious juice, which could be readily withdrawn from it.

At that sight, a sudden memory seemed to flash upon Elsie, and starting up in the bed, "Mammy!" she cried. "Didn't you do that very thing when I was a child?"

"What, honey? Bring de oranges in de mornin'?"

"Yes, I seem to remember your coming in at that door, with just such a waiterful."

"Yes, darlin', de folks allus eats dem 'foah breakfast. Deys jes' lubly, Miss Elsie; massa say so, lubly and delicious." And she brought the waiter to her bedside, holding it out for her young mistress to help herself.

"Yes, mammy dear, they look very tempting, but I won't eat with unwashed hands and face," said Elsie gaily. "And so papa has stolen a march upon me and risen first?"

"Yes, darlin', massa out on the veranda, but he say 'Let your missus sleep long as she will.'"

"My always kind and indulgent father! Mammy, I'll take a bath, and then while you arrange my hair, I'll try the oranges. Go now and ask papa when he will have his breakfast, and tell Aunt Phillis to see that it is ready at the hour he names."

Chloe obeyed, and an hour later Elsie met her father in the breakfast-room so glad, so gay, so bright, that his heart swelled with joy and pleasure in his child, and all fears that she had over-fatigued herself vanished from his mind.

She was full of plans for the comfort and profit of her people, but all to be subject to his approval. "Papa dear," she said as soon as their morning greetings had been exchanged, "I think of sending for a physician to examine Suse and tell us whether there is reason for her complaints. She must not be forced to work if she is really ill."

"I think it will be well," he replied. "There is an excellent physician living about three miles from here."

Elsie was prompt in action by both nature and training, and instantly summoning a servant, dispatched him at once on the proposed errand.

"And now what next?" smilingly inquired her father.

"Well, papa, after breakfast and prayers—how some of the old servants seemed to enjoy them last night—I think of going down to the quarter to see what may be needed there. Unless you have some other plan for me," she added quickly.

"Suppose we first mount our horses and ride over the estate, to learn for ourselves whether Mr. Spriggs has been as faithful as he would have us believe."

"Ah yes, papa; yours is always the better plan."

Their ride in the clear, sweet morning air was most delightful, and both felt gratified with the fine appearance of the crops and the discovery that Spriggs' boast was no idle one; everything being in the nicest order.

They took the quarter on the way to the house, and dismounting, entered one neatly whitewashed cabin after another, kindly inquiring into the condition and wants of the inmates, Elsie making notes on the tablets that nothing might be forgotten.

Everywhere the visit was received with joy and gratitude, and an almost worshipful homage paid to the sweet young mistress whom they seemed to regard as akin to the angels—probably in a great measure because of her extraordinary likeness to her mother, of whom, for so many years they had been accustomed to think and speak as one of the heavenly host.

Spriggs' victim of the previous day was in bed, complaining much of the misery in back and head and limbs.

"De doctah hab been heyah," she said, "an' leff me dese powdahs to take," drawing a tiny package from under her pillow.

Elsie spoke soothingly to her; said she should have some broth from the house, and should be excused from work till the doctor pronounced her quite fit for it again; and left her apparently quite happy.

It was the intention of our friends to spend some weeks at Viamede.

"I want you to have every possible enjoyment while here, my darling," Mr. Dinsmore said, as they sat together resting after their ride, in the wide veranda at the front of the house, looking out over the beautiful lawn, the bayou, and the lovely scenery beyond. "There are pleasant neighbors who will doubtless call when they hear of our arrival."

"I almost wish they may not hear of it then," Elsie said half laughing; "I just want to be left free from the claims of society for this short time, that I may fully enjoy being alone with my father and attending to the comfort of my people. But excuse me, dear papa, I fear I interrupted you."

"I excuse you on condition that you are not again guilty of such a breach of good manners. I was going on to say there are delightful drives and walks in the vicinity, of which I hope we will be able to make good use; also, we will have a row now and then on the bayou, and many an hour of quiet enjoyment of the contents of the library."

"Yes, papa, I hope so. I do so enjoy a nice book, especially when read with you. But I think that, for the present at least, I must spend a part of each day in attending to the preparation of winter clothing for house-servants and field hands."

"I won't have you doing the actual work, the cutting out and sewing, I mean," he answered decidedly. "The head work, calculating how much material is needed, what it will cost, etc., may be yours; but you have servants enough to do all the rest."

"But, papa, consider; over three hundred to clothe, and I want it all done while I am here to oversee."

"Have not some of the house-servants been trained as seamstresses?"

"Yes, sir, two of them, mammy tells me."

"Very well; she knows how to run a sewing-machine. Send for one when you order your material; both can be had in the in the nearest town. Aunt Chloe can soon teach the girls how to manage it—Uncle Joe, too. He has had no regular work assigned him yet, and the four can certainly do all without anything more than a little oversight from you; yes, without even that."

"What a capital planner you are, papa," she said
brightly. "I never thought of getting a machine or setting
Uncle Joe to running it; but I am sure it's just the thing
to do. Mammy can cut and the girls baste, and among
them the machine can easily be kept going from morning to night. I'll make out my orders and send for the
things at once."

"That is right, daughter. It pleases me well to note
how you put in practice the lesson of promptness I have
always tried to teach you. I will help you in making your
estimate of quantities needed, prices to be paid, etc.,
and I think we can accomplish the whole before dinner.
Come to the library and let us to work."

"You dear, kind father, always trying to help me and
smooth the least roughness out of my path, and make
life as enjoyable to me as possible," she said, laying her
hand on his arm and looking up into his face with eyes
beaming with filial love, as they rose and stood together
for a moment.

"A good daughter deserves a good father," he
answered, smoothing with soft caressing motion the
shining hair. "But have you the necessary data for our
estimates?"

"The number to be clothed, papa? I know how many
house-servants, how many babies and older children at
the quarter, but not the number of field hands."

"That will be easily ascertained. I will send a note to
Spriggs, who can tell us all about it."

Mr. Dinsmore's plans were carried out to the letter,
and with entire success. This was Saturday; the orders
were sent that afternoon, and on Monday morning the
work began. Aunt Chloe proved fully equal to the cutting of the garments, and Uncle Joe an apt scholar
under her patient, loving teaching, and a willing worker
at his new employment. There was scarcely need of even
oversight on the part of the young mistress. She would
drop in occasionally, commend their industry, and
inquire if anything were wanting; then felt free for

books, rides or walks, music or conversation with her father.

But she was often down at the quarter visiting the sick, the aged and infirm, seeing that their wants were supplied, reading the Bible to them, praying with them, telling of the better land where no trouble or sorrow can come, and trying to make the way to it, through the shed blood of Christ, very plain and clear. Then she would gather the children about her and tell them of the blessed Jesus and his love for little ones.

"Does He lub niggahs, missus?" queried one grinning little wooly head.

"Yes, if they love him: and they won't be negroes in heaven."

"White folks, missus? Oh, dat nice! Guess I go dar; ef dey let me in."

But we are anticipating somewhat, though Elsie found time for a short visit to the sick and aged on the afternoon of even that first day at Viamede. The next was the Sabbath, and as lovely a day as could be desired. The horses were ordered for an early hour, and father and daughter rode some miles together to morning service, then home again.

As the shadows began to lengthen in the afternoon, Elsie was sitting alone on the veranda, her father having left her side but a moment before, when an old negro, familiarly known as Uncle Ben, came round the corner of the house, and slowly approached her.

Very sweet and fair, very beautiful she looked to his admiring eyes. She held a Bible in her hand, and was so intent upon its perusal that she was not aware of his coming until he had drawn quite near. Ascending the steps, and standing at a respectful distance, hat in hand, he waited till she should notice and address him.

Glancing up from her book, "Ah, Uncle Ben, good evening," she said. "What can I do for you?"

"Missus," he answered, making a slow salaam, "all de darkies is gadered togedder under a tree 'round de house yondah, and dey 'pint me committee to come an' ax de young missuss would she be so kind for to come an' read the Bible to dem, an' talk, an' pray, an' sing like she do for de sick ones down to de quarter? Dey be berry glad, missus, an' more dan obliged."

"Indeed I will, uncle," Elsie said, rising at once and going with him, Bible in hand. "I had been thinking of doing this very thing."

She found a rustic seat placed for her under a giant oak, and garlanded with fragrant flowers. Aunt Phillis, Aunt Chloe, Uncle Joe, and the rest of the house-servants gathered in a semicircle around it, while beyond, the men, women, and children from the quarter sat or lay upon the grass, enjoying the rest from the toils of the week, the quiet, the balmy air laden with the fragrance of the magnolia and orange, and all the sweet sights and sounds of rural life in that favored region.

Everyone rose at the appearance of their young mistress, and there were murmurs of delight and gratitude coming from all sides. "Now bress de Lord, she read the good book for us." "She good an' lubly as de angels." "Missus berry kind, de darkies neber forget."

Elsie acknowledged it all with a smile and a few kindly words, then commanding silence by a slight motion of the hand, addressed them in a clear, melodious voice, which, though not loud, could be distinctly heard by every one of the now almost breathless listeners.

"I shall read to you of Jesus and some of his own words," she said, "but first we will ask him to help us to understand, to love, and to obey his teachings."

Then folding her hands and lifting her eyes to the clear blue sky above, she led them in a prayer so simple and childlike, so filial and loving in spirit and expression, that the dullest understood it, and felt that she spoke to One who was very near and dear to her.

After that she read with the same distinct utterance the third chapter of John's Gospel, and commented briefly upon it. "You all want to go to heaven?" she said, closing the book.

"Yes, Miss Elsie." "Yes missus, we all does."

"But to be able to go there you must know the way, and now I want to make sure that you do know it. Can you tell me what you must do to be saved?"

There were various answers: "Be good;" "Mine de rules an' do 'bout right;" "Pray to de Lord;" etc., etc.

Elsie shook her head gravely. "All that you must do, and more besides. What does Jesus say? 'God so loved the world, that he gave his only begotten Son, that whosoever believeth in him should not perish, but have everlasting life.' We must believe in Jesus—believe all that the Bible tells us about him, that He was very God and very man, that he came down from heaven, was born a little babe and laid in a manger, that he grew up to be a man, went about doing good, and at last suffered and died the cruel death on the cross; and all to save poor lost sinners.

"But even that is not enough: the devils believe so much; they know it is all true. But beside this, we must believe on Christ Jesus. He offers to be our Saviour. 'Come unto Me...and I will give you rest.' 'Him that cometh unto Me, I will in no wise cast out.' And you must come, you must take the eternal life he offers you; you must rest on him and him only.

"Suppose you were out on the bayou yonder, and the boat should upset and float beyond your reach, or be swept away from you by the wind and waves, and you couldn't swim; but just as you are sinking, you find it strong and large enough to bear your weight, and you throw yourself upon it and cling to it for life. Just so you must cast yourself on Jesus, and cling to him with all your strength, and he will save you; for he is able and willing 'to save to the uttermost all that come unto God by him.'

"He will wash away your sins in his own precious blood, and dress you in the beautiful robe of his perfect righteousness; that is, set his goodness to your account, so that you will be saved just as if you had been as good and holy as he was. Then you will love him and try to do right to please him; not to buy heaven; you cannot do that, for 'all our righteousness are as filthy rags,' and we cannot be saved unless we trust only in Jesus and his righteousness."

Something in the faces before her caused Elsie to turn her head. Her father stood with grave, quiet air, but a few feet from her.

"Papa," she said, in an undertone, and blushing slightly, "I did not know you were here. Will you not speak to them? You can do it so much better than I."

She sat down, and stepping to her side he made a brief and simply worded address on the necessity of repentance and faith in Jesus, "the only Saviour of sinners," his willingness to save all who came to him, and the great danger of delay in coming. Then with a short prayer and the singing of a hymn, they were dismissed.

With murmured thanks and many a backward look of admiring love at their already almost idolized young mistress, and her father, who had won their thorough respect and affection years ago, they returned to their homes.

"You must have a shawl and hat, for the air begins to grow cool," said Mr. Dinsmore to his daughter.

"Yes, massa, I'se brought dem," said Chloe, hurrying up almost out of breath, with the required articles in her hand.

"Thank you, mammy, you are always careful of your nursling," Elsie said, smilingly, as the shawl was wrapped carefully about her shoulders and the hat placed upon her head.

Her father drew her hand within his arm and led her across the lawn.

"There is one spot, very dear to us both, which we have not yet visited," he said, low and feelingly, "and I have rather wondered at your delay in asking me to take you there."

She understood him. "Yes, sir," she said, "I should have done so last evening, but that you looked weary. It has hardly been out of my mind since we came, and I have only waited for a suitable time."

"None could be better than the present," he

answered.

On a gently sloping hillside, and beneath the shade of a beautiful magnolia, they found what they sought: a grave, with a headstone on which was carved the inscription:

Fell asleep in Jesus,
March 15, 18—
Elsie, Wife of Horace Dinsmore,
and only remaining child of
William and Elspeth Grayson,
Aged 16 years, and 2 weeks.
'Blessed are the dead who die in the Lord.'

They read it standing side by side.

"How young," murmured the daughter, tears filling her eyes, "how young to be wife, a mother, and to die and leave husband and child! Oh, papa, how I used to long for her, and dream of her—my own precious mamma!"

"When, my darling?" he asked in moved tones, drawing her tenderly to him and passing an arm about her waist.

"Before I knew you, papa, and before you began to love me so dearly and be father and mother both, to me, as you have been for so many years." The low, sweet voice was tremulous with emotion, and the soft eyes lifted to his were brimming over with tears of mingled grief and joy, gratitude and love.

"I have tried to be," he said, "but no one could supply her place. What a loving, tender mother she would have been! But let us forget our loss in the bliss of knowing that it is so well with her."

It was a family burying-ground. There were other graves: those of our Elsie's grandparents, and several of their sons and daughters who had died in infancy or early youth; and in the midst uprose a costly monument, placed there by Mr. Grayson after the death of his wife. The spot showed the same care as the rest of the estate, and was lovely with roses and other sweet flowers and shrubs.

"My mother's grave!" said Elsie, bending over it

again. "Papa, let us kneel down beside it and pray that we may meet her in heaven."

He at once complied with the request, giving thanks for the quiet rest of her who slept in Jesus, and asking that, when each of them had done and suffered all God's holy will here on earth, they might be reunited to her above, and join in her glad song of praise to redeeming love.

Elsie joined fervently in the "Amen," and rising, they lingered a moment longer, then wended their way in sweet and solemn silence to the house.

They sat together in the library after tea, each occupied with a book. But Elsie seemed little interested in hers, looking off the page now and then, as if in deep and troubled thought. At length closing it, she stole round to the side of her father's easy chair, and taking possession of a footstool, laid her head on his knee.

"I have my little girl again tonight," he said, passing his hand caressingly over her hair and cheek.

"I almost wish it was, papa."

"Why? Is anything troubling you, dearest?" And he pushed his book aside, ready to give his whole attention to her.

"I am anxious about my poor people, papa. They are so ignorant of the truths necessary to salvation, and what can I teach them in three to four weeks? I have almost decided that I ought—that I must stay as many months."

"And that without even consulting your father? Much less considering his permission necessary to your action?" Though the words seemed to convey reproach, if not reproof, his tone was gentle and tender.

"No, no, papa! I must cease to think it my duty if you forbid it."

"As I do most positively. I cannot stay, and I should never think for a moment of leaving you here!"

"But papa, how then am I to do my duty by these poor ignorant creatures? How can I let them perish for lack of knowledge whom Christ has put into my care?"

"Procure a chaplain, who shall hold regular services for them every Sabbath, and do pastoral work among them through the week. You will not grudge him his salary."

"Papa, what an excellent idea! Grudge him his salary? No, indeed; if I can get the right man to fill the place, he shall have a liberal one. And then he will be a check upon Mr. Spriggs, and inform me if the people are abused. But how shall I find him?"

"What do you do when in want of something you do not know exactly how to procure?"

"Pray for direction and help," she answered, low and reverently.

"We will both do that, asking that the right man may be sent us; and I will write tomorrow to some of the presidents of the theological seminaries, asking them to recommend someone suited for the place."

"Papa," she cried, lifting a very bright face to his, "what a load you have taken from my mind."

CHAPTER EIGHTH

A mighty pain to love it is
And 'tis a pain that pain to miss;
But of all pains, the greatest pain
It is to love, but love in vain.

—COWLEY

ONE LOVELY AFTERNOON in the second week of their stay at Viamede, Mr. Dinsmore and his daughter were seated in the shade of the trees on the lawn, she busied with some fancy-work while her father read aloud to her.

As he paused to turn a leaf, "Papa," she said, glancing off down the bayou, "there is a steamer coming, the same that brought us, I think, and see, it is rounding to at our landing. Can it be bringing us a guest?"

"Yes, a gentleman is stepping ashore. Why, daughter, it is Harold Allison."

"Harold! Oh, how delightful!" And rising, they hastened to meet and welcome him with truly Southern warmth of hospitality.

"Harold! How good of you!" cried Elsie. "Mamma wrote us that you were somewhere in this region, and if I'd had your address, I should have sent you an invitation to come and stay as long as possible."

"And you have done well and kindly by us to come without waiting for that," Mr. Dinsmore said, shaking the hand of his young brother-in-law with a warmth of cordiality that said more than his words.

"Many thanks to you both," he answered gaily. "I was conceited enough to feel sure of a welcome, and did not wait, as a more modest fellow might, to be invited. But what a lovely place! A paradise upon earth! And, Elsie, you, in those dainty white robes, look the fit presiding genius."

Elsie laughed and shook her head. "Don't turn flatterer, Harold—though I do not object to praise of Viamede."

"I have not heard from Rose in a long time," he said, addressing Mr. Dinsmore. "She and the little folks are well, I hope?"

"I had a letter this morning, and they were all in good health when it was written."

The servants had come trooping down from the house, and seizing Harold's baggage had it all ready in the guest-chamber to which Aunt Phillis ordered it. Aunt Chloe now drew near to pay her respects to "Massa Harold," and tell him that his room was ready.

"Will you go to it at once? Or sit down here and have a little chat with papa and me first?" asked Elsie.

"Thank you; I think I shall defer the pleasure of the chat till I have first made myself presentable for the evening."

"Then let me conduct you to your room," said Mr. Dinsmore, leading the way to the house.

Elsie had come in the course of years to look upon the older brothers of her stepmother as in some sort her uncles, but for Harold, who was so much nearer her own age, she entertained a sincere sisterly regard. And he was worthy of it and of the warm place his many noble qualities had won for him in Mr. Dinsmore's heart.

They did all they could to make his visit to Viamede a pleasant one. There were daily rides and walks, moonlight and early morning excursions on the bayou, rowing parties—oftenest of the three alone, but sometimes in company with gallant chivalrous men and refined, cultivated women and charming young girls from the neighboring plantations.

One of these last, a beautiful brunette, Elsie had selected in her own mind for Harold, and she contrived to throw them together frequently.

"Don't you admire Miss Durand?" she asked, after they had met several times. "I think she is lovely; as good, too, as she is beautiful, and would make you a charming wife."

He flushed hotly. "She is very handsome, very fascinating and talented," he said; "but would never suit me. Nor do I suppose I could win her if I wished."

"Indeed! If you are so hard to please, I fear there will be nothing for you but old bachelorhood," laughed Elsie. "I have picked her out for you, and I believe you could win her if you tried, Harold, but I shall not try to become a match-maker."

"No, I must select for myself. I couldn't let even you choose for me."

"Choose what?" asked Mr. Dinsmore, stepping out upon the veranda, where Harold stood leaning against a vine-wreathed pillar, his blue eyes fixed with a sort of wistful, longing look upon Elsie's graceful figure and fair face, as she sat in a half-reclining posture on a low couch but a few feet from him.

"A wife," he answered, compelling himself to speak lightly.

"Don't let her do it," said Mr. Dinsmore, taking a seat by his daughter's side. "I've warned her more than once not to meddle with match-making." And he shook his head at her with mock gravity.

"I won't any more, papa. I'll leave him to his own devices, since he shows himself so ungrateful for my interest in his welfare," Elsie said, looking first at her father and then at Harold with a merry twinkle in her eye.

"I don't think I've asked how you like your new home and prospects, Harold," said Mr. Dinsmore, changing the subject.

"Very much, thank you, except that they take me so far from the rest of the family."

A few months before this, Harold had met with a

piece of rare good fortune, looked at from a worldly point of view, in being adopted as his sole heir by a rich and childless Louisiana planter, a distant relative of Mrs. Allison.

"Ah, that is an objection," returned Mr. Dinsmore, "but you will be forming new and closer ties, that will doubtless go far to compensate for the partial loss of the old. I hope you are enjoying yourself here?"

"I am indeed, thank you." This answer was true, yet Harold felt himself flush as he spoke, for there was one serious drawback upon his felicity: he could seldom get a word alone with Elsie. She and her father were so inseparable that he scarcely saw the one without the other. And Harold strongly coveted an occasional monopoly of the sweet girl's society. He had come to Viamede with a purpose entirely unsuspected by her or her apparently vigilant guardian.

He should perhaps, have confided his secret to Mr. Dinsmore first, but his heart failed him; and "What would be the use?" he asked himself, "if Elsie is not willing? Ah, if I could but be alone with her for an hour!"

The coveted opportunity offered itself at last, quite unexpectedly. Coming out upon the veranda one afternoon, he saw Elsie sitting alone under a tree far down on the lawn. He hastened toward her.

"I am glad to see you," she said, looking up with a smile and making room for him on the seat by her side. "You see I am 'lone and lorn,' Mr. Durand having carried off papa to look at some new improvement in his sugar-house machinery."

"Ah! And when will your father return?"

"In about an hour, I presume. Shall you attend Aunt Adie's wedding?" she asked.

"Yes, I think so. Don't you sometimes feel as if you'd like to stay here altogether?"

"Yes, and no. It's very lovely, and the more charming I believe, because it is my own, but—there is so much more to bind me to the Oaks, and I could never live far away from papa."

"Couldn't you? I hoped—Oh, Elsie, couldn't you possibly love someone else better even than you love him? You're more to me than father, mother, and all the world beside. I have wanted to tell you so for years, but while I was comparatively poor your fortune sealed my lips. Now I am rich, and I lay all I have at your feet; myself included, and—"

"Oh, Harold, hush!" she cried in trembling tones, flushing and paling by turns, and putting up her hand as if to stop the torrent of words he was pouring forth so unexpectedly that astonishment had struck her dumb for an instant. "Oh! Don't say any more, I—I thought you surely knew that—that I am already engaged."

"No. To whom?" he asked hoarsely, his face pale as death, and lips quivering so that he could scarcely speak.

"To Mr. Travilla. It has been only for a few weeks, though we have loved each other for years. Oh, Harold, Harold, do not look so wretched! You break my heart, for I love you as a very dear brother."

He turned away with a groan, and without another word hastened back to the house, while Elsie, covering her face with her hands, shed some very bitter tears.

Heart-broken, stunned, feeling as if every good thing in life had suddenly slipped from his grasp, Harold sought his room, mechanically gathered up his few effects, packed them into his valise, then sat down by the open window and leant his head upon his hand.

He couldn't think, he could only feel that all was lost, and that he must go away at once, if he would not have everybody know it, and make the idol of his heart miserable with the sight of his wretchedness.

Why had he not known of her engagement? Why had no one told him? Why had he been such a fool as to suppose he could win so great a prize? He was not worthy of her. How plainly he saw it now, how sorely repented of the conceit that had led him on to the avowal of his passion.

He had a vague recollection that a boat was to pass that afternoon. He would take passage in that, and he hoped Mr. Dinsmore's return might be delayed till he was gone. He would away without another word to Elsie; she should not be disturbed by any further unmanly manifestation of his bitter grief and despair.

The hour of the passing of the boat drew near, and valise in hand, he left his room and passed down the stairs. But Elsie was coming in from the lawn, and they met in the lower hall.

"Harold," she cried, "you are not going? You must not leave us so suddenly."

"I must," he said in icy tones, the stony eyes gazing into vacancy. "All places are alike to me now, and I cannot stay here to trouble you and Horace with the sight of a wretchedness I cannot hide."

Trembling so that she could scarcely stand, Elsie leaned against the wall for support, the hot tears coursing down her cheeks. "Oh, Harold!" she sobbed, "What an unhappy creature I am to have been the cause of such sorrow to you! Oh why should you ever have thought of me so?"

Dropping his valise, his whole manner changing, he turned to her with passionate vehemence. "Because I couldn't help it! Even as a boy I gave up my whole heart to you, and I cannot call it back. Oh, Elsie, why did I ever see you?" and he seized both her hands in a grasp that almost forced a cry of pain from her white, quivering lips. "Life is worthless without you. I'd rather die knowing that you loved me than live to see you in the possession of another."

"Harold, Harold, a sister's love I can, I do give you; and can you not be content with that?"

"A sister's love!" he repeated scornfully. "Offer a cup with a drop of water in it, to a man perishing, dying with thirst. Yes, I'm going away, I care not whither; all places are alike to him who has lost all interest in life."

He threw her hands from him almost with violence, half turned away, then suddenly catching her in his arms, held her close to his heart, kissing passionately, forehead, cheek, and lips. "Oh, Elsie, Elsie, light of my eyes, core of my heart, why did we ever meet to part like this? I don't blame you. I have been a fool. Good-bye, darling." And releasing her, he was gone ere she could recover breath to speak. It had all been so sudden she had had no power, perhaps no will, to resist, so sore was the tender, loving heart for him.

He was barely in time to hail the boat as it passed, and at the instant he was about to step aboard, Mr. Dinsmore rode up, and springing from the saddle, throwing the reins to his servant, cried out in astonishment, "Harold! You are not leaving us? Come, come, what has happened to hurry you away? Must you go?"

"Yes, I must," he answered with half-averted face. "Don't call me a scoundrel for making such a return for your hospitality. I couldn't help it. Good-bye. Try to forget that I've been here at all; for Rose's sake, you know."

He sprang into the boat. It pushed off, and was presently lost to sight among the trees shading the bayou on either hand.

Mr. Dinsmore stood for a moment as if spellbound, then turned and walked thoughtfully towards the house. "What did it all mean?" he asked himself. "Of what unkind return on his or Elsie's hospitality could the lad have been guilty? Elsie! Ha! Can it be possible?" and quickened his pace, glancing from side to side in search of her as he hurried on.

Entering the hall, the sound of a half-smothered sob guided him to a little parlor or reception-room seldom used. Softly he opened the door. She was there half-reclining upon a sofa, her face buried in the cushions. In a moment he had her in his arms, the weary, aching head on his breast, while he tenderly wiped away the fast-falling tears.

"My poor darling, my poor little pet, don't take it so to heart. It is nothing; he will probably get over it before he is a month older."

"Papa, is it my fault? Did I give him undue encouragement? Am I a coquette?" she sobbed.

"Far from it! Did he dare to call you that?"

"No, no, oh, no; he said he did not blame me, it was all his own folly."

"Ah! I think the better of him for that; though 'twas no more than just."

"I thought he knew of my engagement."

"So did I. And the absurdity of the thing! Such a mixture of relationships as it would have been! I should never have entertained the thought for a moment. And he ought to have spoken to me first, and spared you all this. No, you needn't fret. He deserves all he suffers, for what he has inflicted upon you, my precious one."

"I hardly think that, papa. He was very generous to take all the blame to himself, but oh, you have eased my heart of half its load. What should I ever do without you, my own dear, dear father!"

The pleasure of our friends, during the rest of their stay at Viamede, was somewhat dampened by this unfortunate episode, though Elsie, for her father's sake, did her best to rally from its effect on her spirits, and to be cheerful and gay as before.

Long, bright, loving letters from home and Ion coming the next day, were a great help. Then the next day brought a chaplain, who seemed in all respects so well suited to his place as to entirely relieve her mind in regard to the future welfare of her people. He entered into all her plans for them, and promised to carry them out to the best of his ability.

So it was with a light heart, though not without some lingering regrets for the sad ones and the loveliness left behind, that she and her father set out on their homeward way.

Mr. Dinsmore's man John, Aunt Chloe, and Uncle Joe, went with them; and it was a continual feast for master and mistress to see the happiness of the poor old couple, especially when their grandchild Dinah, their only living descendant so far as they could learn, was added to the party—Elsie purchasing her, according to promise, as they passed through New Orleans on their return trip.

Dinah was very grateful to find herself installed as assistant to her grandmother, who, Elsie said, must begin to take life more easily now in her old age. Yet that Aunt Chloe found it hard to do, for she was very jealous of having any hands but her own busied about the person of her idolized young mistress.

A glad welcome awaited them at home, where they arrived in due season for Adelaide's wedding.

Sophie and Harry Carrington had returned from their wedding trip, and were making their home with his parents, at Ashlands. Richard, Fred, and May Allison, came with their brother Edward, but Harold, who was to meet them at Roselands, was not there. He had engaged to act as second groomsman, Richard being first, and there was much wondering over his absence. Many regrets were expressed, and some anxiety felt.

But Elsie and her father kept their own counsel, and breathed no word of the episode at Viamede, which would have explained all.

Harold's coming was still hoped for by the others until the last moment, when Fred took his place, and the ceremony passed off as satisfactorily as if there had been no failure on the part of any expected, to participate in it.

It took place in the drawing-room at Roselands, in presence of a crowd of aristocratic guests, and was considered a very grand affair. A round of parties followed for the next two weeks, and then the happy pair set sail for Europe.

Chapter Ninth

My plots fall short, like darts which rash hands throw
With an ill aim, and have too far to go.

—Sir Robert Howard

"I'M SO GLAD it's all over at last!"

"What, my little friend?" and Mr. Travilla looked fondly into the sweet face so bright and happy, where the beauties of rare intellect and moral worth were as conspicuous as the lesser ones of exquisite contour and coloring.

"The wedding and all the accompanying round of dissipation. Now I hope we can settle down to quiet home pleasures for the rest of the winter."

"So do I, and that I shall see twice as much of you as I have of late. You can have no idea how I missed you while you were absent. And I am more than half envious of our bride and groom. Shall our trip be to Europe, Elsie?"

"Are we to take a trip?" she asked with an arch smile.

"That will be as you wish, dearest, of course."

"I don't wish it now, nor do you, I know, but we shall have time enough to settle all such questions."

"Plenty; I only wish we had not so much. Yet I don't mean to grumble; the months will soon slip away and bring the time when I may claim my prize."

They were riding toward the Oaks. The sun had just set, and the moon was still below the horizon.

Elsie suddenly reined in her horse, Mr. Travilla

instantly doing likewise, and turned a pale, agitated face upon him. "Did you hear that?" she asked low and tremulously.

"What, dear child? I heard nothing but the sound of our horses' hoofs, the sighing of the wind in the tree-tops, and our own voices."

"I heard another—a muttered oath and the words, 'You shall never win her. I'll see to that.' The tones were not loud but deep, and the wind seemed to carry the sounds directly to my ear," she whispered, laying a trembling little hand on his arm, and glancing nervously from side to side.

"A trick of the imagination, I think, dearest; but from whence did the sounds seem to come?"

"From yonder thicket of evergreens and—I knew the voice for that of your deadly foe, the man from whom you and papa rescued me in Lansdale."

"My child, he is expiating his crime in a Pennsylvania penitentiary."

"But may he not have escaped, or have been pardoned out? Don't, oh don't, I entreat you!" she cried, as he turned his horse's head in the direction of the thicket. "You will be killed."

"I am armed, and a dead shot," he answered, taking a revolver from his breast pocket.

"But he is in ambush, and can shoot you down before you can see to aim at him."

"You are right, if there is really an enemy concealed there," he answered, returning the revolver to its former resting-place; "but I feel confident that it was either a trick of the imagination with you, or that someone is playing a practical joke upon us. So set your fears at rest, dear child, and let us hasten on our way."

Elsie yielded to his better judgment, trying to believe it nothing worse than a practical joke; but had much ado to quiet her agitated nerves and recover her composure before a brisk canter brought them to the Oaks, and she must meet her father's keen eye.

They found Arthur in the drawing room, chatting

with Rose. He rose with a bland, "Good evening," and gallantly handed Elsie to a seat. Arthur was a good deal changed since his recall from college, and in nothing more than in his manner to Elsie. He was now always polite, often cordial, even when alone with her. He was not thoroughly reformed, but had ceased to gamble and seldom drank to intoxication.

"Thank you; but indeed I must go at once and dress for tea;" Elsie said, consulting her watch. "You are not going yet?"

"No, he will stay to tea," said Rose.

"But must go soon after, as I have an engagement," added Arthur.

Elsie met her father in the hall. "Ah, you are at home again," he remarked with a pleased look. "That is well; I was beginning to think you were making it very late."

"But you are not uneasy when I am in such good hands, papa?"

"No, not exactly; but like better to take care of you myself."

The clock was just striking eight as Arthur mounted and rode away from his brother's door. It was not a dark night, or yet very light, for though the moon had risen, dark clouds were scudding across the sky, allowing but an occasional glimpse of her face, and casting deep shadows over the landscape.

In the partial obscurity of one of these, and only a few rods ahead of him, when about halfway between the Oaks and Roselands, Arthur thought he discovered the figure of a man standing by the roadside, apparently waiting to halt him as he passed.

"Ha! You'll not take me by surprise, my fine fellow, whoever you may be," muttered Arthur between his set teeth, drawing a revolver and cocking it. "Halloo there! Who are you; and what d'ye want?" he called, as his horse brought him nearly opposite the suspicious looking object.

"Your money or your life, Dinsmore," returned the other with a coarse laugh. "Don't pretend not to know me, old chap."

"You!" exclaimed Arthur, with an oath, but half under his breath. "I thought you were safe in—"

"State prison, eh? Well, so I was, but they've pardoned me out. I was a reformed character, you see; and then my vote was wanted at the last election, ha, ha! And so I've come down to see how my old friends are getting along."

"Friends! Don't count me among them!" returned Arthur, hastily. "Jail-birds are no mates for me."

"No, I understand that, the disgrace is in being caught. But you'd as well keep a civil tongue in your head, for if you're covering me with a revolver, I'm doing the same by you."

"I'm not afraid of you, Tom," answered Arthur, with a scornful laugh, "but I'm in a hurry; so be good enough to move out of the way and let me pass." For the other had now planted himself in the middle of the road, and laid a heavy hand upon the horse's bridle-rein.

"When I've said my say; no sooner. So that pretty niece of yours, my former fiancée, is engaged to Travilla? The man whom, of all others, I hate with a hatred bitterer than death. I would set my heel upon his head and grind it into the earth as I would the head of a venomous reptile."

"Who told you?"

"I overheard some o' their sweet talk as they rode by here not two hours ago. He robbed me of her that he might snatch the prize himself; I saw his game at the time. But he shall never get her," he concluded, grinding his teeth with rage.

"Pray, how do you suppose to prevent it?"

"I'll call him out."

Arthur's laugh rang out mockingly upon the still night air. "Southern gentlemen accept a challenge only from gentlemen; and as for Travilla, besides being a dead shot, he's too pious to fight a duel, even with his own class."

"He'll meet me in fair fight, or I'll shoot him down,

like a dog, in his tracks." The words, spoken in low tone, of concentrated fury, were accompanied with a volley of horrible oaths.

"You'd better not try it!" said Arthur. "You'd be lynched and hung on the nearest tree within an hour."

"They'd have to catch me first."

"And they would. They'd set their bloodhounds on your track, and there'd be no escape. As to the lady having been your fiancée—she never was. She would not engage herself without my brother's consent, which you were not able to obtain. And now you'd better take yourself off out of this neighborhood, after such threats as you've made!"

"That means you intend to turn informer, eh?"

"It means nothing of the kind, unless I'm called up as a witness in court; but you can't prowl about here long without being seen and arrested as a suspicious character, an abolitionist, or some other sort of scoundrel— which last you know you are," Arthur could not help adding in a parenthesis. "So take my advice, and retreat while you can. Now out o' the way, if you please, and let me pass."

Jackson sullenly stood aside, letting go the rein, and Arthur galloped off.

In the meantime, the older members of the family at the Oaks were quietly enjoying themselves in the library, where bright lights, and a cheerful wood-fire snapping and crackling on the hearth, added to the sense of comfort imparted by handsome furniture, books, paintings, statuary, rich carpet, soft couches, and easy chairs.

The children had been sent to bed. Mr. and Mrs. Dinsmore sat by the centre table, the one busy with the evening paper, the other sewing, but now and then casting a furtive glance at a distant sofa, where Mr. Travilla and Elsie were seated side by side, conversing in an undertone.

"This is comfort, having you to myself again," he was saying, as he watched admiringly the delicate fingers busied with a crochet needle, forming bright meshes of scarlet zephyr. "How I missed you when you were gone! And yet, do you know, I cannot altogether regret the short separation, since otherwise I should have missed my precious budget of letters."

"Ah," she said, lifting her merry brown eyes to his face for an instant, then dropping them again, with a charming smile and blush, "do you think that an original idea, or rather that it is original only with yourself?"

"And you are glad to have mine? Though not nearly so sweet and fresh as yours." How glad he looked as he spoke.

"Ah!" she answered archly. "I'll not tell you what I have done with them, lest you grow conceited. But I have a confession to make," and she laughed lightly. "Will you absolve me beforehand?"

"Yes, if you are penitent, and promise to offend no more. What is it?"

"I see I have aroused your curiosity. I shall not keep you in suspense. I am corresponding with a young gentleman. Here is a letter from him, received today." Drawing it from her pocket as she spoke, she put it into his hand.

"I have no wish to examine it," he said gravely, laying it on her lap. "I can trust you fully, Elsie."

"But I should like you to read it. 'Tis from Mr. Mason, my chaplain at Viamede, and gives a lengthy, and very interesting account of the Christmas doings there."

"Which I should much prefer to hear from your lips, my little friend."

"Ah, read it, please; read it aloud to me. I shall then enjoy it as much as I did the first time; and you will learn how truly good and pious Mr. Mason is, far better than from my telling. Not that he talks of himself, but you perceive it from what he says to others."

He complied with her request, reading in the undertone in which they had been talking.

"A very well-written and interesting letter," he remarked, as he refolded and returned it. "Yes, I should judge from it that he is the right man in the right place. I presume the selection of gifts so satisfactory to all parties must have been yours?"

"Yes, sir. Being with them, I was able to ascertain their wants and wishes, by questioning one in regard to another. Then I made out the list, and left Mr. Mason to do the purchasing for me. I think I can trust him again, and it is a great relief to my mind to have someone there to attend to the welfare of their souls and bodies."

"Have you gotten over your fright of this evening?" he inquired tenderly, bending towards her, and speaking lower than before.

"Almost if—if you have not to return to Ion tonight. Must you, really?"

"Yes; mother would be alarmed by my absence, and she seldom retires till I am there to bid her good-night."

"Then promise me to avoid that thicket," she pleaded anxiously.

"I cannot think there is any real danger," he said, with a reassuring smile, "but I shall take the other road. 'Tis but a mile further round, and it would pay me to travel fifty to spare you a moment's anxiety, dearest."

She looked her thanks.

He left at ten, his usual hour, bidding her have no fear for him, since no real evil can befall those who put their trust in him whose watchful, protecting care is ever about his chosen ones.

"Yes," she whispered, as for a moment, his arm encircled her waist, "'What time I am afraid, I will trust in thee.' It is comparatively easy to trust for myself, and God will help me to do it for you also."

She stood at the window watching his departure, her heart going up in silent prayer for his safety. Then, saying to herself, "Papa must not be disturbed with my idle fancies," she turned to receive his good-night with a face so serene and unclouded, a manner so calm and peaceful, that he had no suspicion of anything amiss.

Nor was it an assumed peace and calmness, for she had not now to learn to cast her care on the Lord, whom she had loved and served from her very infancy, and her head had not rested many moments upon her pillow, ere she fell into a deep, sweet sleep, that lasted until morning.

While Elsie slept, and Mr. Travilla galloped homeward by the longer route, the moon, peering through the cloud curtains, looked down upon a dark figure, standing behind a tree not many yards distant from the thicket Elsie had besought her friend to shun. The man held a revolver in his hand, ready cocked for instant use. His attitude was that of one listening intently for some expected sound.

He had stood thus for hours, and was growing very weary. "Curse the wretch!" he muttered. "Does he court all night? How many hours have I been here waiting for my chance for a shot at him? It's getting to be no joke, hungry, cold, tired enough to lie down here on the ground. But I'll stick it out, and shoot him down like a dog. He thinks to enjoy the prize he snatched from me, but he'll find himself mistaken, or my name's n—" The sentence ended with a fierce grinding of the teeth. Hark! Was that the distant tread of a horse? He bent his ear to the earth, and almost held his breath to listen. Yes, faint but unmistakable; the sounds filled him with a fiendish joy. For years he had nursed his hatred of Travilla, whom he blamed almost exclusively for his failure to get possession of Elsie's fortune.

He sprang up and again placed himself in position to fire. But what had become of the welcome sounds? Alas for his hoped-for-revenge, they had died away entirely. The horse and his rider must have taken some other road. More low-breathed, bitter curses: yet perchance it was not the man for whose life he thirsted. He would wait and hope on.

But the night waned: one after another the moon and stars set and day began to break in the east. The birds waking in their nests overhead grew clamorous with joy, yet their notes seemed to contain a warning tone for him, bidding him begone ere the coming of the light hated by those whose deeds are evil. Chilled by the frosty air, and stiff and sore from long standing in a constrained position, he limped away, and disappeared in the deeper shadows of the woods.

Arthur's woods warning had taken their desired effect, and cowardly, as base, wicked, and cruel, the man made haste to flee from the scene of his intended crime, imagining at times that he even heard the bloodhound already on his track.

CHAPTER TENTH

At last I know thee—and my soul,
From all thy arts set free,
Abjures the cold consummate art
Shrin'd as a soul in thee.

—SARAH J. CLARK

THE REST OF THE WINTER passed quietly and happily with our friends at Ion and the Oaks—Mr. Travilla spending nearly half his time at the latter place, and in rides and walks with Elsie, whom he now and then coaxed to Ion for a call upon his mother.

Their courtship was serene and peaceful: disturbed by no feverish heat of passion, no doubts and fears, no lover's quarrels, but full of a deep, intense happiness, the fruit of their long and intimate friendship, their full acquaintance with, and perfect confidence in each other, and their strong love. Enna sneeringly observed that "they were more like some staid old married couple than a pair of lovers."

Arthur made no confidant in regard to his late interview with Jackson; nothing more was heard or seen of the scoundrel, and gradually Elsie came to the conclusion that Mr. Travilla, who occasionally rallied her good-naturedly on the subject of her fright, had been correct in his judgment that it was either the work of imagination or of some practical joker.

Arthur, on his part, thought that fear of the terrors he

had held up before him would cause Jackson—whom he knew to be an arrant coward—to refrain from adventuring himself again in the neighborhood.

But he miscalculated the depth of the man's animosity towards Mr. Travilla, which so exceeded his cowardice as at length to induce him to return and make another effort to destroy either the life of that gentleman or his hopes of happiness; perhaps both.

Elsie was very fond of the society of her dear ones, yet occasionally found much enjoyment in being alone, for a short season, with Nature or a book. A very happy little woman, as she had every reason to be, and full of gratitude and love to the Giver of all good for his unnumbered blessings, she loved now and then to have a quiet hour in which to count them over, as a miser does his gold, to return her heartfelt thanks, tell her best, her dearest Friend of all, how happy she was, and seek help from him to make a right use of each talent committed to her care.

Seated in her favorite arbor one lovely spring day, with thoughts thus employed, and eyes gazing dreamily upon the landscape spread out at her feet, she was startled from her reverie by someone suddenly stepping in and boldly taking a seat by her side.

She turned her head. Could it be possible? Yes, it was indeed Tom Jackson, handsomely dressed and looking, to a casual observer, the gentleman she had once believed him to be. She recognized him instantly.

A burning blush suffused her face, dyeing even the fair neck and arms. She spoke not a word, but rose up hastily with the intent to fly from his hateful presence.

"Now don't, my darling, don't run away from me," he said, intercepting her. "I'm sure you couldn't have the heart, if you knew how I have lived for years upon the hope of such a meeting: for my love for you, dearest Elsie, has never lessened, the ardor of my passion has never cooled—"

"Enough, sir!" she said, drawing herself up, her eyes kindling and flashing as he had never thought they could. "How dare you insult me by such words, and by your presence here? Let me pass."

"Insult you, Miss Dinsmore?" he cried, in affected surprise. "You were not wont, in past days, to consider my presence an insult, and I could never have believed fickleness a part of your nature. You are now of age, and have a right to listen to my defense, and my suit for your heart and hand."

"Are you mad? Can you still suppose me ignorant of your true character and your history for years past? Know then that I am fully acquainted with them; that I know you to be a lover of vice and the society of the vicious—a drunkard, profane, a gambler, and one who has stained his hands with the blood of a fellow-creature," she added with a shudder. "I pray God you may repent and be forgiven; but you are not and can never be anything to me."

"So with all your piety you forsake your friends when they get into trouble," he remarked with a bitter sneer.

"Friend of mine you never were," she answered quietly. "I know it was my fortune and not myself you really wanted. But though it were true that you loved me as madly and disinterestedly as you professed, had I known your character, never, never should I have held speech with you, much less admitted you to terms of familiarity—a fact which I look back upon with the deepest mortification. Let me pass, sir, and never venture to approach me again."

"No you don't, my haughty miss! I'm not done with you yet," he exclaimed between his clenched teeth, and seizing her rudely by the arm as she tried to step past him. "So you're engaged to that fatherly friend of yours, that pious sneak, that deadly foe to me?"

"Unhand me, sir!"

"Not yet," he answered, tightening his grasp, and at the same time taking a pistol from his pocket. "I swear you shall never marry that man: promise me on your oath that you'll not, or—I'll shoot you through the heart; the heart that's turned false to me. D'ye hear," and he held the muzzle of his piece within a foot of her breast.

Every trace of color fled from her face, but she stood like a marble statue, without speech or motion of a muscle, her eyes looking straight into his with firm defiance.

"Do you hear me?" he repeated, in a tone of exasperation. "Speak! Promise that you'll never marry Travilla, or I'll shoot you in three minutes—shoot you down dead on the spot, if I swing for it before night."

"That will be as God pleases," she answered low and reverently. "You can have no power at all against me except it be given you from above."

"I can't, hey? Looks like it; I've only to touch the trigger here, and your soul's out o' your body. Better promise than die."

Still she stood looking him unflinchingly in the eye; not a muscle moving, no sign of fear except that deadly pallor.

"Well," lowering his piece, "you're a brave girl, and I haven't the heart to do it," he exclaimed in admiration. "I'll give up that promise; on condition that you make another—that you'll keep all this a secret for twenty-four hours, so I can make my escape from the neighborhood before they get after me with their blood-hounds."

"That I promise, if you will begone at once."

"You'll not say a word to any one of having seen me, or suspecting I'm about here?"

"Not a word until the twenty-four hours are over."

"Then good-bye. Your pluck has saved your life—but remember, I've not said I won't shoot him or your father, if chance throws them in my way," he added, looking back over his shoulder with a malicious leer, as he left the arbor, then disappearing from sight among the trees and shrubbery beyond.

Elsie's knees shook and trembled under her. She sank back into her seat, covering her face and bowing her head upon her lap, while she sent up silent, almost agonizing petitions for the safety of those two so inexpressibly dear to her. Some moments passed thus, then she rose and hastened, with a quick nervous step, to the house. She entered her boudoir, and lay down upon a couch trembling in every fibre, every nerve quivering with excitement. The shock had been terrible.

"What de matter wid my chile? What ails you, honey?" asked Aunt Chloe, coming to her side full of concern.

"I think one of my bad headaches is coming on, mammy. But oh, tell me, is Mr. Travilla here? And papa—where is he?"

"Here, daughter," his voice answered, close at hand, "and with a note for you from Mr. Travilla, who has not shown himself today."

She shook it eagerly, but with a hand that trembled as if with sudden palsy, while the eyes, usually so keen-sighted, saw only a blurred and confused jumble of letters in place of the clear, legible characters really there.

"I cannot see," she said, in a half-frightened tone, and pressing the other hand to her brow.

"And you are trembling like an aspen leaf," he said, bending over her in serious alarm. "My child, when did this come on? And what has caused it?"

"Papa, I cannot tell you now, or till tomorrow, at this hour; I will then. But oh, papa dear, dear papa!" she cried, putting her arm about his neck and bursting into hysterical weeping. "Promise me, if you love me promise me, that you will not leave the house till I have told you. I am sick, I am suffering; you will stay by me? You will not leave me?"

"My darling, I will do anything I can to relieve you, mentally or physically," he answered in tones of tenderest love and concern. "I shall not stir from the house, while to do so would increase your suffering. I perceive there has been some villainy practiced upon you, and a promise extorted, which I shall not ask you to break, but rest assured, I shall keep guard over my precious one."

"And Mr. Travilla!" she gasped. "Oh, papa, if I only knew he was safe!"

"Perhaps the note may set your mind at rest on that point. Shall I read it for you?"

"Yes, sir," she said, putting it into his hand with a slight blush. "He never writes what I should be ashamed or afraid to have my father see."

It was but short, written merely to explain his absence, and dated from a neighboring plantation, where he had gone to assist in nursing a sick friend whom he should not be able to leave for some days. There were words of deep, strong affection, but as she had foreseen, nothing that she need care to have her father know or see.

"Does not this news allay your fears for him?" Mr. Dinsmore asked tenderly.

"Yes, papa," she answered, the tears streaming from her eyes. "Oh, how good God is to me! I will trust him, trust him for you both, as well as myself." She covered her face with her hands, while shudder after shudder shook her whole frame.

Mr. Dinsmore was much perplexed, and deeply concerned. "Shall I send for Dr. Barton?" he asked.

"No, no, papa! I am not ill; only my nerves have had a great, a terrible shock. They seem all unstrung, and my temples are throbbing with pain."

"My poor, poor darling! Strange that with all my care and watchfulness you should have been subjected to such a trial. Some ruffian has been trying to extort money from you, I presume, by threatened violence to yourself, Travilla, and me. Where were you?"

"In my arbor, sir."

"And alone?"

"Yes, papa; I thought myself safe there."

"I forbid you to go there or to any distance from the house, alone, again. You must always have someone within call, if not close at your side."

"And my father knows I will obey him," she said, tremulously lifting his hand to her lips.

He administered an anodyne to relieve the tortured nerves, then sitting down beside her, passed his hand soothingly over hair and cheek, while with the other he held one of hers in loving, tender clasp. Neither spoke, and at length she fell asleep; yet not a sound, refreshing slumber, but disturbed by starts and moans, and frequent wakings to see and feel that he was still there. "Papa, don't go away; don't leave me!" was her constant cry.

"My darling, my precious one, I will not," was his repeated assurance. "I will stay with you while this trouble lasts."

And all that day and night he never left her side, while Rose came and went, full of anxiety and doing everything that could be done for the sufferer's relief.

It was a night of unrest to them all; but morning found her free from pain, though weak and languid, and still filled with distress if her father was absent for more than a few moments from her side. She inquired of him at what hour she had come in the day before: then watched the time and, as soon as released from her promise, told them all.

Great was his indignation; and, determined that, if possible, the villain should be apprehended and brought to justice, he sent word at once to the magistrates. A warrant was issued, and several parties were presently out in different directions in hot pursuit.

But with the twenty-four hours' start Jackson had made good his escape, and the only advantage gained was the relief of knowing that he no longer infested the neighborhood.

"But when may he not return?" Elsie said with a shudder. "Papa, I tremble for you, and for—Mr. Travilla."

"I am far more concerned for you," he answered, gazing upon her pale face with pitying, fatherly tenderness. "But let us cast this care, with all others, upon our God. 'Thou wilt keep him in perfect peace whose mind is stayed on Thee; because he trusteth in thee.'"

CHAPTER ELEVENTH

*Of truth, he truly will all styles deserve
Of wise, good, just; a man both soul and nerve.*

—SHIRLEY

THE STORY REACHED Mr. Travilla's ears that evening, and finding he could be spared from the sick-room, he hastened to the Oaks. His emotions were too big for utterance as he took his "little friend" in his arms and clasped her to his beating heart.

"God be thanked that you are safe!" he said at last. "Oh, my darling, my darling, what peril you have been in and how bravely you met it! You are the heroine of the hour," he added with a faint laugh, "all, old and young, male and female, black and white, are loud in praise of your wonderful firmness and courage. And, my darling, I fully agree with them, and exult in the thought that this brave lady is mine own."

He drew her closer as he spoke, and just touched his lips to the shining hair and the pure white forehead resting on his breast.

"Ah!" she murmured low and softly, a dewy light shining in her eyes. "Why should they think it anything wonderful or strange that I felt little dread or fear at the prospect of a sudden transit from earth to heaven—a quick summons home to my Father's house on high, to be at once freed from sin and forever with the Lord? I have a great deal to live for, life looks very bright and sweet to me; yet but for you and papa, I think it would have mattered little to me had he carried out his threat."

"My little friend, it would have broken my heart. To lose you were worse than a thousand deaths."

They were alone in Elsie's boudoir, but when an hour had slipped rapidly away there came a message from Mr. Dinsmore to the effect that their company would be very acceptable in the library.

They repaired thither at once, and found him and Rose laying out plans for a summer trip. The matter was under discussion all the rest of the evening and for some days after, resulting finally in the getting up a large party of tourists, consisting of the entire families of the Oaks and Ion, with the addition of Harry and Sophie Carrington, and Lora with her husband and children, servants of course included.

They kept together for some time, visiting different points of interest in Virginia, Pennsylvania, and New York, spending several weeks at Cape May, where they were joined by the Allisons of Philadelphia—Mr. Edward and Adelaide among the rest, they having returned from Europe shortly before.

At length they separated, some going in one direction, some in another. Lora went to Louise, Rose to her father's, Mrs. and Mr. Travilla to friends in Cincinnati and its suburbs, and Elsie to pay a long-promised visit to Lucy in her married home, a beautiful country-seat on the banks of the Hudson. Her father saw her safely there, then left her for a fortnight, their fears in regard to Jackson having been allayed by the news that he had been again arrested for burglary, and Lucy and her husband promising to guard their precious charge with jealous care.

At the end of the fortnight Mr. Dinsmore returned for his daughter, and they went on together to Lansdale to visit Miss Stanhope.

Elsie had set her heart on having her dear old aunt spend the fall and winter with them in the "sunny South," and especially on her being present at the wedding; and Miss Stanhope, after much urging and many protestations that she was too old for such a journey, had at last yielded, and given her promise, on condition that her nephew and niece should come for her, and first spend a week or two in Lansdale. She entreated that Mr. Travilla and his mother might be of the party: he was a great favorite of hers, and she was sure his mother must be a woman in a thousand.

They accepted the kindness as cordially as it was proffered, met the others at the nearest point of connection, and all arrived together.

It was not Lottie King who met them at the depot this time, but a fine-looking young man with black moustache and roguish dark eye, who introduced himself as Harry Duncan, Miss Stanhope's nephew.

"Almost a cousin! Shall we consider you quite one?" asked Mr. Dinsmore, warmly shaking the hand held out to him in cordial greeting.

"Thank you, I shall feel highly honored," the young man answered in a gratified tone, and with a glance of undisguised admiration and a respectful bow directed towards Elsie. Then turning with an almost reverential air and deeper bow to Mrs. Travilla, "And, madam, may I have the privilege of placing you alongside of my dear old aunt, and addressing you by the same title?"

"You may, indeed," was the smiling rejoinder. "And my son here, I suppose, will take his place with the others as cousin. No doubt we are all related, if we could only go back far enough in tracing out our genealogies."

"To Father Adam, for instance," remarked Mr. Travilla, laughingly.

"Or good old Noah, or even his son Japheth," rejoined Harry, leading the way to a family carriage sufficiently roomy to hold them all comfortably.

"Your checks, if you please, aunt and cousins, and Simon here will attend to your luggage. Servants' also."

Elsie turned her head to see a young colored man, bowing, scraping, and grinning from ear to ear, in whom she perceived a faint resemblance to the lad Simon of four years ago.

"You hain't forgot me, miss?" he said. "I'm still at de ole place wid Miss Wealthy."

She gave him a smile and a nod, dropping a gold dollar into his hand along with her checks; the gentlemen said, "How d'ye do," and were equally generous, and he went off chuckling.

As they drew near their destination, a quaint little figure could be seen standing at the gate in the shade of a maple tree, whose leaves of mingled green and scarlet, just touched by the September frosts, made a brilliant contrast to the sober hue of her dress.

"There she is! Our dear old auntie!" cried Elsie with eager delight, that brought a flush of pleasure to Harry's face.

Miss Stanhope's greetings were characteristic. "Elsie! My darling! I have you again after all these years! Mrs. Vanilla too! How kind! But you tell me your face is always that. Horace, nephew, that is good of you! And Mr. Torville, I'm as glad as the rest to see you. Come in, come in, all of you, and make yourselves at home."

"Does Mrs. Schilling still live opposite to you, Aunt Wealthy?" asked Elsie as they sat about the tea-table an hour later.

"Yes, dearie; though she's lost all commercial value," laughed the old lady. "She's taken a second wife at last; not Mr. Was though, but a newcomer, Mr. Smearer."

"Dauber, auntie," corrected Harry, gravely.

"Well, well, child, the meaning's about the same," returned Miss Stanhope, laughing afresh at her own mistake, "and I'd as soon be the other as one."

"Mrs. Dauber wouldn't though," said Harry. "I noticed her face grow as red as a beet the other day when you called her Mrs. Smearer."

"She didn't mind being Mrs. Sixpence, I think," said Elsie.

"Oh yes, she did. It nettled her a good deal at first, but she finally got used to it, after finding out how innocent auntie was, and how apt to miscall other names."

"But I thought she would never be content with anybody but Mr. Wert."

"Well, she lost all hope there, and dropped him at once as soon as Dauber made his appearance."

Mr. Dinsmore inquired about the Kings. Elsie had done so in a private chat with her aunt, held in her room directly after their arrival.

"The doctor's as busy as ever, killing people all round the country; he's very successful at it," replied Miss Stanhope. "I've the utmost confidence in his skill."

"You are a warm friend of his, I know, auntie," said Mr. Dinsmore, smiling, "but I would advise you not to try to assist his reputation among strangers."

"Why not, nephew?"

"Lest they should take your words literally, auntie."

"Ah, yes, I must be careful how I use my stumbling tongue," she answered with a good-humored smile. "I ought to have always by, somebody to correct my blunders. I've asked Harry to do me that kindness, and he often does."

"It is quite unnecessary with us; for we all know what you intend to say," remarked Mrs. Travilla, courteously.

"Thank you, dear madam," said Miss Stanhope. "I am not at all sensitive about it, fortunately, as my nephew knows, and my blunders afford as much amusement to any one else as to me, when I'm made aware of them."

"Nettie King is married, papa," said Elsie

"Ah! Lottie also?"

"No, she's at home and will be in, with her father and mother, this evening," said Aunt Wealthy. "I've been matching to make a hope between her and Harry, but find its quite useless."

"No, we're the best of friends, but don't care to be anything more," remarked the young gentleman, coloring and laughing.

"No," said Mr. Travilla, "it is said by someone that two people with hair and eyes of the same color should beware of choosing each other as partners for life."

"And I believe it," returned Harry. "Lottie and I are

too much alike in disposition. I must look for a blue-eyed, fair-haired maiden, whose mental and moral characteristics will supply the deficiencies in mine."

"Gray eyes and brown; that will do very well, won't it?" said the old lady absently, glancing from Elsie to Mr. Travilla and back again.

Both smiled, and Elsie cast down her eyes with a lovely blush, while Mr. Travilla answered cheerily, "We think so, Miss Stanhope."

"Call me Aunt Wealthy; almost everybody does, and you might as well begin now as any time."

"Thank you, I shall avail myself of the privilege in future."

The weather was warm for the time of year, and on leaving the table the whole party repaired to the front porch, where Harry quickly provided everyone with a seat.

"That is a beautiful maple yonder," remarked Mr. Travilla.

"Yes, sir," returned Harry. "We have a row of them all along the front of the lot, and as Mrs. Dauber says, they are 'perfectly gordeous' in the fall."

"The maple is my favorite among the shade leaves," remarked Miss Stanhope, joining in the talk. "From the time it trees out in the spring till the bare become branches in the fall. Through this month and next they're a perpetual feast to the eye."

"Aunt, how did you decide in regard to that investment you wrote to consult me about?" asked Mr. Dinsmore, turning to her.

"Oh, I concluded to put in a few hundreds, as you thought it safe, on the principle of not having all my baskets in one egg."

"Small baskets they would have to be, auntie," Harry remarked quietly.

"Yes, my eggs are not so many, but quite enough for an old lady like me."

As the evening shadows crept over the landscape the air began to be chilly, and our friends adjourned to the parlor.

Here all was just as when Elsie last saw it: neat as wax, everything in place, and each feather-stuffed cushion beaten up and carefully smoothed to the state of perfect roundness in which Miss Stanhope's soul delighted.

Mrs. Travilla, who had heard descriptions of the room and its appointments from both her son and Elsie, looked about her with interest: upon the old portraits, the cabinet of curiosities, and the wonderful sampler worked by Miss Wealthy's grandmother. She examined with curiosity the rich embroidery of the chair cushions, but preferred a seat upon the sofa.

"Dr. and Mrs. King and Miss Lottie!" announced Simon's voice from the doorway, and the three entered.

Lively, cordial greetings followed, especially on the part of the two young girls. Mrs. Travilla was introduced, and all settled themselves for a chat—Lottie and Elsie, of course, managing to find seats side by side.

"You dearest girl, you have only changed by growing more beautiful than ever," cried Lottie, squeezing Elsie's hand which she still held, and gazing admiringly into her face.

Elsie laughed low and musically.

"Precisely what I was thinking of you, Lottie. It must be your own fault that you are still single. But we won't waste time in flattering each other, when we have so much to say that is better worthwhile."

"No, surely. Aunt Wealthy has told me of your engagement."

"That's right; it is no secret, and should not be from you if it were from others. Lottie, I want you to be one of my bridesmaids. We're going to carry Aunt Wealthy off to spend the winter with us, and I shall not be content unless I can do the same by you."

"A winter in the 'sunny South'—and with you! How delightful! You dear, kind creature, to think of it, and to ask me. Ah, if I only could!"

"I think you can, though of course I know your father and mother must be consulted. And if you come, you will grant my request?"

"Yes, yes indeed! Gladly."

Aunt Chloe, always making herself useful wherever she went, was passing around the room with a pile of plates, Phillis following with cakes and confections, while Simon brought in a waiter with saucers and spoons, and two large moulds of ice cream.

"Will you help the cream, Harry?" said Miss Stanhope. "There are two kinds, you see, travilla and melon. Ask Mrs. Vanilla which she'll have, or if she'll take both."

"Mrs. Travilla, may I have the pleasure of helping you to ice cream?" he asked. "There are two kinds, vanilla and lemon. Let me give you both."

"If you please," she answered, with a slightly amused look; for though Aunt Wealthy had spoken in an undertone, the words had reached her ear.

"Which will you have, dearies?" said the old lady, drawing near the young girls' corner, "travilla cream or melon?"

"Lemon for me, if you please, Aunt Wealthy," replied Lottie.

"And I will take Travilla," Elsie said, low and mischievously, and with a merry twinkle in her eye.

"But you have no cake! Your plate is quite empty and useless," exclaimed the aunt. "Horace," turning towards her nephew, who was chatting with the doctor at the other side of the room, "some of this cake is very plain; you don't object to Elsie eating a little of it?"

"She is quite grown up now, aunt, and can judge for herself in such matters," he answered smiling, then turned to finish what he had been saying to the doctor.

"You will have some then, dear, won't you?" Miss Stanhope inquired in her most coaxing tone.

"A very small slice of this sponge cake, if you please, auntie."

"How young Mr. Travilla looks," remarked Lottie, "younger I think, than he did four years ago. Happiness, I presume. It's said to have that effect. I believe I was vexed when I first heard you were engaged to him, because I thought he was too old, but really he doesn't look so. A man should be considerably older than his wife, that she may find it easier to look up to him, and he know the better how to take care of her."

"I would not have him a day younger, except that he would like to be nearer my age, or different in any way from what he is," Elsie said, her eyes involuntarily turning in Mr. Travilla's direction.

They met the ardent gaze of his. Both smiled, and rising he crossed the room and joined them. They had a half hour of lively chat together, then Mrs. King rose to take leave.

Mr. Travilla moved away to speak to the doctor, and Lottie seized the opportunity to whisper to her friend, "He's just splendid, Elsie! I don't wonder you look so happy, or that he secured your hand and heart after they had been refused to dukes and lords. You see Aunt Wealthy has been telling me all about your conquests in Europe," she added, in answer to Elsie's look of surprise.

"I am, indeed, very happy, Lottie," Elsie replied in the same low tone. "I know Mr. Travilla so thoroughly, and have not more perfect confidence in papa's goodness and love to me, than in his. It is very restful thing to have such a friend."

Dr. King's circumstances had greatly improved in the last four years, so that he was quite able to give Lottie the pleasure of accepting Elsie's invitation, and at once gave his cordial consent. Mrs. King at first objected that the two weeks of our friends' intended stay in Lansdale would not give sufficient time for the necessary additions to Lottie's wardrobe, but this difficulty was overcome by a suggestion from Elsie. She would spend two or three weeks in Philadelphia, attending to the purchasing and making up of her trousseau, she said, and Lottie's dresses could be bought and made at the same time and place.

The two weeks allotted to Lansdale of course passed very rapidly, especially to Harry, to whom the society of these new-found relatives was a great pleasure, and who on their departure would be left behind, with only Phillis for his housekeeper.

The latter received so many charges from Aunt Wealthy in regard to careful attention to "Mr. Harry's" health and comfort, that at length she grew indignant, and protested that she loved Mr. Harry as if he was her own child—didn't she "nuss him when he was a little feller?" And there was "no 'casion for missus to worry an' fret as if she was leavin' him to a stranger."

It was not for want of a cordial invitation to both the Oaks and Ion that Harry was left behind, but business required his presence at home, and he could only promise himself a week's holiday at the time of the wedding.

CHAPTER TWELFTH

Bring flowers, fresh flowers for the bride to wear;
They were born to blush in her shining hair;
She's leaving the home of her childhood's mirth;
She hath bid farewell to her father's hearth;
Her place is now by another's side;
Bring flowers for the locks of the fair young bride.

—Mrs. Hemans

A FAIR OCTOBER DAY is waning, and as the shadows deepen and the stars shine out here and there in the darkening sky, the grounds at the Oaks glitter with colored lamps, swinging from the branches of the trees that shade the long green alleys, and dependent from arches wreathed with flowers. In doors and out everything wears a festive look; almost the whole house is thrown open to the guests who will presently come thronging to it from nearly every plantation for miles around.

The grand wedding has been talked of, prepared for, and looked forward to for months past, and few, if any, favored with an invitation, will willingly stay away.

The spacious entrance hall is brilliantly lighted, and on either hand wide-open doors give admission to long suites of richly, tastefully furnished rooms, beautiful with rare statuary, paintings, articles of vertu, and flowers scattered everywhere, in bouquets, wreaths, festoons, filling the air with their delicious fragrance.

These apartments, waiting for the guests, are almost

entirely deserted, but in Elsie's dressing-room a bevy of gay young girls, in white tarlatan and with flowers in their elaborately dressed hair, are laughing and chatting merrily, and now and then offering a suggestion to Aunt Chloe and Dinah, whose busy hands are arranging their mistress for her bridal.

"Lovely!" "Charming!" "Perfect!" the girls exclaim in delighted, admiring chorus, as the tirewomen having completed their labors, Elsie stands before them in a dress of the richest white satin, with an overskirt of point lace, a veil of the same, enveloping her slender figure like an airy cloud, or morning mist, reaching from the freshly gathered orange blossoms wreathed in the shining hair to the tiny white satin slipper just peeping from beneath the rich folds of the dress. Flowers are her only ornament tonight, and truly she needs no other.

"Perfect! Nothing superfluous, nothing wanting," says Lottie King.

Rose, looking almost like a young girl herself, so sweet and fair in her beautiful evening dress, came in at that instant to see if all was right in the bride's attire. Her eyes grew misty while she gazed, her heart swelling with a strange mixture of emotions: love, joy, pride, and a touch of sadness at the thought of the partial loss that night was to bring to her beloved husband and herself.

"Am I all right, mamma?" asked Elsie.

"I can see nothing amiss," Rose answered, with a slight tremble in her voice. "My darling, I never saw you so wondrously sweet and fair," she whispered, adjusting a fold of the drapery. "You are very happy?"

"Very, mamma dear; yet a trifle sad too. But that is a secret between you and me. How beautiful you are tonight."

"Ah, dear child, quite ready, and the loveliest bride that ever I saw, from the sole of your head to the crown of your foot," said a silvery voice, as a quaint little figure came softly in and stood at Mrs. Dinsmore's side. "No, I mean from the crown of your foot to the sole of your head. Ah, funerals are almost as sad as weddings. I don't know how people can ever feel like dancing at them."

"Well, auntie dear, there'll be no dancing at mine," said Elsie, smiling slightly.

"I must go and be ready to receive our guests," said Rose, hearing the rumble of carriage wheels. "Elsie, dear child," she whispered, "keep calm. You can have no doubts or fears in putting your future in—"

"No, no, mamma, not the slightest," and the fair face grew radiant.

As Rose passed out at one door, Miss Stanhope following, with a parting injunction to the bride not to grow frightened or nervous, Mr. Dinsmore entered by another.

He stood a moment silently gazing upon his lovely daughter; then a slight motion of his hand sent all others from the room, the bridesmaids passing into the boudoir, where the groom and his attendants were already assembled, the tirewomen vanishing by a door on the opposite side.

"My darling!" murmured the father, in low, half tremulous accents, putting his arm about the slender waist. "My beautiful darling! How can I give you to another?" and again and again his lips were pressed to hers in long, passionate kisses.

"Papa, please don't make me cry," she pleaded, the soft eyes lifted to his, filled almost to overflowing.

"No, no, I must not," he said, hastily taking out his handkerchief and wiping away the tears before they fell. "It is shamefully selfish in me to come and disturb your mind thus just now."

"No, papa, no, no; I will not have you say that. Thank you for coming. It would have hurt me had you stayed away. But you would not have things different now if you could? Have no desire to?"

"No, daughter, no. Yet, unreasonable as it is, the thought will come, bringing sadness with it, that tonight you resign my name, and my house ceases to be your only home."

"Papa, I shall never resign the name dear to me because inherited from you: I shall only add to it. Your house shall always be one of my dear homes, and I shall be your own, own daughter, your own child, as truly as I ever have been. Is it not so?"

"Yes, yes, my precious little comforter."

"And you are not going to give me away—ah, papa, I could never bear that any more than you. You are taking a partner in the concern," she added with playful tenderness, smiling archly through gathering tears.

Again he wiped them hastily away. "Did ever father have such a dear daughter?" he said, gazing fondly down into the sweet face. "I ought to be the happiest of men. I believe I am—"

"Except one," exclaimed a joyous voice, at sound of which Elsie's eyes brightened and the color deepened on her cheek. "May I come in?"

"Yes, Travilla," said Mr. Dinsmore; "you have now an equal right with me."

Travilla thought his was superior, or would be after the ceremony, but generously refrained from saying so. And had Mr. Dinsmore been questioned on the subject, he could not have asserted that it had ever occurred to him that Mr. Allison had an equal right with himself in Rose. But few people are entirely consistent.

Mr. Travilla drew near the two, still standing together, and regarded his bride with a countenance beaming with love and delight. The sweet eyes sought his questioningly, and meeting his ardent gaze the beautiful face sparkled all over with smiles and blushes.

"Does my toilet please you, my friend?" she asked. "And you, papa?"

"The general effect is charming," said Mr. Travilla; "but," he added, in low, tender tones saying far more that the words, "I've been able to see nothing else for the dear face that is always that to me."

"I can see no flaw in face or attire," Mr. Dinsmore said, taking a more critical survey. "You are altogether pleasing in your doting father's eyes, my darling. But you must not stand any longer. You will need all your strength for your journey." And he would have led her to a sofa.

But she gently declined. "Ah, I am much too fine to sit down just now, my dear, kind father. I should crush my lace badly. So please let me stand. I am not conscious of weariness."

He yielded, saying with a smile, "That would be a pity; for it is very beautiful. And surely you ought to be allowed your own way tonight if ever."

"Tonight and ever after," whispered the happy groom in the ear of his bride.

A loving, trustful look was her only answer.

A continued rolling of wheels without, and buzz of voices coming from veranda, hall, and reception rooms, could now be heard.

"The house must be filling fast," said Mr. Dinsmore, "and as host I should be present to receive and welcome my guests. Travilla," and his voice trembled slightly, as he took Elsie's right hand and held it for a moment closely clasped in his, "I do not fear to trust you with what to me is a greater treasure than all the gold of California. Cherish my darling as the apple of your eye; I know you will."

He bent down for another silent caress, laid the hand in that of his friend, and left the room.

"And you do not fear to trust me, my little friend?" Travilla's tones, too, were tremulous with deep feeling.

"I have not the shadow of a fear," she answered, her eyes meeting his with an earnest, childlike confidence.

"Bless you for those words, dearest," he said. "God helping me you never shall have cause to regret them."

A door opened, and a handsome, dark-eyed boy, a miniature likeness of his father, came hurrying in. "Elsie! Papa said I might come and see how beautiful you are!" he cried, as if resolutely mastering some strong emotion. "But I'm not to say anything to make you cry. I'm not to hug you hard and spoil your dress. Oh, but you do look like an angel, only without the wings. Mr. Travilla, you'll be good, good to her, won't you?" and the voice almost broke down.

"I will, indeed, Horace; you may be sure of that. And you needn't feel as if you are losing her, she'll be back again in a few weeks, please God."

"But not to live at home any more!" he cried impetuously. "No, no, I wasn't to say that, I—"

"Come here and kiss me, my dear little brother," Elsie said tenderly; "and you shall hug me, too, as hard as you like, before I go."

He was not slow to accept the invitation, and evidently had a hard struggle with himself, to refrain from giving the forbidden hug.

"You may hug me instead, Horace, if you like," said Mr. Travilla. "You know we're very fond of each other, and are going to be brothers now."

"Yes, that I will, for I do like you ever so much," cried the boy, springing into the arms held out to him, and receiving and returning a warm embrace, while the sister looked on with eyes glistening with pleasure.

"Now, in a few minutes I'll become your brother Edward, and that's what I want you to call me in future. Will you do it?"

"Yes, sir, if papa doesn't forbid me."

A light tap at the door leading into the boudoir, and Walter put in his head. "The company, the clergyman, and the hour have come. Are the bride and groom ready?"

"Yes."

Releasing the child, Mr. Travilla drew Elsie's hand within his arm. For an instant he bent his eyes with earnest, questioning gaze upon her face. It wore an expression that touched him to the heart, so perfectly trustful, so calmly, peacefully happy, yet with a deep tender solemnity mingling with and subduing her joy. The soft eyes were misty with unshed tears as she lifted them to his.

"It is for life," she whispered; "and I am but young and foolish. Shall you never regret?"

"Never, never, unless you grow weary of your choice."

The answering smile was very sweet and confiding. "I have not chosen lightly, and do not fear because it is for life," was its unspoken language.

And truly it was no hasty, ill-considered step she was taking, but one that had been calmly, thoughtfully pondered in many an hour of solitude and communion with that unseen Friend whom from earliest youth she had acknowledged in all her ways, and who had, according to his promise, directed her paths. There was no excitement, no nervous tremor, about her then or during the short ceremony that made them no more twain but one flesh. So absorbed was she in the importance and solemnity of the act she was performing, that little room was left for thought of anything else—her personal appearance, or the hundreds of pairs of eyes fixed upon her. Even her father's presence, and the emotions swelling in his breast were for the time forgotten. Many marked the rapt expression of her face, and the clear and distinct though low tones of the sweet voice as she pledged herself to "love, honor, and obey." Mr. Travilla's promise "to love, honor, and cherish to life's end," was given no less earnestly and emphatically.

The deed was done, and relatives and friends gathered about them with kindly salutations and good wishes.

Mr. Dinsmore was the first to salute the bride. "God bless and keep you, my daughter," were his tenderly whispered words.

"Dear, dear papa," was all she said in response, but her eyes spoke volumes. "I am yours still, your very own, and glad it is so," they said.

Then came Rose with her tender, silent caress, half-sorrowful, half-joyful, and Mrs. Travilla with her altogether joyous salutation, "My dear daughter, may your cup of happiness be ever filled to overflowing;" while Mr. Dinsmore, to hide his emotion, turned jocosely to Travilla with a hearty shake of the hand, and "I wish you joy, my son."

"Thank you, father," returned the groom gravely, but with a twinkle of merriment in his eye.

Aunt Wealthy, standing close by awaiting her turn to greet the bride, shook her head at her nephew. "Ah you are quite too old for that, Horace. Mr. Vanilla, I wish you joy; but what am I to call you now?"

"Edward, if you please, Aunt Wealthy."

"Ah, yes, that will do nicely. It's a good name—so easily forgotten. Elsie, dearie, you went through it brave as a lion. May you never wish you'd lived your lane like your auld auntie."

"As if single blessedness could ever be real blessedness!" sneered Enna, coming up just in time to catch the last words.

"Our feelings change as we grow older," returned Miss Stanhope, in her gentle, refined tones, "and we come to look upon quiet and freedom from care as very desirable things."

"And I venture to say that old age is not likely to find Mrs. Percival so happy and contented as is my dear old maiden aunt, " remarked Mr. Dinsmore.

"Yet we will hope it may, papa," said Elsie, receiving Enna's salutation with kindly warmth.

But the list of relatives, near connections and intimate friends, is too long for particular mention of each. All the Dinsmores were there, both married and single; also most of the Allisons. Harold had not come with the others, nor had he either accepted or rejected the invitation.

On first raising her eyes upon the conclusion of the ceremony, had Elsie really seen, far back in the shadow of the doorway, a face white, rigid, hopeless with misery as his when last they met and parted? She could not tell; for if really there, it vanished instantly.

"Did Harold come?" she asked of Richard when he came to salute the bride and groom.

"I think not; I haven't seen him. I can't think what's come over the lad to be so neglectful of his privileges."

Harry Duncan was there, too, hanging upon the smiles of merry, saucy, blue-eyed May Allison, while her brother Richard seemed equally enamored with the brunette beauty and sprightliness of Lottie King.

Stiffness and constraint found no place among the guests, after the event of the evening was over.

In the great dining-room a sumptuous banquet was laid; and thither, after a time, guests and entertainers repaired.

The table sparkled with cut-glass, rare and costly china, and solid silver and gold plate. Every delicacy from far and near was to be found upon it; nothing wanting that the most fastidious could desire, or the most lavish expenditure furnish. Lovely, fragrant flowers were there also in the utmost profusion, decorating the board, festooning the windows and doorways, in bouquets upon the mantels and antique stands, scattered here and there through the apartment, filling the air with their perfume; while a distant and unseen band discoursed sweetest music in soft, delicious strains.

The weather was warmer far than at that season in our northern clime, the outside air balmy and delightful, and through the wide-open doors and windows glimpses might be caught of the beautiful grounds, lighted here and there by a star-like lamp shining out among the foliage. Silent and deserted they had been all the earlier part of the evening, but now group after group, as they left the bountiful board, wandered into their green alleys and gay parterres; low, musical tones, light laughter, and merry jests floating out upon the quiet night air and waking the echoes of the hills.

But the bride retired to her own apartments, where white satin, veil, and orange blossoms were quickly exchanged for an elegant traveling dress, scarcely less becoming to her rare beauty.

She reappeared in the library, which had not been thrown open to the guests, but where the relations and bridesmaids were gathered for the final good-bye.

Mr. Dinsmore's family carriage, roomy, easy-rolling, and softly cushioned, stood at the door upon the drive, its spirited gray horses pawing the ground with impatience to be gone. It would carry the bride and groom—

and a less pretentious vehicle their servants—in two hours to the seaport where they were to take the steamer for New Orleans, for their honeymoon was to be spent at Viamede, Elsie still adhering to the plan of a year ago.

Here adieus were gaily given to one and another, beginning with those least dear; very very affectionately to Mrs. Travilla, Aunt Wealthy, Rose and the little Horace (sleeping Rosebud had already been softly kissed in her crib).

Her idolized father only remained, and now all her gaiety forsook her, all her calmness gave way, and clinging about his neck, "Papa, papa, oh papa!" she cried, with a burst of tears and sobs.

Holy and pure are the drops that fall,
When the young bride goes from her father's hall;
She goes unto love yet untried and new—
She parts from love which hath still been true.

It was his turn now to comfort her. "Darling daughter," he said, caressing her with exceeding tenderness, "we do not part for long. Should it please God to spare our lives, I shall have my precious one in my arms in a few short weeks. Meantime we can have a little talk on paper every day. Shall we not?"

"Yes, yes, dear, dear, precious father."

Mr. Travilla stood by with a face full of compassionate tenderness. Putting one hand into her father's, Elsie turned, gave him the other, and together they led her to the carriage and placed her in it. There was a hearty, lingering hand-shaking between the two gentlemen. Mr. Travilla took his seat by Elsie's side, and amid a chorus of good-byes they were whirled rapidly away.

"Cheer up, my dear," said Rose leaning affectionately on her husband's arm. "It is altogether addition and not subtraction; you have not lost a daughter but gained a son."

"These rooms tell a different tale," he answered with a sigh. "How desolate they seem. But this is no time for the indulgence of sadness. We must return to our guests, and see that all goes merry as a marriage bell with them till the last has taken his departure."

CHAPTER THIRTEENTH

My bride,
My wife, my life. O we will walk this world
Yok'd in all exercise of noble aim
And so through those dark gates across the wild
That no man knows.

—TENNYSON'S PRINCESS

ELSIE'S TEARS were falling fast, but an arm as strong and kind as her father's stole quietly about her, a hand as gentle and tender as a woman's drew the weary head to a resting-place on her husband's shoulder, smoothed back the hair from the heated brow, and wiped away the falling drops.

"My wife! My own precious little wife!"

How the word, the tone, thrilled her! Her very heart leaped for joy through all the pain of parting from one scarcely less dear. "My husband," she murmured, low and shyly—it seemed so strange to call him that, so almost bold and forward—"my dear, kind friend, to be neither hurt nor angry at my foolish weeping."

"Not foolish, dear one, but perfectly natural and right. I understand it; I who know so well what your father has been to you these many years."

"Father and mother both."

"Yes; tutor, friend, companion, confidant, everything. I know, dear little wife, that you are sacrificing much for me, even though the separation will be but partial. And how I love you for it, and for all you are to me, God only knows."

The tears had ceased to flow; love, joy, and thankfulness were regaining their ascendancy in the heart of the youthful bride. She became again calmly, serenely happy.

The journey was accomplished without accident. They were favored with warm, bright days, clear, starlit nights, and on as lovely an afternoon as was ever known in that delicious clime, reached Viamede.

Great preparations had been made for their reception. Banners were streaming, and flags flying from balconies and tree-tops. Mr. Mason met them at the pier with a face beaming with delight; Spriggs with a stiff bow. A gun was fired and a drum began to beat as they stepped ashore. Two pretty mulatto girls scattered flowers in their path, and passing under a grand triumphal arch they presently found themselves between two long rows of smiling, bowing negroes, whose fervent ejaculations: "God bless our dear young missus an' her husband!" "God bless you, massa an' missus!" "Welcome home!" "Welcome to Viamede!" "We've not forgot you, Miss Elsie; you's as welcome as de daylight!" affected our tender-hearted heroine almost to tears.

She had a kind word for each, remembering all their names, and inquiring after their "miseries;" everyone was permitted to take her small white hand, many of them kissing it with fervent affection. They were introduced to their "new master," too—that was what she called him—and shaken hands with by him in a cordial, interested way that won their hearts at once.

Aunt Phillis was in her glory, serving up a feast the preparation of which had exhausted the united skill of both Aunt Sally and herself. Their efforts were duly appreciated and praised, the viands evidently greatly enjoyed, all to their intense delight.

Mr. Mason was invited to partake with the bride and groom, and assigned the seat of honor at Mr. Travilla's right hand. Elsie presided over the tea-urn with the same gentle dignity and grace as when her father occupied the chair at the opposite end of the table, now filled by her husband. Her traveling dress had been exchanged for one of simple white, and there were white flowers in her hair and at her throat. Very sweet and charming she looked, not only in the eyes of her husband, who seemed to find her fair face a perpetual feast, but in those of all others who saw her.

On leaving the table they repaired to the library, where Mr. Mason gave a report of the condition of the people and his work among them, also assuring Mrs. Travilla that Spriggs had carefully carried out her wishes, that the prospect for the crops was fine, and everything on the estate in excellent order.

She expressed her gratification, appealing to Mr. Travilla for his approval, which was cordially given; said she had brought a little gift for each of the people, and desired they should be sent up to the house about sunset the next evening to receive it.

The chaplain promised that her order should be attended to, then retired, leaving husband and wife alone together.

"All very satisfactory, my little friend, was it not?" said Mr. Travilla.

"Yes, sir, very. I'm so glad to have secured such a man as Mr. Mason to look after the welfare of these poor helpless creatures. And you like the house, Mr. Travilla, do you not?"

"Very much, so far as I have seen it. This is a beautiful room, and the dining-room pleased me equally well."

"Ah, I am eager to show you all!" she cried, rising quickly and laying her hand on the bell-rope.

"Stay, little wife, not tonight," he said. "You are too much fatigued.

She glided to the back of the easy chair in which he sat, and leaning over him, said laughingly, "I'm not conscious of being fatigued, but I have promised to obey and—"

"Hush, hush!" he said flushing. "I meant to have that left out. And did I not tell you you were to have your own way that night and ever after? You've already done enough obeying to last you a lifetime. But please come round where I can see you better." Then, as she stepped to his side, he threw an arm about her and drew her to his knee.

"But it wasn't left out," she said, shyly returning his fond caress. "I promised and must keep my word."

"Ah, but if you can't, you can't. How will you obey when you get no orders?"

"So you don't mean to give me any?"

"No, indeed. I'm your husband, your friend, your protector, your lover, but not your master."

"Now, Mr. Travilla—"

"I asked you to call me Edward."

"But it seems so disrespectful."

"More so than to remind me of the disparity of our years? Or than to disregard my earnest wish? Then I think I'll have to require the keeping of the promise in this one thing. Say Edward, little wife, and never again call me Mr. Travilla when we are alone."

"Well, Edward, I will try to obey; and if I use the wrong word through forgetfulness you must please excuse it. But ah, I remember papa would say that was no excuse."

"But I shall not be so strict—unless you forget too often. I have sometimes thought my friend too hard with his tender-hearted, sensitive little daughter."

"Don't blame him—my dear, dear father!" she said, low and tremulously, her face growing grave and almost sad for the moment. "He was very strict, it is true, but none too strict in the matter of requiring prompt and implicit obedience, and oh, so kind, so loving, so tender, so sympathizing. I could, and did go to him with every little childish joy and sorrow, every trouble, vexation, and perplexity, always sure of sympathy, and help, too, if needed. Never once did he repulse me, or show himself an uninterested listener.

"He would take me on his knee, hear all I had to say, clasp me close to his heart, caress me, call me pet names, joy, sorrow with, or counsel me as the case required, and bid me always come freely to him so, assuring me that nothing which concerned me, one way or another, was too trivial to interest him, and he would be glad to know I had not a thought or feeling concealed from him. I doubt if even you, my friend, have ever known all that papa has been and is to me: father, mother, everything—but husband," she added with a blush and smile, as her eyes met the kindly, tender look in his.

"Ah, that is my blessed privilege," he whispered, drawing her closer to him. "My wife, my own precious little wife! God keep me from ever being less tender, loving, sympathizing to you than your father has been."

"I do not fear it, my husband. Oh, was ever woman so blessed with love as I! Daughter, and wife! They are the sweetest of all names when addressed to me by papa's lips and yours."

"I ought not to find fault with training, seeing what credit you do it. However, you seemed to me as near perfection as possible before he began. Ah, my little friend, for how many years I loved you with scarcely a hope it would ever be returned in the way I wished. Indeed I can hardly believe fully in my own happiness," he concluded with a joyous laugh.

The next day Elsie had the pleasure of showing her husband over the house first, and then the estate. Their life at Viamede, for the few weeks of their stay, seemed much like a repetition of her visit there the year before with her father. They took the same rides, walks and drives; glided over the clear waters of the bayou in the same boat; sought out each spot of beauty or interest he had shown her; were, if possible, even more constantly together, reading, writing, or engaged with music in library or drawing-room, seated side by side on veranda or lawn enjoying conversation, book or periodical; or, it might be, silently musing, hand in hand, by the soft moonlight that lent such a witchery to the lovely landscape. A pleasanter honeymoon could hardly have been devised.

In one thing, however, they were disappointed: they had hoped to be left entirely to each other. But it was impossible to conceal their presence at Viamede from the hospitable neighbors, and calls and invitations had to be received and returned. But, both being eminently fitted to shine in society, and each proud to display the other, this state of things did not, after all, so greatly interfere with their employment.

In fact, so delightful did they find their life in that lovely country that they lingered week after week till nearly six had slipped away, and letters from home began to be urgent for their return. Mr. Dinsmore was wearying for his daughter, Mrs. Travilla for her son, and scarcely less for the daughter so long vainly hoped for.

Every day a servant was dispatched to the nearest post-office with their mail, generally returning as full handed as he went. Mr. Dinsmore's letters were, as he had promised, daily, and never left unanswered. The old love was not, could not be forgotten in the new. Elsie was no less a daughter because she had become a wife; but Edward was always a sharer in her enjoyment, and she in his.

They were sitting on the veranda one morning when Uncle Ben rode up and handed the mail-box to his master. Mr. Travilla hastened to open it, gave Elsie her letter and began to perusal of his own.

A softly breathed sigh called to his attention to her.

"What is it, little wife?" he asked. "Your face is grave almost to sadness."

"I was thinking," she answered, with her eye still upon her father's letter open in her hand. "Papa says," and she read aloud from the sheet, "how long you are lingering in Viamede. When will you return? Tell Travilla I am longing for a sight of the dear face his eyes are feasting upon, and he must remember his promise not to part us.

"I am writing in your boudoir. I have been thinking of the time (it seems but yesterday) when I had you here a little girl, sitting on my knee reciting your lessons or listening with almost rapt attention to my remarks and explanations. Never before had tutor so dear, sweet, and interesting a scholar!"

"A fond father's partiality," she remarked, looking up with a smile and blush. "But never, I am sure, was such another tutor; his lucid explanations, intense interest in the subject and his pupil, apt illustrations, and fund of information constantly opened up to me, made my lessons a delight."

"He has made you wonderfully well informed and thorough," her husband said.

She colored with pleasure.

"Such words are very sweet, coming from your lips. You appreciate papa."

"Yes, indeed, and his daughter too, I hope," he answered, smiling fondly upon her. "Yes, your father and I have been like brothers since we were little fellows. It seems absurd to think of him in any other relation."

"But what about going home? Isn't it time, as papa thinks?"

"That you shall decide, ma chere. Our life here has been very delightful to me, and to you also, I hope."

"Very, if we had your mother and papa and mamma and the children here, I should like to stay all winter. But as it is I think we ought to return soon." He assented, and after a little more consultation they decided to go soon—not later than the middle of the next week, but the day was not set.

CHAPTER FOURTEENTH

The low reeds by the streamlet's side,
And hills to the thunder peal replied:
The lightening burst on its fearful way
While the heavens were lit in its red array.

—WILLIS GAYLORD CLARK

Thither, full fraught with mischievous revenge
Accurs'd, and in a cursed hour he hies.

—MILTON'S PARADISE LOST

THEY WERE ALL ALONE that evening, and retired earlier than usual. They had been quietly sleeping for some time when Elsie was wakened by a sudden gust of wind that swept round the house, rattling doors and windows; then followed the roll and crash of thunder, peal on peal, accompanied with vivid flashes of lightening.

Elsie was not timid in regard to thunder and lightening. She knew so well that they were entirely under the control of her Father, without whom not a hair of her head could perish. She lay listening to the war of the elements, thinking of the words of the Psalmist, "The clouds poured out water: the skies sent out a sound; thine arrows also went abroad. The voice of thy thunder was in the heaven; the lightenings lightened the world, the earth trembled and shook."

But another sound startled her. Surely she heard some stealthy step on the veranda upon which the windows of the room opened (long windows reaching from the floor almost to the ceiling), and then a hand at work with the fastenings of the shutters of the one farthest from the bed.

Her husband lay sleeping by her side. She half raised herself in the bed, put her lips to his ear, and shaking him slightly, whispered, "Edward, someone is trying to get in at the window!"

He was wide-awake in an instant, raised himself and while listening intently took a loaded revolver from under his pillow and cocked it ready for use.

"Lie down, darling," he whispered. "It will be safer, and should the villain get in, this will soon settle him, I think."

"Don't kill him, if you save yourself without," she answered, in the same low tone and with a shudder.

"No; if I could see, I should aim for his right arm."

A moment of silent waiting, the slight sound of the burglar's tool faintly heard amid the noise of the storm, then the shutter flew open, a man stepped in. At that instant a vivid flash of lightening showed the three to each other, and the men fired simultaneously.

A heavy, rolling crash of thunder followed close upon the sharp crack of the revolvers; the robber's pistol fell with a loud thump upon the floor and he turned and fled along the veranda, this time moving with more haste than caution. They distinctly heard the flying footsteps.

"I must have hit him," said Mr. Travilla. "Dearest, you are not hurt?"

"No, no; but you?"

"Have escaped also, thank God," he added, with earnest solemnity.

Elsie, springing to the bell-rope, sent peal after peal resounding through the house. "He must be pursued, if possible!" she cried. "For oh, Edward, your life is in danger as long as he is at large. You recognized him?"

"Yes, Tom Jackson. I thought him safe in prison at the North, but probably he has been bailed out—perhaps by one of his own gang—for so are the ends of justice often defeated."

He was hurrying on his clothes as he spoke. Elsie had hastily donned dressing-gown and slippers, and now struck a light.

Steps and voices were heard in the hall without, while Aunt Chloe coming in from the other side, asked in tones tremulous with affright, "What's de matter? What's de matter, darlin'? Is you hurted?"

"No, mammy, but there was a burglar here a moment since," said Elsie. "He and Mr. Travilla fired at each other, and he must be pursued instantly. Send Uncle Joe to rouse Mr. Spriggs and the boys, and go after him with all speed."

Meantime Mr. Mason was knocking at the door opening into the hall, asking what was wrong and offering his services; a number of negro men's voices adding, "Massa and missus, we's all heyah and ready to fight for ye."

Mr. Travilla opened the door, briefly explained what had happened, and repeated Elsie's order for an immediate and hot pursuit.

"I myself will head it," he was adding, when she interposed.

"No, no, no, my husband, surely you will not think of it. He may kill you yet. Or he might return from another direction, and what could I do with only the women to help me? Oh, Edward, don't go! Don't leave me!" And she clung to him trembling and with tears in the soft, entreating eyes.

"No, dearest, you are right. I will stay here to protect you, and Spriggs may lead the boys," he answered, throwing an arm about her. "I think I wounded the fellow," he added to Mr. Mason. "Here, Aunt Chloe. bring the light nearer."

Yes, there lay a heavy revolver, and beside it a pool of blood on the carpet where the villain had stood; and there was a bloody trail all along the veranda where he had run, and on the railing and pillar by which he had swung himself to the ground. Indeed, they could track him by it for some distance over the lawn, where the trees kept the ground partially dry; but beyond that the rain coming down in sheets, had helped the fugitive by washing away the tell-tale stains.

Elsie shuddering and turning pale and faint at the horrible sight, ordered an immediate and thorough cleansing of both carpet and veranda.

"Dere's hot water in de kitchen," said Aunt Phillis. "You, Sal an' Bet, hurry up yah wid a big basin full, an' soap an' sand an' house-cloths. Glad 'nuff dat massa shot dat ole debbil, but Miss Elsie's house not to be defiled wid his dirty blood."

"Cold watah fust, Aunt Phillis," interposed Chloe. "Cold watah fust to take out blood-stain, den de hot after dat."

"Mammy knows; do as she directs," said Elsie, hastily retreating into her dressing-room.

"My darling, this has been too much for you," her husband said tenderly, helping her to lie down on a sofa.

Chloe came hurrying in with a tumbler of cold water in one hand, a bottle of smelling salts in the other, her dusky face full of concern.

Travilla took the articles from her. "That is right, but I will attend to your mistress," he said in a kindly tone; "and do you go and prepare a bed for her in one of the rooms on the other side of the hall."

"It is hardly worthwhile, dear," said Elsie; "I don't think I can sleep again tonight."

"Yet perhaps you may. It is only two o'clock," he said, as the timepiece on the mantle struck the hour, "and at least you may rest a little better than you could here."

"And perhaps you may sleep. Yes, mammy, get the bed ready as soon as you can."

"My darling, how pale you are!" Mr. Travilla said with concern, as he knelt by her side, applying the restoratives. "Do not be alarmed. I am quite sure the man's right arm is disabled, and therefore the danger is past, for the present at least."

She put her arm about his neck and relieved her full heart with a burst of tears. "Pray, praise," she whispered.

"Oh, thank the Lord for your narrow escape. The ball must have passed very near your head; I heard it whiz over mine and strike the opposite wall."

"Yes, it just grazed my hair and carried away a lock, I think. Yes, let us thank the Lord." And he poured out a short but fervent thanksgiving, to every word of which her heart said, "Amen!"

"Yes, there is a lock gone, sure enough," she said, stroking his hair caressingly as he bent over her. "Ah, if we had not lingered so long here, this would not have happened."

"Not here, but elsewhere perhaps."

"That is true, and no doubt all has been ordered for the best."

Aunt Chloe presently returned, with the announcement that the bed was ready; and they retired for the second time, leaving the house in the care of Uncle Joe and the women servants.

It was some time before Elsie could compose herself to sleep, but near daybreak she fell into a deep slumber that lasted until long past the usual breakfast hour. Mr. Travilla slept late also, while the vigilant Aunts Chloe and Phillis and Uncle Joe took care that no noise should be made, no intruder allowed access to their vicinity to disturb them.

The first news that greeted them on leaving their room, was of the failure of the pursuit after the burglar. He had managed to elude the search, and to their chagrin Spriggs and his party had been obliged to return empty-handed. The servants were the first to tell the tale, then Spriggs came in with a fuller report.

"The scoundrel!" he growled. "How he contrived to do it I can't tell. If we'd had hounds, he couldn't. We've none on the place, but if you say so, I'll borrow—"

"No, no! Mr. Travilla, you will not allow it?" cried Elsie, turning an entreating look upon him.

"No, Spriggs, the man must be greatly weakened by the loss of blood, and, unable to defend himself, might be torn to pieces by them before you could prevent it."

"Small loss to the rest of the world if he was," grumbled the overseer.

"Yes, but I wouldn't have him die such a death as that; or hurried into eternity without a moment for repentance."

"But might it not be well to have another search?" suggested Elsie. "He had better be given up to justice, even for his own good, than die in the woods of weakness and starvation."

"Hands are all so busy with the sugar-cane just now, ma'am, that I don't see how they could be spared," answered Spriggs. "And tell you what, ma'am"—as if struck with a sudden thought—"the rascal must have a confederate that's helped him off."

"Most likely," said Mr. Travilla. "Indeed, I think it must be so. And you need give yourself no further anxiety about him, my dear."

Chapter Fifteenth

Revenge at first though sweet.
Bitter ere long, back on itself recoils.

—MILTON'S PARADISE LOST

AT THE INSTANT of discharging his revolver, Jackson felt a sharp stinging pain in his right arm, and it dropped useless at his side. He hoped he had killed both Mr. Travilla and Elsie; but, an arrant coward and thus disabled, did not dare to remain a moment to learn with certainty the effect of his shot, but rushing along the veranda, threw himself over the railing, and sliding down a pillar, by the aid of the one hand, and with no little pain and difficulty, made off with all speed across the lawn.

But he was bleeding at so fearful a rate that he found himself compelled to pause long enough to improvise a tourniquet by knotting his handkerchief above the wound—tying it as tightly as he could with the left hand aided by his teeth. He stooped and felt on the ground in the darkness and rain, for a stick, by means of which to tighten it still more; for the bleeding, though considerably checked, was by no means stanched. But sticks, stones, and every kind of litter, had long been banished thence. His fingers came in contact with nothing but the smooth, velvety turf, and with a muttered curse, he rose and fled again, for the flashing of lights, the loud ringing of a bell, peal after peal, and sounds of running feet and many voices in high excited tones, told him there was danger of a quick and hot pursuit.

Clearing the lawn, he presently struck into a bridle-path that led to the woods. Here he again paused to search for the much-needed stick, found one suited to his purpose, and by its aid succeeded in decreasing still more the drain upon his life current, yet could not stop the flow entirely.

But sounds of pursuits began to be heard in the distance, and he hastened on again, panting with weakness, pain and affright. Leaving the path, he plunged deeper into the woods, ran for some distance along the edge of a swamp, and leaping in up to his knees in mud and water, doubled on his track, then turned again, and penetrating farther and farther into the depths of the morass, finally climbed a tree, groaning with the pain the effort cost him, and concealed himself among the branches.

His pursers came up to the spot where he had made his plunge into the water; here they paused, evidently at fault. He could hear the sound of their footsteps and voices, and judge of their movements by the gleam of the torches many of them carried.

Some now took one direction, some another, and he perceived with joy that his stratagem had been at least partially successful. One party, however, soon followed him into the swamp. He could hear Spriggs urging them on and anathematizing him as "a scoundrel, robber, burglar, murderer, who ought to be swung up to the nearest tree."

Every ticket was undergoing a thorough search, heads were thrown back and torches held high that eager blacks eyes might scan the tree-tops, and Jackson began to grow sick with the almost certainty of being taken, as several stout negroes drew nearer and nearer his chosen hiding-place.

He uttered a low, breathed imprecation upon his useless right arm, and the man whose sure aim had made it so. "But for you," he muttered, grinding his teeth, "I'd sell my life dear."

But the rain, which had slackened for a time, again

poured in torrents, the torches sputtered and went out, and the pursuers turned back in haste to gain the firmer soil, where less danger was to be apprehended from alligators, panthers, and poisonous reptiles.

The search was kept up for some time longer, with no light but an occasional flash from the skies; but finally abandoned, as we have seen.

Jackson passed several hours most uncomfortably and painfully on his elevated perch, quaking with fear of both man and reptile, not daring to come down or to sleep in his precarious position, or able to do so for the pain of his wound, and growing hour by hour weaker from the bleeding which it was impossible to cheek entirely.

Then his mind was in a state of great disturbance. His wound must be dressed, and that speedily. Yet how could it be accomplished without imperiling life and liberty? Perhaps he had now two new murders on his hands: he did not know, but he had at least attempted to take life, and the story would fly on the wings of the wind. Such stories always did.

He had been lurking about the neighborhood for days, and had learned that Dr. Balis, an excellent physician and surgeon, lived on the plantation, some two or three miles eastward from Viamede. He must contrive a plausible story, and go to him at break of day, before the attack on Viamede would be likely to reach him. It would be a risk, but what better could be done? He might succeed in quieting the doctor's suspicions, and yet make good his escape from the vicinity.

The storm had spent itself before the break of day, and descending from his perch with the first faint rays of light that penetrated the gloomy recesses of the swamp, he made his way out of it, slowly and toilsomely, with weary, aching limbs, suffering intensely from the gnawings of hunger and thirst, the pain of his injury, and the fear of being overtaken by the avengers of his innocent victims. Truly, as the Bible tells us, "The way of transgressors is hard."

The sun was more than an hour high when Dr. Balis, ready to start upon his morning round, and pacing thoughtfully to and fro upon the veranda of his dwelling while waiting for his horses, saw a miserable-looking object coming up the avenue: a man almost covered from head to foot with blood and mud; a white handkerchief, also both bloody and muddy, knotted around the right arm, which hung apparently useless at his side. The man reeled as he walked, either from intoxication or weakness and fatigue.

The doctor judged the latter, and called to a servant, "Nap, go and help that man into the office." Then hurrying thither himself, got out lint, bandages, instruments, whatever might be needed for the dressing of a wound. With the assistance of Nap's strong arm, the man tottered in, then sank, half fainting, into a chair.

"A glass of wine, Nap, quick!" cried the doctor, sprinkling some water in his patient's face, and applying ammonia to his nostrils.

He revived sufficiently to swallow with eager avidity the wine Nap held to his lips.

"Food, for the love of God," he gasped. "I'm starving!"

"Bread, meat, coffee, anything that is on the table, Nap," said the master. "And don't let the grass grow under your feet."

Then to the stranger, and taking gentle hold of the wounded limb: "But you need this flow of blood stanched more than anything else. You came to me for surgical aid, of course. Pistol-shot wound, eh? And a bad one at that."

"Yes, I—"

"Never mind; I'll hear your story after your arm's dressed and you've had your breakfast. You haven't strength for talk right now."

Dr. Balis had his own suspicions, as he ripped up the coat sleeve, bared the swollen limb, and carefully dressed the wound, but kept them to himself. The stranger's clothes, though much soiled and torn in several places by contact with thorns and briers, were of good material, fashionable cut, and not old or worn; his manners were gentlemanly, and his speech was that of an educated man. But all this was no proof that he was not a villain.

"Is that mortification?" asked the sufferer, looking ruefully at the black, swollen hand and forearm, and wincing under the doctor's touch as he took up the artery and tied it.

"No, no; only the stagnation of the blood."

"Will the limb ever be good for anything again?"

"Oh yes; neither the bone nor nerve has suffered injury. The ball has glanced from the bone, passed under the nerve, and cut the humeral artery. Your tourniquet has saved you from bleeding to death. 'Tis well you knew enough to apply it. The flesh is much torn where the ball passed out, but that will heal in time."

The doctor's task was done. Nap had set a plate of food within reach of the stranger's left hand, and he was devouring it like a hungry wolf.

"Now, sir," said the good doctor, when the meal was finished, "I should like to hear how you came by that ugly wound. I can't deny that things look suspicious. I know everybody, high and low, rich and poor, for miles in every direction, and so need no proof that you do not belong to this neighborhood."

"No; a party of us, from New Orleans last, came out to visit this beautiful region. We were roaming through the forest yesterday, looking for the game, when I somehow got separated from the rest, lost my way, darkness came on, and wandering hither and thither in the vain effort to find my comrades, tumbling over logs and fallen trees, scratched and torn by brambles, almost eaten up by mosquitoes, I thought I was having a dreadful time of it. But worse was to come, for I presently found myself in a swamp up to my knees in mud and water, and in the pitchy darkness tumbling over another fallen tree, struck my revolver, which I had foolishly been carrying in my coat pocket. It went off and shot me in the arm, as you see. That must have been early in the night; and what with loss of blood, pain, fatigue, and long fasting, I had but little strength when daylight came and I could see to get out of swamp and woods, and come on here."

The doctor listened in silence, his face telling nothing of his thoughts.

"A bad business," he said, rising and beginning to draw on his gloves. "You are not fit to travel, but are welcome to stay her for the present; had better lie down on the sofa there and take a nap while I am away visiting my patients. Nap, clean the mud and the blood from the gentleman's clothes; take his boots out and clean them too; and see that he doesn't want for attention while I am gone. Good-morning, sir; make yourself at home." And the doctor walked out, giving Nap a slight sign to follow him.

"Nap," he said, when they were out of earshot of the stranger, "watch that man and keep him here if possible, till I come back."

"Yes, sah."

Nap went back into the office while the doctor mounted and rode away.

"Humph," he said, half aloud, as he cantered briskly along. "Took me for a fool, did he? Thought I couldn't tell where the shot went in and where it came out, or where it would go in or out if caused in that way. No, sir, you never gave yourself that wound; but the question is who did? And what for? Have you been housebreaking or some other mischief?" Dr. Balis was traveling the direction of Viamede, intending to call there too, but having several patients to visit on the way, did not arrive until the late breakfast of its master and mistress was over.

They were seated together on the veranda, her hand in his, the other arm thrown lightly about her waist, talking earnestly, and so engrossed with each other and the subject of their conversation, that they did not at first observe the doctor's approach.

Uncle Joe was at work on the lawn, clearing away the leaves and twigs blown down by the storm.

"Mornin', Massa Doctah; did you heyah de news,

sah?" he said, pulling off his hat and making a profound obeisance, as he stepped forward to take the visitor's horse.

"No, uncle, what is it?"

"Burglah, sir, burglah broke in de house las' night, an' fire he revolvah at massa an' Miss Elsie. Miss dem dough, an' got shot hisself."

"Possible!" cried the doctor in great excitement, springing from the saddle and hurrying up the steps of the veranda.

"Ah, doctor, good-morning. Glad to see you, sir," said Mr. Travilla, rising to give the physician a hearty shake of the hand.

"Thank you, sir. How are you after your fright? Mrs. Travilla, you are looking a little pale; and no wonder. Uncle Joe tells me you had a visit from a burglar last night?"

"A murderer, sir, one whose object was to take my husband's life," Elsie answered with a shudder, and in low tremulous tones, leaning on Edward's arm, and gazing into his face with eyes swimming with tears of love and gratitude.

"My wife's also, I fear," Mr. Travilla said with emotion, fondly stroking her sunny hair.

"Indeed! Why this is worse and worse! But he did not succeed in wounding either of you?"

"No; his ball passed over our heads, grazing mine so closely as to cut off a lock of my hair. But I wounded him, must have cut an artery, I think, from the bloody trail he left behind him."

"An artery?" cried the doctor, growing more and more excited. "Where? Do you know where your ball struck?"

"A flash of lightening showed us to each other and we fired simultaneously, I aiming for his right arm. I do not often miss my aim: we heard his revolver fall to the floor and he fled instantly, leaving it and a trail of blood behind him."

"You had him pursued promptly, of course?"

"Yes; but they did not find him. I expected to see them return with his corpse, thinking he must bleed to death in a very short time. But I presume he had an accomplice who was able to stanch the flow of blood and carry him away."

"No, I don't think he had, and if I'm not greatly mistaken I dressed his wound in my office this morning and left him there in charge of my boy Nap, bidding him keep the fellow there, if possible, till I came back. I'd better return at once, lest he should make his escape. Do you know the man? And can you describe him?"

"I do; I can," replied Mr. Travilla. "But, my little wife, how you are trembling! Sit down here, dearest, and lean on me," leading her to a sofa. "And doctor, take that chair.

"The man's name is Tom Jackson. He is a noted gambler and forger, has been convicted of manslaughter and other crimes, sent to the penitentiary and pardoned out. He hates me because I have exposed his evil deeds, and prevented the carrying out of some of his wicked designs. He has before this threatened both our lives. He is about your height and build, doctor; can assume the manners and speech of a gentleman; has dark hair, eyes, and whiskers, regular features, and but for a sinister look would be very handsome."

"It's he and no mistake!" cried Dr. Balis, rising in haste. "I must hurry home and prevent his escape. Why, it's really dangerous to have him at large. If he wasn't so disabled I'd tremble for the lives of my wife and children.

"He trumped up a story to tell me—had his revolver in his coat pocket, set it off in tumbling over a log in the dark, and so shot himself. Of course I knew 'twas a lie, because in that case the ball would have entered from below, at the back of the arm, and come out above, while the reverse was the case."

"But how could you tell where it entered or where it passed out, doctor?" inquired Elsie.

"How, Mrs. Travilla? Why, where it goes in it makes merely a small hole—you see nothing but a blue mark—

but a much larger opening in passing out, often tearing the flesh a good deal, as in this case.

"Ah, either he was a fool or thought I was. But good-bye. I shall gallop home as fast as possible and send back word whether I find him there or not."

"Don't take the trouble, doctor," said Mr. Travilla. "We will mount and follow you at once, to identify him if he is to be found. Shall we not, wife?"

"If you say so, Edward, and are quite sure he cannot harm you now?"

"No danger, Mrs. Travilla," cried the doctor, looking back as he rode off.

CHAPTER SIXTEENTH

Oft those whose cruelty makes many mourn
Do by the fires which they first kindle burn.

—EARL OF STIRLING

As crimes do grow, justice shall rouse itself.

—JOHNSON'S CATILINE

JACKSON THOUGHT he read suspicion in the doctor's eye as the latter left the office; also he felt sure the physician would not ride far before hearing of the attack on Viamede, and would speedily come at the truth by putting that and that together; perhaps return with a party of avengers, and hang him in the tree in the adjacent forest.

"I must get out o' this before I'm an hour older," said the scoundrel to himself. "Oh, for the strength I had yesterday!"

"Why don't you lie down, sah, as Massa Doctah tole ye?" asked Nap, returning. "Massa always 'spects folks to do prezactly as he tells dem."

"Why, Sambo, I'm too dirty to lie on that nice sofa," replied Jackson, glancing down at his soiled garments.

"Sambo's not my name, sah," said the negro, drawing himself up with dignity. "I'se Napoleon Boningparty George Washington Marquis de Lafayette, an' dey calls me Nap for short. If ye'll take off dat coat, sah, an' dem boots, I'll take 'em out to de kitchen yard an' clean 'em."

"Thank you; if you will I'll give you a dollar. And if you'll brush the mud from my pants first, I'll try the sofa, for I'm nearly dead for sleep and rest."

"All right, sah," and Nap went to a closet, brought out a whisk, and using it vigorously upon the pantaloons, soon brushed away the mud, which the sun had made very dry. A few blood stains were left, but there was no help for that at present. The coat was taken off with some difficulty on account of the wounded arm, then the boots, and Jackson laid himself down on the sofa and closed his eyes.

Nap threw the coat over his arm, and taking the boots in the other hand went softly out, closing the door behind him. "Safe 'nuff now, I reckon," he chuckled to himself. "Guess he not trabble far widout dese."

He was hardly gone, however, when Jackson roused himself and forced his weary eyes to unclose. "As dangerous as to go to sleep when freezing," he muttered. He rose, stepped to the closet door, and opened it.

A pair of boots stood on the floor, a coat hung on a peg. He helped himself to both, sat down and drew on the boots, which were a little too large but went on all the more readily for that. Now for the coat. It was not new, but by no means shabby. He took out his knife, hastily ripped up the right sleeve and put it on. It fitted even better than the boots.

Nap had brought a bottle of wine and left it on the office table, forgetting to carry it back to the dining-room. Jackson took it up, and placing it to his mouth drained the last drop. Then putting on his hat, he stole softly from the house and down the avenue.

To his great joy a boat was just passing in the direction to take him farther from Viamede. He signaled it, and was taken aboard.

"Been getting Dr. Balis to patch up a wound, eh, stranger?" said the skipper, glancing at the disabled arm.

"Yes," and Jackson repeated the story already told to the surgeon.

The skipper sympathized and advised a rest in the

cabin.

"Thank you," said Jackson, "but I'm only going a few miles, when I'll reach a point where, by taking to the woods again, I'll be likely to find my friends, who are doubtless anxious to know what has become of me."

"Very well, sir, when we come to the right place, just let us know and we'll put you off."

Evidently the skipper had heard nothing to arouse his suspicions. Jackson was landed at the spot he pointed out—a lonely one on the edge of a forest, without question or demur, and the boat went on its way.

He watched it till it disappeared from view, then plunging into the woods, presently found a narrow footpath, pursuing which for an hour or so he came out into a small clearing. At the farther side, built just on the edge of the forest, was a rude log cabin. A slatternly woman stood in the open doorway.

"So ye did get back at last?" she remarked, as he drew near. "I'd most give ye up. What ails your arm now?"

He briefly repeated his story to the doctor and skipper, then asked hurriedly, "Is my horse all right?"

The woman nodded. "I've tuck good care of her. Now where's the gold ye promised me?"

"Here," he said, taking out, and holding up before her delighted eyes, several shining half-eagles. "Have my horse saddled and bridled and brought round to the door here as quickly as possible, and these are yours."

"I'll do it. Bill," to a half-grown youth who sat on a rude bench within lazily smoking a pipe—"run and fetch the gentleman's hoss. But what's yer hurry, mister?"

"This," he answered, pointing to the disabled limb. "It's growing worse, and I'm in haste to get home, where I can be nursed by mother and sisters, before I quite give out."

"She's a awful spirited cratur, and you'll have a hard job o' it to manage her, with one hand."

"I must try it nevertheless. I believe I can do it too, for she knows her master."

"She'll go like lightnin'," said the boy, as he brought the animal to the door. "She's been so long in the stable, she's as wild and scary as a bird."

Jackson threw the gold into the woman's lap, turned about and taking the bridle from the boy, stroked, patted, and talked soothingly to the excited steed, who was snorting and pawing the ground in a way that boded danger to anyone attempting to mount.

His caresses and kindly tones seemed, however, to have a calming effect; she grew comparatively quiet, he sprang into the saddle and was off like an arrow from the bow.

It was about that time the doctor returned to his office to find it deserted. Nap was summoned.

"What's become of the man I left here in your charge, sirrah?" asked the doctor sternly.

"Dunno, sah, Massa Doctah," answered Nap, glancing in astonishment from side to side. "To't he heyah, sah; 'deed I did. Took he coat an' boots to clean 'em. To't he safe till I fotch 'em back; wouldn't go off without dem."

The doctor stepped to the closet. "Yes, my coat and boots gone, bottle of wine emptied, no fee for professional aid—a fine day's work for me."

"Massa Doctah! You don't say de rascal done stole yer coat an' boots? Oh, ef I cotch him, I—" and Napoleon Bonaparte George Washington Marquis de Lafayette looked unutterable things.

"Better take care I don't get hold of you!" cried the irate master. "Go and tell Cato to saddle and bridle Selim and bring him to the door as quickly as possible, and do you find out if anybody saw which way the rascal went. He must be caught, for he's a burglar and murderer!"

Nap lifted his hands and opened mouth and eyes wide in surprise and horror.

"Begone!" cried the doctor, stamping his foot. "And don't stand gaping there while the scoundrel escapes."

Nap shuffled out, leaving his master pacing the office to and fro with angry, impatient strides.

"What is it, my dear? What has gone wrong?" asked his wife, looking in upon him.

"Come, sit down on the sofa here and I'll tell you," he

said, his excited manner quieting somewhat at sight of her pleasant face.

She accepted the invitation, and seating himself beside her he briefly related all that he knew of Jackson and his attack on Mr. Travilla.

He had hardly finished when Nap returned with the news that several of the negro children had seen a man go down the avenue and get aboard a passing boat.

"Ah ha!" cried the doctor, jumping up. "And which way was the boat going?"

"Dat way, sah," replied Nap, indicating the direction by a flourish of his right hand.

At that moment Mr. and Mrs. Travilla rode up, and Dr. and Mrs. Balis hastened out to greet them.

"He's gone; took the morning boat," cried the doctor.

"Good!" said Mr. Travilla. "We have only to head him with a telegram, and he'll be arrested on stepping ashore, or on board the boat."

"Unless he should land in the next town, Madison, which the boat, having a good hour's start of us, would reach before the swiftest messenger we could send; probably has already reached."

"Then the best plan for me will be to ride on to Madison, give notice to the authorities, have it ascertained whether our man has landed there, and if not telegraph to the next town and have them ready to board the boat, with a warrant for his arrest, as soon as it arrives."

"Yes; and I'll mount Selim and go with you," answered the doctor. "I probably know the road better than you do. And our wives may keep each other company till we return.

"What do you say, Elsie?" asked Mr. Travilla.

"That I will go or stay as you think best."

"We must ride very fast; I think it would fatigue you too much, so advise you to stay with Mrs. Balis, and I will call for you on my return."

"Do, Mrs. Travilla! I should be delighted to have you," urged Mrs. Balis; "and you can tell me all about last night. What a trial to your nerves! I don't wonder you are looking a little pale this morning."

"Thank you, I will stay," said Elsie; and instantly her husband, giving his horse into Nap's charge for a moment, sprang to the ground and lifted her from the saddle. "Don't be anxious, little wife," he whispered, as the soft eyes met with his with a fond wistful look, "I am not likely to be in danger, and you know the sweet words, 'Not a hair of your head shall fall to the ground without your Father.'"

"Yes, yes, I know, and I will trust you in his hands, my dear husband," was the low-breathed response.

Another moment and the two gentlemen were galloping rapidly down the avenue side by side. The ladies stood on the veranda, watching till they were out of sight, then went into the house.

"Now, my dear Mrs. Travilla, shall I just treat you as one of ourselves, and take you into my own breezy room?" asked Mrs. Balis, regarding Elsie with an affectionate, admiring look.

"It is just what I shall like, Mrs. Balis," Elsie answered, with a smile so sweet that her hostess put her arm about her and kissed her.

"I can't help it," she said. "You take my heart by storm with your beauty, grace, and sweetness."

"Thank you, and you need not apologize," Elsie said, returning the embrace. "Love is too precious a gift to be rejected."

"I think Mr. Travilla a very fortunate man, and so does my husband."

"And am I not a fortunate woman, too?"

"Ah, yes, Mr. Travilla is most agreeable and entertaining, handsome too; and indeed I should think everything one could wish in a husband, as mine is," she added laughingly. "I presume neither of us would consent to an exchange of partners. Are you fond of children, Mrs. Travilla?"

"Very."

"Shall I show you mine?"

"I should like to see them, if you please."

Mrs. Balis at once led the way to the nursery, where she exhibited, with much motherly pride and delight, her three darlings; the eldest five, the second three years of age, the third a babe in the arms. They were bright-eyed, rosy-cheeked children, full of life and health; but to Elsie's taste not half so sweet and pretty as Rosebud.

Mrs. Balis next conducted her guest to her boudoir; a servant brought in refreshments, consisting of a variety of fruits, cakes, and confections, with wine sugaree and lemonade. After partaking of these, the ladies had a long talk while awaiting the return of their husbands. The gentlemen were gone much longer than had been anticipated, and I am not sure the wives did not grow a little uneasy. At all events they left the boudoir for the front veranda, which gave them a view of the avenue and some hundred yards of the road beyond in the direction from which the travelers must come. And when at length the two were descried approaching, in a more leisurely manner than they went, there was a simultaneous and relieved exclamation, "Oh, there they are at last."

The ladies stood up and waved their handkerchiefs. There was no response. The gentlemen's faces were toward each other and they seemed to be engaged in earnest converse.

"Unsuccessful," said Mrs. Balis.

"How do you know?" asked Elsie.

"There's an air of dejection about them."

"I don't see it," returned Elsie, smiling. "They seem to me only too busy talking to notice out little attention."

But Mrs. Balis was correct in her conjecture. The boat had passed Madison some time before the gentlemen arrived there, had paused but a few minutes and landed no such passenger. Learning this they then telegraphed the authorities of the next town, waited some hours, and received a return telegram to the effect that the boat had been boarded, no person answering the description found; but the captain gave the information that such a man had been taken on board at Dr.

Balis' plantation, and set ashore at the edge of a forest half-way between that place and Madison.

On receiving this intelligence, Mr. Travilla and the doctor started for home, bringing with them a posse of mounted men headed by some of the police of Madison.

Dr. Balis had taken with him to Madison the blood-stained coat of Jackson. From this the hounds took the scent, and on arriving at the wood mentioned by the skipper, soon found the trail and set off in hot pursuit, the horsemen following close at their heels.

Our gentlemen did not join in the chase, but having seen it well begun, continued on their homeward way.

"And you did consent to the use of hounds?" Elsie said inquiringly, and with a slightly reproachful look at her husband.

"My dear," he answered gently, "having been put into the hands of the police it has now become a common-wealth case, and I have no authority to dictate their mode of procedure."

"Forgive me, dearest, if I seemed to reproach you," she whispered, the sweet eyes seeking his with a loving, repentant look, as for a moment they were left alone together.

He drew her to him with a fond caress. "My darling, I have nothing to forgive."

In the cabin at whose door Jackson had made his call and remounted his steed, a woman—the same with whom his business had been transacted—was stooping over an open fire, frying fat pork and baking hoe-cake. Bill sat on his bench smoking as before, while several tow-headed children romped and quarreled, chasing each other round and round the room with shouts of "You quit that ere!" "Mammy, I say, make her stop."

"Hush!" cried the woman, suddenly straightening herself, and standing in a listening attitude, as a deep sound came to the ear, borne on the evening breeze.

"Hounds! Blood-hounds!" cried Bill, springing to his feet with unwonted energy. "And they're a comin' this way, makin' straight for the house," he added, glancing from the door, then shutting it with a bang. "They're after that man, you may depend. He's a 'balitionist, or a horse-thief, or somethin'."

The children crouched, silent, pale, and terror-stricken, in a corner, while outside, the deep baying of the hounds drew nearer and nearer, and mingling with it came other sounds of horses' hoofs and the gruff voices of men. Then a loud "Halloo the house!"

"What's wanted?" asked Bill, opening the one window and putting out his head.

"The burglar you're hiding from justice and the hounds have tracked to your door. A fellow with his right arm disabled by a pistol-shot."

"He isn't here, didn't step inside at all' don't ye see the hounds are turning away from the door? But you kin come in an' look for yourself."

One of the men dismounted and went in.

"Look round sharp now," said the woman. "I only wish he was here fur ye to ketch um. If I'd know'd he was a burglar, he would never hev got off so easy. He jest come for his beast that he left with us four days ago, and mounted there at the door and was of like a shot."

"Which way?" asked the man.

She pointed in a southerly direction. "It's the way to Texas, aint it? An' he's got four or five hours the start o' ye, an' on a swift horse. He'll be over the border line afore ye kin ketch up to him."

"I'm afraid so, indeed; but justice can follow him even there," replied the officer, hastening out, already satisfied that the one bare room did not contain his quarry.

He sprang into the saddle, and the whole party galloped away in the wake of the dogs, who had found the trail again and started off in full cry.

The party had a hard ride of some hours, the hounds never faltering or losing the scent; but at length they were at fault. They had reached a brook and here the trail was lost. It was sought for on both sides of the stream for a considerable distance both up and down, then abandoned in despair.

The wily burglar had made his steed travel the bed of the stream, which was nowhere very deep, for several miles. Then taking to the open country again and traveling under cover of the darkness of a cloudy night, at length, in a condition of utter exhaustion, reached a place of safety among some of his confederates—for he had joined himself to a gang of villains who infested that part of the country.

But "Though hand join in hand, the wicked shall not be unpunished." Few if any of them would escape a violent and terrible death at the last, and—"after that the judgment," from which none may be excused.

Chapter Seventeenth

His house she enters, there to be a light
Shining within, when all without is night;
A guardian angel o'er his life presiding,
Doubling his pleasure, and his cares dividing.

—Rogers' Human Life

At the set time our friends turned their faces homeward, leaving their loving dependents of Viamede all drowned in tears. In the six weeks of their stay, "Massa" an' "Missus" had become very dear to those warm, childlike hearts.

Elsie could not refrain from letting fall some bright sympathetic drops, though the next moment her heart bounded with joy at the thought of home and father. The yearning to hear again the tones of his loved voice, to feel the clasp of his arm and the touch of his lip upon brow and cheek and lip, increased with every hour of the rapid journey.

Its last stage was taken in the Ion family carriage, which was found waiting for them at the depot.

Elsie was hiding in her own breast a longing desire to go first to the Oaks, chiding herself for the wish, since her husband was doubtless fully as anxious to see his mother, and wondering why she had not thought of asking for a gathering of both families at the one place or the other.

They had left the noisy city far behind, and were

bowling smoothly along a very pleasant part of the road, bordered with greensward and shaded on either side by noble forest trees, she with her mind filled with these musings, sitting silent and pensive, gazing dreamily from the window.

Suddenly her eyes encountered a well-known noble form, seated on a beautiful spirited horse, which he was holding in with a strong and resolute hand.

"Papa!" she exclaimed, with a joyous, ringing cry; and instantly he had dismounted—his servant taking Selim's bridle-reins—the carriage had stopped, and springing out, she was in his arms.

"My dear father, I was so hungry to see you," she said, almost crying for joy. "How good of you to come to meet us, and so much nicer here than in the crowded depot."

"Good of me," he answered, with a happy laugh. "Of course, as I was in no haste to have my darling in my arms. Ah, Travilla, my old friend, I am very glad to see your pleasant face again." And he shook hands warmly. "Many thanks to you—and to a higher power—" he added reverently, "for bringing her safely back to me. She seems to have been well taken care of—plump and bright and rosy."

"I have been, papa; even you could not be more tender and careful of me than—my husband is."

Her father smiled at the shy, half-hesitating way in which the last word slipped from the rich red lips, and the tender, loving light in the soft eyes as they met the fond, admiring gaze of Travilla's.

"No repentance on either side yet, I see," he said laughingly. "Travilla, your mother is in excellent health and spirits, but impatient to embrace both son and daughter, she bade me say. We all take tea by invitation at Ion today—that is, we of the Oaks, including Aunt Wealthy and Miss King."

"Oh, how nice! How kind!" cried Elsie.

"And tomorrow you are all to be at the Oaks!" added her father. "Now shall I ride beside your carriage? Or take a seat in it with you?"

The latter, by all means," answered Travilla, Elsie's sparkling eyes saying the same, even more emphatically.

"Take Selim home, and see that both he and the family carriage are at Ion by nine this evening," was Mr. Dinsmore's order to his servant.

"Ah, papa! So early!" Elsie interposed, in a tone that was half reproach, half entreaty.

"We must not keep you up late after your journey, my child," he answered, following her into the carriage, Mr. Travilla stepping in after.

"The seats are meant for three. Let me sit between you, please," requested Elsie.

"But are you not afraid of crushing your dress?" asked her father jocosely, making room for her by his side.

"Not I," she answered gaily, slipping into her chosen place with a light, joyous laugh, and giving a hand to each. "Now I'm the happiest woman in the world."

"As you deserve to be," whispered her husband, clasping tight the hand he held.

"Oh, you flatterer!" she returned. "Papa, did you miss me?"

"Every day, every hour. Did I not tell you so in my letters? And you? Did you think often of me?"

"Oftener than I can tell."

"I have been wondering," he said, looking gravely into her eyes, "why you both so carefully avoided the slightest allusion to that most exciting episode of your stay at Viamede."

Elsie blushed. "We did not wish to make you uneasy, papa."

"Of course, you must have seen a newspaper account?" observed Mr. Travilla.

"Yes; and now suppose you let me hear your report. Did the villain's shot graze Elsie's forehead and carry a tress of her beautiful hair?"

"No, no, it was only a lock of her unworthy husband's hair—a much slighter loss," Travilla said, laughing. "But perhaps the reporter would justify his misrepresentation on the plea that man and wife are one."

"Possibly. And did your shot shatter the bone in the rascal's arm?"

"No; Dr. Balis told me the ball glanced from the bone, passed under the nerve and severed the humeral artery."

"It's a wonder he didn't bleed to death."

"Yes; but it seems he had sufficient knowledge and presence of mind to improvise a tourniquet with his handkerchief and a stick."

"What rooms were you occupying?" asked Mr. Dinsmore. "Come, just tell me the whole story as if I had heard nothing of it before."

Travilla complied, occasionally appealing to Elsie to assist his memory, and they had hardly done with the subject when the carriage turned into the avenue at Ion.

"My darling, welcome to your home," said Travilla low and tenderly, lifting the little gloved hand to his lips.

An involuntary sigh escaped from Mr. Dinsmore's breast.

"Thank you, my friend," Elsie replied to her husband, the tone and the look saying far more than the words. Then turning to her father, "And tomorrow, papa, you will welcome me to the other of my two dear homes."

"I hope so, daughter. Sunlight is not more welcome than you will always be."

What joyous greetings now awaited our travelers. Elsie had hardly stepped from the carriage ere she found herself in Mrs. Travilla's arms, the old lady rejoicing over her as the most precious treasure Providence could have sent her.

Then came Rose, with her tender, motherly embrace, and joyous "Elsie, dearest, how glad I am to have you with us again."

"Oh, but you've missed us sadly!" said Aunt Wealthy, taking her turn. "The house seemed half gone at the Oaks. Didn't it, Horace?"

"Yes; the absence of our eldest daughter made a very wide gap in the family circle," answered Mr. Dinsmore.

And "Yes, indeed!" cried Horace junior, thinking himself addressed. "I don't believe I could have done without her at all if she hadn't written me those nice little letters."

"Don't you thank me for bringing her back then, my little brother?" asked Mr. Travilla, holding out his hand to the child.

"Yes, indeed, Brother Edward. Papa says I may call you that, as you asked me to, and I'll give you another hug as I did that night, if you'll let me."

"That I will, my boy!" And opening wide his arms he took the lad into a warm embrace, which was returned as heartily as given.

"Now, Elsie, it's my turn to have a hug and kiss from you," Horace said, as Mr. Travilla released him. "Everybody's had a turn but me. Miss King and Rosebud and all."

Elsie had the little one in her arms, caressing it fondly.

"Yes, my dear little brother," she said, giving Rosebud to her mammy, "you shall have as hard a hug as I can give, and as many kisses as you want. I love you dearly, dearly, and am as glad to see you as you could wish me to be."

"Are you much fatigued, Elsie dear?" asked Rose, when the greetings were over, even to the kindly shake of the hand and pleasant word to each of the assembled servants.

"Oh, no, mamma, we have traveled but little at night, and last night I had nine hours of sound, refreshing sleep."

"That was right," her father said, with an approving glance at Travilla.

Mrs. Travilla led the way to a suite of beautiful apartments prepared for the bride.

Elsie's taste had been consulted in all the refitting and refurnishing, and the whole effect was charming. This was, however, her first sight of the rooms since the changes had been begun.

The communicating doors were thrown wide, giving a

view of the whole suite at once, from the spot where Elsie stood between Mr. Travilla and his mother. She gazed for a moment, then turned to her husband a face sparkling with delight.

"Does it satisfy you, my little wife?" he asked, in tones that spoke intense enjoyment of her pleasure.

"Fully, in every way; but especially as an evidence of my husband's love," she answered, suffering him to throw an arm about her and fold her to his heart.

There had been words of welcome and a recognition of the younger lady as now mistress of the mansion, trembling on the mother's tongue, but she now stole quietly away and left them to each other.

In half an hour the two rejoined their guests, "somewhat improved in appearance," as Mr. Travilla laughingly said he hoped they would be found.

"You are indeed," said Aunt Wealthy. "A lily or a rose couldn't look lovelier than Elsie does in that pure white, and with the beautiful flowers in her hair. I like her habit of wearing natural flowers in her hair."

"And I," said her husband. "They seem to me to have been make for her adornment."

"And your money-hoon's over, Elsie. How odd it seems to think you've been so long married. And did you get through the money-hoon without a quarrel? But of course you did."

Elsie, who had for a moment looked slightly puzzled by the new word, now answered with a smile of comprehension, "Oh, yes, auntie; surely we should be a sad couple if even the honeymoon were disturbed by a disagreement. But Edward and I never mean to quarrel."

Mr. Dinsmore turned in his chair, and gave his daughter a glance of mingled surprise and disapprobation.

"There, papa, I knew you would think me disrespectful," she exclaimed with a deep blush, "but he insisted, indeed ordered me, and you know I have promised to obey."

"It is quite true," assented Mr. Travilla, coloring in his turn. "But I told her it was the only order I ever meant to give her."

"Better not make rash promises," said Mr. Dinsmore, laughing. "These wives are sometimes inclined to take advantage of them."

"Treason! Treason!" cried Rose, lifting her hands. "To think you'd say that before me!

'Husband, husband, cease your strife
No longer idly rove, sir;
Tho' I am your wedded wife,
Yet I am not your slave, sir.'

There was a general laugh, in the midst of which the tea-bell rang.

"Come," said the elder Mrs. Travilla good-humoredly, "don't be setting a bad example to my children, Mr. and Mrs. Dinsmore, but let us all adjourn amicably to the tea-room, and try the beneficial effect of meat and drink upon our tempers."

"That's a very severe reproof, coming from so mild a person as yourself, Mrs. Travilla," said Rose. "My dear, give your arm to Aunt Wealthy, or our hostess. The ladies being so largely in the majority, the younger ones should be left to take care of themselves—of course excepting our bride. Miss King, will you take my arm?"

"Sit here, my daughter," said Mrs. Travilla, indicating the seat before the tea-urn.

"Mother, I did not come here to turn you out of your rightful place," objected Elsie, blushing painfully.

"My dear child, it is your own place. As the wife of the master of the house, you are its mistress. And if you knew how I long to see you actually filling that position, how glad I am to resign the reins to such hands as yours, you need not to hesitate or hold back."

"Yes, take it, wife," said Mr. Travilla, in tender, reassuring tones, as he led her to the seat of honor. "I know my mother is sincere—she is never anything else—and she told me long ago, even before she knew who was to be her daughter, how glad she would be to resign the cares of mistress of the household." Elsie yielded, making no further objection, and presided with the same modest ease, dignity, and grace with which she had filled the like position at Viamede. The experience there had accustomed her to the duties of the place, and after the first moment she felt quite at home in it.

Mr. Dinsmore's carriage was announced at the early hour he had named. The conversation in the drawing-room had been general for a time, but now the company had divided themselves into groups, the two older married ladies and Aunt Wealthy forming one, Mr. Travilla and Miss King another, while Mr. Dinsmore and his daughter had sought out the privacy of a sofa, at a distance from the others, and were in the midst of one of the long, confidential chats they always enjoyed so much.

"Ah, papa, don't go yet," Elsie pleaded. "We're not half done our talk, and it's early."

"But the little folks should have been in their nests long before this," he said, taking out his watch.

"Then send them and their mammies home, and let the carriage return for you and the ladies, unless they wish to go now."

He looked at her smilingly. "You are not feeling the need of rest and sleep?"

"Not at all, papa, only the need of a longer chat with you."

"Then, since you had so good a rest last night, it shall be as you wish."

"Are you ready, my dear?" asked Rose, from the other side of the room.

"Not yet, wife. I shall stay half an hour longer, and if you ladies like to do the same we will send the carriage home with the children and their mammies, and let it return for you."

"What do you say, Aunt Wealthy and Miss Lottie?" inquired Mrs. Dinsmore.

"I prefer to stay and talk out my finish with Mrs. Travilla," said Miss Stanhope.

"I cast my vote on the same side," said Miss King. "But, my dear Mrs. Dinsmore, don't let us keep you."

"Thanks, no; but I, too, prefer another half hour in

this pleasant company."

The half hour flew away on swift wings, to Elsie especially.

"But why leave us at all tonight, auntie and Lottie?" she asked, as the ladies began their preparations for departure. "You are to be my guests for the rest of the winter, are you not?" Then turning, with a quick vivid blush, to Mrs. Travilla, "Mother, am I transcending my rights?"

"My dearest daughter, no; did I not say you were henceforth mistress of this house?"

"Yes, from its master down to the very horses in the stable and dogs in the kennel," laughed Mr. Travilla, coming softly up and stealing an arm about his wife's waist.

Everybody laughed.

"No, sir; I don't like to contradict you," retorted Elsie, coloring but looking lovingly into the eyes bent so fondly upon her, "but I am—nothing to you but your little wife," and her voice sank almost to a whisper with the last word.

"Ah? Well, dear child, that's enough for me," he said, in the same low tone.

"But, Lottie," she remarked aloud, "you are tying on your hat. Won't you stay?"

"Not tonight, thank you, Mrs. Travilla," answered the gay girl in her merry, lively tones.

"You are to be at the Oaks tomorrow, and perhaps I'll—well, we can settle the time there."

"And you, auntie?"

"Why, dearie, I think you'd better get your housekeeping a little used to your ways first. And it's better for starting out that young folks should be alone."

Mr. Dinsmore had stepped into the hall for his hat, and while the other ladies were making their adieus to her new mother, Elsie stole softly after him.

"My good-night kiss, papa," she whispered, putting her arms about his neck.

"My dear darling! My precious, precious child! How

glad I am to be able to give it to you once more, and to take my own from your own sweet lips," he said, clasping her closer. "God bless you and keep you, and ever cause his face to shine upon you."

CHAPTER EIGHTEENTH

O what passions then
What melting sentiments of kindly care,
On the new parents seize."

—THOMSON'S AGAMEMNON

There is none
In all this cold and hollow world, no fount
Of deep, strong, deathless love, save that within
A mother's heart!

—MRS. HEMANS

FINDING IT SO EVIDENTLY the wish of both her husband and his mother, Elsie quietly and at once assumed the reins of government.

But with that mother to go to for advice in every doubt and perplexity, and with a dozen or more of well-trained servants at her command, her post, though no sinecure, did not burden her with its duties. She still could find time for the cultivation of mind and heart, for daily walks and rides, and the enjoyment of society both at home and abroad.

Shortly after the return of the newly married pair, there was a grand party given in their honor at Roselands, another at Ashlands, one at Pinegrove, at the Oaks, and several other places; then a return was made by a brilliant affair of the kind at Ion.

But when at last this rather wearying round was over, they settled down to the quiet home life much more congenial to both. Always ready to entertain with unbounded hospitality, and ignoring none of the legitimate claims of the outside world, they were yet far more interested in the affairs of their own little one, made up of those nearest and dearest.

They were an eminently Christian household, carefully instructing their dependents in the things pertaining to godliness, urging them to faith in Jesus evidenced by good works; trying to make the way of salvation very clear to their often dull apprehension, and to recommend it by their own pure, consistent lives.

Night and morning all were called together—family and house servants—and Mr. Travilla read aloud a portion of Scripture, and led them in prayer and praise. Nor was a meal ever eaten without God's blessing having first been asked upon it.

There was but one drawback to Elsie's felicity—that she no longer dwelt under the same roof with her father; yet that was not so great, as a day seldom passed in which they did not meet once or oftener. It must be very urgent business, or a severe storm, that kept him from riding or driving over to Ion, unless his darling first appeared at the Oaks.

Aunt Wealthy and Lottie came to Ion within a fortnight after the return from Viamede, and while the former divided the rest of her stay at the South between Ion and the Oaks, Lottie spent nearly the whole of hers with Elsie.

In May, Harry Duncan came for his aunt, and Miss King returned with them to her paternal home. Our friends at Ion and the Oaks decided to spend their summer at home this year.

"We have traveled so much of late years," said Rose, "that I am really tired of it."

"And home is so dear and sweet," added Elsie. "I mean both Ion and the Oaks, Edward and papa—for somehow they seem to me to be both included in that one dear word."

"That is right," responded her father.

"Yes; we seem to be all one family," said Mr. Travilla, contentedly, fondling Rosebud, whom he had coaxed to a seat upon his knee; "and like a good spouse, I vote on the same side with my wife."

"I too," said his mother, looking affectionately upon them both. "I have no inclination to travel, and shall be much happier for having you all about me."

The summer glided rapidly by, and vanished, leaving at Ion a priceless treasure.

It was a soft, hazy, delicious September morning. Elsie sat in her pretty boudoir, half-reclining in the depths of a large velvet-cushioned easy chair. Her husband had left her a minute before, and she was—no, not quite alone, for her eyes were turning with a sweet, new light in them, upon a beautiful rosewood crib where, underneath the silken covers and resting on pillows of eiderdown, lay a tiny form, only a glimpse of the pink face and one wee doubled-up fist to be caught through the lace curtains so carefully drawn about the little sleeper.

A familiar step was heard in the outer room. The door opened quietly, and Elsie looking up cried, "Papa," in a delighted yet subdued tone.

"My darling," he said, coming to her and taking her in his arms. "How nice to see you up again; but you must be careful, very, very careful, not to overexert yourself."

"I am, my dear father, for Edward insists on it, and watches over me, and baby too, as if really afraid we might somehow slip away from him."

"He is quite right. There, you must not stand, recline in your chair again, while I help myself to a seat by your side. How are you today?"

"I think I never felt better in my life, papa; so strong and well that it seems absurd to be taking such care of myself."

"Not at all; you must do it. You seem to be alone with your babe. I hope you never lift her?"

"No, sir, not yet. That I shall not has been my husband's second order. Mammy is within easy call, just in the next room, and will come the instant she is wanted."

"Let me look at her—unless you think it will disturb her rest."

"Oh, no, sir." And the young mother gently drew aside the curtain of the crib.

The two bent over the sleeping babe, listening to its gentle breathing.

"Ah, papa, I feel so rich! You don't know how I love her!" whispered Elsie.

"Don't I, my daughter? Don't I know how I love you?" And his eyes turned with yearning affection upon her face, then back to that of the little one. "Six weeks old today, and a very cherub for beauty. Aunt Chloe tells me she is precisely my daughter over again, and I feel as if I had now an opportunity to recover what I lost in not having my first-born with me from her birth. Little Elsie, grandpa feels that you are his; his precious treasure."

The young mother's eyes grew misty with a strange mixture of emotion, in which love and joy were the deepest and strongest. Her arm stole round her father's neck.

"Dear papa, how nice of you to love her so—my precious darling. She is yours, too, almost as much as Edward's and mine. And I am sure if we should be taken away and you and she be left, you would be the same good father to her you have been to me."

"Much better, I hope. My dear daughter, I was far too hard with you at times. But I know you have forgiven it all long ago."

"Papa, dear papa, please don't ever talk of—of forgiveness from me. I was your own, and I believe you always did what you thought was for my good; and oh, what you have been, and are to me, not tongue can tell."

"Or you to me, my own beloved child," he answered with emotion.

The babe stirred, and opened its eyes with a little, "Coo, coo."

"Let me take her," said Mr. Dinsmore, turning back

the cover and gently lifting her from her cozy nest.

Elsie lay back among her cushions again, watching with delighted eyes as her father held and handled the wee body as deftly as the most competent child's nurse.

It was a very beautiful babe; the complexion soft, smooth, and very fair, with a faint pink tinge; the little, finely formed head covered with rings of golden hair that would some day change to the darker shade of her mother's, whose regular features and large, soft brown eyes she inherited also.

"Sweet little flower blossomed into his world of sin and sorrow! Elsie, dearest, remember that she is not yours, her father's, or mine, but only lent you a little while to be trained up for the Lord."

"Yes, papa, I know," she answered with emotion, "and I gave her to him even before her birth."

"I hope she will prove as like you in temper and disposition as she bids fair to be in looks."

"Papa, I should like her to be much better than I was."

He shook his head with a half-incredulous smile. "That could hardly be, if she has any human nature at all."

"Ah, papa, you forget how often I used to be naughty and disobedient, how often you had to punish me, particularly in that first year after you returned from Europe."

A look of pain crossed his features. "Daughter, dear, I am full of remorse when I think of that time. I fully deserved the epithet Travilla once bestowed upon me in his righteous indignation at my cruelty to my gentle, sensitive little girl."

"What was that, papa?" she asked, with a look of wonder and surprise.

"Dinsmore, you're a brute!"

"Papa, how could he say that!" and the fair face flushed with momentary excitement and anger towards the father of her child, whom she so thoroughly respected and so dearly loved.

"Ah, don't be angry with him," said Mr. Dinsmore. "I was the culprit. You cannot have forgotten your fall from the piano-stool which came so near making me childless? It was he who ran in first, lifted you, and laid you on the sofa with the blood streaming from the wounded temple over your curls and your white dress. Ah, I can never forget the sad sight, or the pang that shot through my heart with the thought that you were dead. It was as he laid you down that Travilla turned to me with those indignant words, and I felt that I fully deserved them. And yet I was even more cruel afterward, when next you refused to obey when I bade you offend against your conscience."

"Don't let us think or talk of it anymore, dear father. I love far better to dwell upon the long years that followed, full of the tenderest care and kindness. You certainly can find nothing to blame yourself with in them."

"Yes; I governed you too much. It would probably have ruined a less amiable temper, a less loving heart, than yours. It is well for parents to be sometimes a little blind to trivial faults. And I was so strict, so stern, so arbitrary, so severe. My dear, be more lenient to your child. But of course she will never find sternness in either you or her father."

"I think not, papa; unless she proves very headstrong. But you surely cannot mean to advise us not to require the prompt, cheerful, implicit obedience you have always exacted from all your children?"

"No, daughter; though you might sometimes excuse or pardon a little forgetfulness when the order has not been of vital importance," he answered, with a smile.

There was a moment's silence. Then, looking affectionately into her father's face, Elsie said, "I am so glad, papa, that we have had this talk. Edward and I have had several on the same subject—for we are very, very anxious to train our little one aright—and I find that we all agree. But you must be tired acting the part of nurse. Please lay her in my arms."

"I am not tired, but I see you want her," he answered with a smile, doing as she requested.

"Ah, you precious wee pet! You lovely, lovely little

darling!" the young mother said, clasping her child to her bosom, and softly kissing the velvet cheek. "Papa, is she really beautiful? Or is it only the mother love that makes her so in my eyes?"

"No; she is really a remarkably beautiful babe. Strangers pronounce her so as well as ourselves. Do you feel quite strong enough to hold her?"

"Oh, yes, sir; yes, indeed! The doctor says he thinks there would now be no danger in my lifting her, but—" laughingly, and with a fond look up into her husband's eyes, as at that moment he entered the room, "that old tyrant is so fearful of an injury to this piece of his personal property, that he won't let me."

"That old tyrant, eh?" he repeated, stooping to take a kiss from the sweet lips, and to bestow one on the wee face resting on her bosom

"Yes, you know you are," she answered, her eyes contradicting her words. "The idea of you forbidding me to lift my own baby!"

"My baby, my little friend," he said gaily.

Elsie laughed a low, silvery, happy laugh, musical as a chime of bells. "Our baby," she corrected. "But you have not spoken to papa."

"Ah, we said good morning out in the avenue. Dinsmore, since we are all three here together now, suppose we get Elsie's decision in regard to that matter we were consulting about."

"Very well."

"What matter?" she asked, looking a little curious.

"A business affair," replied her husband, taking a seat by her side.

"I have a very good offer for your New Orleans property, daughter," said Mr. Dinsmore. "Shall I accept it?"

"Do you think it advisable, papa? And you, Edward? I have great confidence in your judgments."

"We do. We think the money could be better and more safely invested in foreign stock. But it is for you to decide, and the property is yours."

"More safely invested? I thought I had heard you both say real estate was the safest of all investments."

"Usually," replied her father, "but we fear property there is likely to depreciate in value."

"Well, papa, please do just as you and my husband think best. You both know far more about these things than I do, and so I should rather trust your judgment than my own."

"Then I shall make the sale, and I think the time will come when you will be very glad that I did."

Mr. Dinsmore presently said good-bye and went away, leaving them alone.

"Are not your arms tired, little wife?" asked Mr. Travilla.

"No, dear. Ah, it is so sweet to have her little head lying here, to feel her little form, and know that she is my own, own precious treasure."

He rose, gently lifted her in his arms, put himself in the easy chair and placed her on his knee.

"Now I have you both. Darling, do you know that I love you better today than I ever did before?"

"Ah, but you have said that many times," she answered, with an arch, yet tender smile.

"And it is always true. Each day I think my love as great as it can be, but the next I find it still greater."

"And I have felt angry with you today, for the first time since you told me of your love." Her tone was remorseful and pleading, as though she would crave forgiveness.

"Angry with me, my dearest? In what can I have offended?" he asked, in sorrowful surprise.

"Papa was saying that he had sometimes been too hard with me, and had fully deserved the epithet you once bestowed upon him in your righteous indignation. It was when I fell from the piano-stool. Do you remember?"

"Ah, yes, I can never forget it. And I called him a brute. But you will forgive what occurred so long ago, and in a moment of anger aroused by my great love for you?"

"Forgive you, my husband? Ah, it is I who should crave forgiveness, and I do, though it was but a momentary feeling; and now I love you all the better for the great loving heart that prompted the exclamation."

"We will exchange forgiveness," he whispered, folding her closer to his heart.

CHAPTER NINETEENTH

Sweet is the image of the brooding dove!
Holy as heaven a mother's tender love!
The love of many prayers, and many tears
Which changes not with dim, declining years—
The only love which, on this teeming earth,
Asks no return for passion's wayward birth.

—MRS. NORTON'S DREAM

Death is another life.

—BAILEY

NO MORTAL TONGUE or pen can describe the new, deep fountain of love the birth of her child had opened in our Elsie's heart.

Already a devoted wife and daughter, she was the tenderest, most careful, most judicious of mothers, watching vigilantly over the welfare—physical, moral, and spiritual—of her precious charge.

Often she took it with her to her closet, or kneeling beside its cradle, sent up fervent petitions to him who, while on earth, said, "Suffer the little children, and forbid them not, to come unto Me," that he would receive her little one, and early make her a lamb of his fold.

And even before the child could comprehend, she began to tell it of that dear Saviour and his wondrous love. Then, as soon as it could speak, she taught it to lisp a simple prayer to him.

Little Elsie was almost the idol of her father and grandparents, who all looked upon her as a sort of second edition of her mother, more and more so as she grew in size, in beauty, and intelligence. Our Elsie seemed to find no cloud in her sky during that first year of her motherhood. "I thought I was as perfectly happy as possible in this world, before our darling came," she said to her husband one day, "but I am far happier now, for oh, such a well-spring of joy as she is!"

"I am sure I can echo and reecho your words," he answered, folding the child to his heart. "How rich I have grown in the last two years! My two Elsies, more precious than the wealth of the world! Sometimes I'm half afraid I love you both with an idolatrous affection, and that God will take you from me." His voice trembled with the last words.

"I have had that fear also," she said, coming to his side and laying her hand on his arm. "But Edward, if we put God first, we cannot love each other, nor this wee precious pet, too dearly."

"No, you are right, little wife. But we must not expect to continue always, or very long, so free from trial; for 'we must through much tribulation enter into the kingdom of God.' And 'many are the afflictions of the righteous.'"

"But the Lord delivereth him out of them all," she responded, finishing the quotation.

"Yes, dearest, I know that trials and troubles will come, but not of themselves, and what our Father sends, he will give us strength to bear. "The Lord God is a sun and shield, the Lord will give grace and glory.'"

This conversation was held when the little girl was about a year old.

Early in the following winter Elsie said to the dear old Mrs. Travilla, "Mother, I'm afraid you are not well. You are losing flesh and color, and do not seem so strong as usual. Mamma remarked it to me today, and asked what ailed you."

"I am doing very well, dear," the old lady answered

with a placid smile, and in her own gentle, quiet tones.

"Mother, dear mother, something is wrong. You don't deny that you are ill!" and Elsie's tone was full of alarm and distress, as she hastily seated herself upon an ottoman beside Mrs. Travilla's easy chair, and earnestly scanned the aged face she loved so well. "We must have Dr. Barton here to see you. May I not send at once?"

"No, dearest, I have already consulted him, and he is doing all he can for my relief."

"But cannot cure you?"

The answer came after a moment's pause.

"No, dear, but I had hoped it would be much longer ere my cross cast its shadow over either your or Edward's path."

Elsie could not speak. She only took the pale hands in hers, and pressed them again and again to her quivering lips, while her eyes filled to overflowing.

"Dear daughter," said the calm, sweet voice, "do not grieve that I have got my summons home, for dearly, dearly as I love you all, I am often longing to see the face of my Beloved—of him who hath redeemed me and washed me from my sins in his own precious blood."

Mr. Travilla from the next room had heard it all. Hurrying in, he knelt by her side and folded his arms about her. "Mother," he said, hoarsely, "oh, is it, can it be so? Are we to lose you?"

"No, my son; blessed be God, I shall not be lost, but only gone before. So don't be troubled and sorrowful when you see me suffer. Remember that he loves me far better than you can, and will never give me one unneeded pang.

"Well may I bear joyfully all he sends; for 'our light affliction, which is but for a moment, worketh for us a far more exceeding and eternal weight of glory,' and he has said, 'When thou passeth through the waters, I will be with thee: and through the floods, they shall not overflow thee: when thou walkest through the fire thou shalt not be burned, neither shall the flames kindle upon thee.'"

"And he is faithful to his promises. But we will not let you die yet, my mother, if anything in the wide world can save you. There are more skillful physicians than Dr. Barton; we will consult them—"

"My son, the disease is one the whole profession agree in pronouncing incurable, and to travel would be torture. No, be content to let me die at home, with you and this beloved daughter to smooth my dying pillow, our wee precious pet to while away the pain with her pretty baby ways, and my own pastor to comfort me with God's truth and sweet thoughts of heaven."

Elsie looked the question her trembling lips refused to utter.

"I shall not probably leave you soon," said the old lady. "It is a slow thing, the doctor tells me. It will take some time to run its course."

Elsie could scarce endure the anguish in her husband's face. Silently she placed herself by his side, her arm about his neck, and laid her cheek to his.

He drew her yet closer, the other arm still embracing his mother. "Are you suffering much, dearest mother?"

"Not more than he giveth me strength to bear, and his consolations are not small.

"My dear children, I have tried to hid this from you lest it should mar your happiness. Do not let it do so; it is no cause of regret to me. I have lived my three-score years and ten, and if by reason of strength they should be four-score, yet would their strength be labor and sorrow. I am deeply thankful that our Father has decreed to spare me the infirmities of extreme old age, by calling me home to that New Jerusalem where sin and sorrow, pain and feebleness, are unknown."

"But to see you suffer, mother!" groaned her son.

"Think on the dear Hand that sends the pain—so infinitely less than what he bore for me; that it is but for a moment; and of the weight of glory it is to work for me. Try, my dear children, to be entirely submissive to his will."

"We will, mother," they answered; "and to be cheerful for your sake."

A shadow had fallen upon the brightness of the hitherto happy home—a shadow of a great, coming sorrow—and the present grief of knowing that the dear mother, though ever patient, cheerful, resigned, was enduring almost constant and often very severe pain.

They watched over her with tenderest love and care, doing everything in their power to relieve, strengthen, comfort her, never giving way in her presence to the grief that often wrung their hearts.

Dearly as Mr. Travilla and Elsie had loved each other before, this community of sorrow drew them still closer together—as did their love for, and joy and pride in, their beautiful child.

The consolations of God were not small with any of our friends at Ion and the Oaks, yet was it a winter of trial to all.

For some weeks after the above conversation, Mr. Dinsmore and Rose called every day, and showed themselves sincere sympathizers; but young Horace and little Rosebud were taken with the scarlet fever in its worst form, and the parents being much with them, did not venture to Ion for fear of carrying the infection to wee Elsie.

By God's blessing upon skillful medical advice and attention, and the best of nursing, the children were brought safely through the trying ordeal, the disease leaving no evil effects, as it so often does. But scarcely had they convalesced when Mr. Dinsmore fell ill of typhoid fever, though of a rather mild type.

Then, as he began to go about again, Rose took to her bed with what proved to be a far more severe and lasting attack of the same disease. For weeks her life was in great jeopardy, and even after the danger was past, the improvement was so very slow that her husband was filled with anxiety for her.

Meanwhile the beloved invalid at Ion was slowly sinking to the grave. Nay, rather, as she would have it, journeying rapidly towards her heavenly home, "the land of the leal," the city which hath foundations, whose builder and Maker is God.

She suffered, but with a patience that never failed, a cheerfulness and joyful looking to the end, that made her sick-room a sort of little heaven below.

Her children were with her almost constantly through the day, but Mr. Travilla, watchful as ever over his idolized young wife, would not allow her to lose a night's rest, insisting on her retiring at the usual hour. Nor would he allow her ever to assist in lifting his mother, or any of the heavy nursing. She might smooth her pillows, give her medicines, order dainties prepared to tempt the failing appetite, and oversee the negro women, who were capable nurses, and one of whom was always at hand night and day, ready to do whatever was required.

Elsie dearly loved her mother-in-law, and felt it both a duty and delight to do all in her power for her comfort and consolation, but when she heard that her own beloved father was ill, she could not stay away from him, but made a daily visit to the Oaks and to his bedside. She was uniformly cheerful in his presence, but wept in secret because she was denied the privilege of nursing him in his illness.

Then her sorrow and anxiety for Rose were great, and all the more because, Mrs. Travilla being then at the worst, she could very seldom leave her for even the shortest call at the Oaks.

In the afternoon of a sweet bright Sabbath in March, a little group gathered in Mrs. Travilla's room. Her pastor was there: a man of large heart full of tender sympathy for the sick, the suffering, the bereaved, the poor, the distressed in mind, body, or estate; a man mighty in the Scriptures; with its warnings, its counsels, its assurances, its sweet and precious promises ever ready on his tongue; one who by much study of the Bible, accompanied by fervent prayer for the wisdom promised to him that asks it, had learned to wield wisely and with success "the sword of the Spirit which is the word of God." Like Noah he was a preacher of righteousness, and like Paul could say, "I ceased not to warn every one night and day with tears."

He had brought with him one of his elders, a man of like spirit, gentle, kind, tender, ever ready to obey the command to "weep with those that weep and rejoice with those that rejoice," a man silver-haired and growing feeble with age, yet so meek and lowly in heart, so earnest and childlike in his approaches to our Father, that he seemed on the very verge of heaven.

"Comfort ye, comfort ye my people, saith your God." Often had these two been in that sick-room, comforting the aged saint as she neared "the valley of the shadow of death."

Today they had come again on the same Christ-like errand, and for the last time; for all could see that she stood on Jordan's very brink, its cold waters already creeping up about her feet.

Mr. Dinsmore, Mr. Travilla, and Elsie were present; also, a little withdrawn from the others, Aunt Chloe, Uncle Joe, and a few of the old house servants who were Christians. "The rich and the poor meet together; the Lord is the Maker of them all."

It was a sweetly solemn service, refreshing to the soul of each one there; most of all, perhaps, to that of her who would so soon be casting her crown at the Master's feet. "I am almost home," she said with brightening countenance, her low, sweet voice breaking the solemn stillness of the room. "I am entering the valley, but without fear, for Jesus is with me. I hear him saying to me, 'Fear not; I have redeemed thee; thou art mine.'"

"He is all your hope and trust, dear friend, is he not?" asked her pastor.

"All, all; his blood and righteousness are all my hope. All my righteousnesses are as filthy rags; all my best services have need to be forgiven. I am vile; but his blood cleanseth from all sin, and he has washed me in it and made me mete for the inheritance of the saints in light."

"Dear sister," said the old elder, taking her hand in a

last farewell, "good-bye for a short season. 'Twill not be long till we meet before the throne. Do not fear to cross the river, for he will be with you, and will not let you sink."

"No, the everlasting arms are underneath and around me, and he will never leave nor forsake."

"'Precious in the sight of the Lord is the death of his saints,'" said the pastor, taking the feeble hand in his turn. "Fear not; you shall be more than conqueror through him that loved us."

"Yes, the battle is fought, the victory is won, and I hear him saying to me, 'Come up hither.' Oh, I shall be there very soon—a sinner saved by grace!"

The pastor and elder withdrew, Mr. Travilla going with them to the door. Elsie brought a cordial and held it to her mother's lips, Mr. Dinsmore gently raising her head. "Thank you both," she said, with the courtesy for which she had ever been distinguished. Then, as Mr. Dinsmore settled her more comfortably on her pillows, and Elsie set aside the empty cup, "Horace, my friend, farewell till we meet in a better land. Elsie, darling," laying her pale thin hand on the bowed head, "you have been a dear, dear daughter to me, such a comfort, such a blessing! May the Lord reward you."

Elsie had much ado to control her feelings. Her father passed his arm about her waist and made her rest her head upon his shoulder.

"Mother, how are you now?" asked Mr. Travilla, coming in and taking his place on his wife's other side, close by the bed of the dying one.

"All is peace, peace, the sweetest peace. I have nothing to do but to die. I am in the river, but the Lord upholdeth me with his hand, and I have almost reached the farther shore."

She then asked for the babe, kissed and blessed it,

and bade her son good-bye.

"Sing to me, children, the twenty-third psalm."

Controlling their emotion by a strong effort, that they might minister to her comfort, they sang; the three voices blending in sweet harmony.

"Thank you," she said again, as the last strain died away. "Hark! I hear sweeter, richer melody. The angels have come for me, Jesus is here. Lord Jesus receive my spirit."

There was an enraptured upward glance, an ecstatic smile, then the eyes closed and all was still. Without a struggle or a groan the spirit had dropped its tenement of clay and sped away on its upward flight.

It was like a translation. A deep hush filled the room, while for a moment they seemed almost to see the "glory that dwelleth in Immanuel's land." They scarcely wept, their joy for her, the ransomed of the Lord, almost swallowing up their grief for themselves.

But soon Elsie began to tremble violently, shudder after shudder shaking her whole frame, and in sudden alarm her husband and father led her from the room.

"Oh, Elsie, my darling, my precious wife!" cried Travilla, in a tone of agony, as they laid her upon a sofa in her boudoir. "Are you ill? Are you in pain?"

"Give way, daughter, and let the tears come;" said Mr. Dinsmore, tenderly bending over her and gently smoothing her hair. "It will do you good, bring relief to the overstrained nerves and full heart."

Even as he spoke the barriers which for so many hours had been steadily, firmly resisting the grief and anguish swelling in her breast, suddenly gave way, and tears poured out like a flood.

Her husband knelt by her side and drew her head to a resting-place on his breast, while her father, with one of her hands in his, softly repeated text after text speaking of the bliss of the blessed dead.

She grew calmer. "Don't be alarmed about me, dear Edward, dear papa," she said in her low sweet tones. "I don't think I am ill, and heavy as our loss is, dearest husband, how we must rejoice for her. Let me go and perform the last office of love for her—our precious mother. I am better; I am able."

"No, no, you are not; you must not;" both answered in a breath. "Aunt Dinah and Aunt Chloe will do it all tenderly and lovingly as if she had been of their own flesh and blood," added Mr. Travilla, in trembling tones.

Chapter Twentieth

There are smiles and tears in the mother's eyes,
For her new-born babe beside her lies;
Oh, heaven of bliss! when the heart o'er flows
With the rapture a mother only knows!

—Henry Ware, Jr.

Mrs. Travilla was laid to rest in their own family burial ground, her dust sleeping beside that of her husband, and children who had died in infancy; and daily her surviving son carried his little daughter thither to scatter flowers upon "dear grandma's grave."

It was not easy to learn to live without the dear mother; they missed her constantly. Yet was their sorrow nearly swallowed up in joy for her—the blessed dead who had departed to be with Christ in glory and to go no more out forever from that blissful presence.

Their house was not made dark and gloomy, the sunlight and sweet spring air entered freely as of yore. Nor did they suffer gloom to gather in their hearts or cloud their faces. Each was filled with thankfulness for the spared life of the other, and of their darling little daughter.

And scarce a week had passed away since heaven's portals opened wide to the ransomed soul, when a new voice—that of a son and heir—was heard in the old home, and many hearts rejoiced in the birth of the beautiful boy.

"God has sent him to comfort you in your sorrow,

dearest," Elsie whispered, as her husband brought the babe—fresh from its first robing by Aunt Chloe's careful hands—and with a very proud and happy face laid it in her arms.

"Yes," he said, in moved tones. "Oh, that men would praise the Lord for his goodness, and for his wonderful works to the children of men!"

"If mother could only have seen him!" And tears gathered in the soft, sweet eyes of the young mother gazing so tenderly upon the tiny face on her arm.

"She will, one day, I trust. I have been asking for this new darling that he may be an heir of glory, that he may early be gathered into the fold of the good Shepherd."

"And I, too," she said, "have besought my precious Saviour to be the God of my children also from their birth."

"What do you intend to call your son?"

"What do you?" she asked, smiling up at him.

"Horace, for your father, if you like."

"And I had thought of Edward, for his father and yours. Horace Edward. Will that do?"

"I am satisfied, if you are. But Edward would do for the next."

"But he may never come to claim it," she said, laughing. "Is papa in the house?"

"Yes, and delighted to learn that he has a grandson."

"Oh, bring him here and let me see the first meeting between them."

"Can you bear the excitement?"

"I promise not to be excited; and it always does me good to see my dear father."

Mr. Dinsmore came softly in, kissed very tenderly the pale face on the pillow, then took a long look at the tiny pink one nestling to her side.

"Ah, isn't he a beauty? I have made you two grandfathers now, you dear papa!" she said, indulging in a little jest to keep down the emotions tugging at her heartstrings. "Do you begin to feel old and decrepit, mon père?"

"Not very," he said smiling, and softly smoothing her hair. "Not more so today than I did yesterday. But now I must leave you to rest and sleep. Try, my darling, for all our sakes, to be very prudent, very calm and quiet."

"I will, papa; and don't trouble about me. You know I am in good hands. Ah, stay a moment! Here is Edward bringing wee bit Elsie to take her first peep at her little brother."

"Mamma," cried the child, stretching out her little arms towards the bed. "Mamma, take Elsie."

"Mamma can't, darling; poor mamma is so sick," said Mr. Travilla. "Stay with papa."

"But she shall kiss her mamma, dear, precious little pet," Elsie said. "Please hold her close for a minute, papa, and let her kiss her mother."

He complied under protest, in which Mr. Dinsmore joined, that he feared it would be too much for her; and the soft baby hands patted the wan cheeks, the tiny rosebud mouth was pressed again and again to the pale lips, with rapturous cooings, "Mamma, mamma!"

"There, pet, that will do," said her father. "Now, see what mamma has for you."

"Look, mother's darling," Elsie said with a glad smile, exposing to view the tiny face by her side.

"Baby!" cried the little girl, with a joyous shout, clapping her chubby hands. "Pretty baby Elsie take," and the small arms were held out entreatingly.

"No, Elsie is too little to hold it," said her papa, "but she may kiss it very softly."

The child availed herself of the permission, then gently patting the newcomer, repeated her glad cry, "Baby, pretty baby."

"Elsie's little brother," said her mamma, tenderly. "Now, dearest, let mammy take her away," she added, sinking back on her pillows with a weary sigh.

He complied, then bent over her with a look of concern. "I should not have brought her in," he said anxiously. "It has been too much for you."

"But I wanted so to see her delight. One more kiss,

papa, before you go, and then I'll try to sleep."

Elsie did not recover so speedily and entirely as before—after the birth of her first babe—and those to whom she was so dear grew anxious and troubled about her.

"You want change, daughter," Mr. Dinsmore said, coming in one morning and finding her lying pale and languid on a sofa, "and we are all longing to have you at home. Do you feel equal to a drive over to the Oaks?"

"I think I do, papa," she answered, brightening. "Edward took me for a short drive yesterday, and I felt better for it."

"Then, dearest, come home to your father's house and stay there as long as you can; bring babies and nurses and come. Your own suite of rooms is quite ready for you," he said, caressing her tenderly.

"Ah, papa, how nice to go back and feel at home in my own father's house again," she said, softly stroking his head with her thin white hand as he bent over her, the sweet soft eyes, gazing full into his, brimming over with love and joy. "I shall go, if Edward doesn't object. I'd like to start this minute. But you haven't told me how poor mamma is today?"

"Not well, not very much stronger than you are, I fear," he answered, with a slight sigh. "But your coming will do her a world of good. Where is Travilla?"

"Here, and quite at your service," replied Mr. Travilla's cheery voice, as he came in from the garden with his little daughter in his arms.

He set her down, and while he exchanged greetings with Mr. Dinsmore, she ran to her mother with a bouquet of lovely sweet-scented spring blossoms they had been gathering "for mamma."

"Thank you, mother's darling," Elsie said, accepting the gift and tenderly caressing the giver; "you and papa, too. But see who is here?"

The child turned to look, and with a joyous cry "G'anpa!" ran into his outstretched arms.

"Grandpa's own wee pet," he said, hugging the little

form close and covering the baby face with kisses. "Will you come and live with grandpa in his home for awhile?"

"Mamma? Papa too?" she asked, turning a wistful look on them.

"Oh, yes; yes indeed, mamma and papa too."

"Baby?"

"Yes, baby and mammies and all. Will you come?"

"May Elsie, mamma?"

"Yes, pet; we will all go, if your papa is willing." And her soft eyes sought her husband's face with a look of love and confidence that said she well knew he would never deny her any good in his power to bestow.

"I have been proposing to my daughter to take possession again, for as long a time as she finds it convenient and agreeable, of her old suite of rooms at the Oaks. I think the change would do her good, and perhaps you and the little ones also," Mr. Dinsmore explained.

"Thank you; I think it would. When will you go, little wife?"

"Papa proposes taking me at once."

"My carriage is at the door, and this is the pleasantest part of the day," remarked Mr. Dinsmore.

"Ah, yes; then take Elsie with you, and I will follow shortly with the children and servants. There is no reason in the world why she should not go, if she wishes, and stay as long as she likes."

The change proved beneficial to Elsie. It was so pleasant to find herself again a member of her father's family; and that even without a short separation from her husband and little ones.

Here, too, absent from the scenes so closely associated with the memory of her beloved mother-in-law, she dwelt less upon her loss, while at the same time she was entertained and cheered by constant intercourse with father, Rose, and young brother and sister. It was indeed a cheering thing to all parties to be thus brought together for a time as one family in delightful social intercourse.

Yet, though the invalids improved in spirits, and to

some extent in other respects, they did not regain their usual strength, and the physicians recommending travel, particularly a sea voyage, it was finally decided to again visit Europe for an indefinite period, the length of their stay to depend upon circumstances.

It was in June, 1860, they left their homes; and traveling northward, paid a short visit to relatives and friends in Philadelphia; then took the steamer for Europe.

A few weeks later found them cozily established in a handsome villa overlooking the beautiful bay of Naples.

They formed but one family here as at the Oaks; each couple having their own private suite of apartments, while all other rooms were used in common and their meals taken together; an arrangement preferred by all; Mr. Dinsmore and his daughter especially rejoicing in it, as giving them almost as much of each other's society as before her marriage.

In this lovely spot they planned to remain for some months, perchance a year—little dreaming that five years would roll their weary round ere they should see home and dear native land again.

Chapter Twenty-first

THE SEA VOYAGE had done much for the health of both ladies, and the soft Italian air carried on the cure. Mr. Dinsmore, too, had recovered his usual strength, for the first time since his attack of fever.

There was no lack of good society at their command, good both socially and intellectually. American, English, Italian, French, etc.; many former friends and acquaintances and others desiring to be introduced by these; but none of our party felt disposed at that time to mix much with the outside world.

Elsie's deep mourning was for her sufficient excuse for declining all invitations, while Rose could plead her still precarious state of health.

She wore no outward badge of mourning for Mrs. Travilla, but felt deep and sincere grief at her loss, for the two had been intimate and dear friends for many years, the wide disparity in age making their intercourse and affection much like that of mother and daughter.

The condition of political affairs in their own country was another thing that caused our friends to feel more exclusive and somewhat reluctant to mingle with those of other nationalities. Every mail brought them letters and papers from both North and South, and from their distant standpoint they watched with deep interest and anxiety the course of events fraught with such momentous consequences to their native land.

Neither Mr. Dinsmore nor Mr. Travilla had ever been a politician, but both they and their wives were dear lovers of their country, by which they meant the whole Union. The three who were natives of the South acknowledged that that section was dearer to them than any part; while Rose said she knew no difference—it was all her own beloved native land, to her mind one and indivisible.

They led a cheerful, quiet life in their Italian home, devoting themselves to each other and their children, Mr. Dinsmore acting the part of tutor to young Horace, as he had done to Elsie.

Her little ones were the pets and playthings of the entire household, while she and their father found the sweetest joy in caring for them and watching over and assisting the development of their natures—mental, moral, and physical. Their children would never be left to the care and training of servants, however faithful and devoted.

Nor would those of Mr. Dinsmore and Rose. In the esteem of these wise, Christian parents the God-given charge of their own offspring took undoubted precedence of the claims of society.

Thus placidly passed the summer and autumn, the monotony of their secluded life relieved by the enjoyment of literary pursuits, and varied by walks, rides, drives, and an occasional sail, in bright, still weather, over the waters of the lovely bay.

Elsie entered the drawing-room one morning, with the little daughter in her arms. The child was beautiful as a cherub, the mother sweet and fair as ever, nor a day older in appearance than while yet a girl in her father's house.

She found him sole occupant of the room, pacing to and fro with downcast eyes and troubled countenance. But looking up quickly at the sound of her footsteps he came hastily towards her.

"Come to grandpa," he said, holding out his hands to the little one; then as he took her in his arms, "My dear daughter, if I had any authority over you now—"

"Papa," she interrupted, blushing deeply, while the quick tears sprang to her eyes, "you hurt me! Please don't speak so. I am as ready now as ever to obey your slightest behest."

"Then, my darling, don't carry this child. You are not strong, and I fear will do yourself an injury. She can walk very well now, and if necessary to have her carried, call upon me, her father, or one of the servants. Aunt Chloe, Uncle Joe, Dinah, one or another is almost sure to be at hand."

"I will try to follow out your wishes, papa. Edward has said the same thing to me, and no doubt you are right; but it is so sweet to have her in my arms, and so hard to refuse when she asks to be taken up."

"You mustn't ask mamma to carry you," Mr. Dinsmore said to the child, caressing her tenderly as he spoke. "Poor mamma is not strong, and you will make her sick."

They had seated themselves side by side upon a sofa. The little one turned a piteous look upon her mother, and with a quivering lip and fast-filling eyes, said, "Mamma sick? Elsie tiss her, make her well?"

"No, my precious pet, mother isn't sick; so don't cry," Elsie answered, receiving the offered kiss, as the babe left her grandfather's knee and crept to her; then the soft little hands patted her on the cheeks and the chubby arms clung about her neck.

But catching sight, through the open window, of her father coming up the garden walk, wee Elsie hastily let go her hold, slid to the floor, and ran to meet him.

Mr. Dinsmore seemed again lost in gloomy thought.

"Papa, dear, what is it? What troubles you so?" asked Elsie, moving closer to him, and leaning affectionately on his shoulder, while the soft eyes sought his with a wistful, anxious expression.

He put his arm about her, and just touching her cheek with his lips, heaved a deep sigh. "The papers bring us bad news. Lincoln is elected."

"Ah well, let us not borrow trouble, papa. Perhaps he may prove a pretty good president after all."

"Just what I think," remarked Mr. Travilla, who had come in with his little girl in his arms at the moment of Mr. Dinsmore's announcement, and seated himself on his wife's other side. "Let us wait and see. All may go right with our country yet."

Mr. Dinsmore shook his head sadly. "I wish I could think so, but in the past history of all republics whenever section has arrayed itself against section the result has been either a peaceful separation, or civil war; nor can we hope to be a exception to the rule."

"I should mourn over either," said Elsie. "I cannot bear to contemplate the dismemberment of our great, glorious old Union. Foreign nations would never respect either portion as they do the undivided whole."

"No; and I can't believe either section can be so mad as to go that length," remarked her husband, fondling his baby daughter as he spoke. "The North, of course, does not desire a separation; but if the South goes, will be pretty sure to let her go peaceably."

"I doubt it, Travilla. And even if a peaceable separation should be allowed at first, so many causes of contention would result—such as the control of the navigation of the Mississippi, the refusal of the North to restore runaway negroes, etc., etc.—that it would soon come to blows."

"Horace, you frighten me," said Rose, who had come in while they were talking.

The color faded from Elsie's cheek, and a shudder ran over her, as she turned eagerly to hear her husband reply.

"Why cross the bridge before we come to it, Dinsmore?" he answered cheerily, meeting his wife's anxious look with one so fond and free from care, that her heart grew light. "Surely there'll be no fighting where there is no yoke of oppression to cast off. There can be no effect without a cause."

"The accursed lust of power on the part of a few selfish, unprincipled men, may invent a cause, and for the carrying out of their own ambitious schemes, they may lead the people to believe and act upon it. No one proposes to interfere with our institution where it already exists—even the Republican party has emphatically denied any such intention—yet the hue and cry has been raised that slavery will be abolished by the incoming administration, arms put into the hands of the blacks, and a servile insurrection will bring untold horrors to the hearths and homes of the South."

"Oh, dreadful, dreadful!" cried Rose.

"But, my dear, there is really no such danger: the men—unscrupulous politicians—do not believe it themselves, but they want power, and as they could never succeed in getting the masses to rebel to compass their selfish ends, they have invented this falsehood and are deceiving the people with it."

"Don't put all the blame on one side, Dinsmore," said Mr. Travilla.

"No; that would be very unfair. The framers of our constitution looked to gradual emancipation to rid us of this blot on our escutcheon, this palpable inconsistency between our conduct and our political creed.

"It did so in a number of the States, and probably would ere this in all, but for the fierce attacks of a few ultra-abolitionists, who were more zealous to pull the mote out of their brother's eye than the beam out of their own, and so exasperated the Southern people by their wholesale abuse and denunciations, that all thought of emancipation was given up.

"It is human nature to cling the tighter to anything another attempts to force from you, even though you may have felt ready enough to give it up of your own free will."

"Very true," said Travilla, "and Garrison and his crew would have been at better work repenting of their own sins, than denouncing those of their neighbors."

"But, papa, you don't think it can come to war, a civil war, in our dear country? The best land the sun shines on; and where there is none of the oppression that makes a wise man mad!"

"I fear it, daughter, I greatly fear it, but we will cast this care, as well as all others, upon him who 'doeth according to His will, in the army of heaven and among the inhabitants of the earth.'"

What a winter of uncertainty and gloom to Americans, both at home and abroad, was that of 1860-61. Each mail brought to our anxious friends in Naples news calculated to depress them more and more in view of the calamities that seemed to await their loved land.

State after State was seceding and seizing upon United States property within its limits—forts, arsenals, navy-yards, custom-houses, mints, ships, armories, and military stores—while the government at Washington remained inactive, doubtless fearing to precipitate the civil strife.

Still Mr. Travilla, Rose, and Elsie, like many lovers of the Union, both North and South, clung to the hope that war might yet be averted.

At length came the news of the formation of the Confederacy, Davis's election as its president, then of the firing upon the Star of the West, an unarmed vessel bearing troops and supplies to Fort Sumter.

"Well, the first gun has been fired," said Mr. Dinsmore, with a sigh, as he laid down the paper from which he had been reading the account.

"But perhaps it may be the only one, papa," remarked Elsie hopefully.

"I wish it may," replied her father, rising and beginning to pace to and fro, as was his wont when excited or disturbed.

The next news from America was looked for with intense anxiety. It was delayed longer than usual, and at length a heavy mail came, consisting of letters and papers of various dates from the twelfth to the twentieth of April, and bringing news of the most exciting character in the fall of Fort Sumter, the call of the president for seventy-five thousand troops to defend the capital, the seizure of the United States armory at Harper's Ferry by the Confederates, the attack on the Massachusetts troops while passing through Baltimore, and lastly the seizure of Norfolk Navy-yard.

Dinner was just over at the villa, the family still chatting over the dessert, children and all in an unusually merry mood, when this mail was brought in by a servant, and handed to Mr. Dinsmore.

He promptly distributed it, took up the paper of the earliest date, and glancing over the headings, exclaimed, with a groan, "It has come!"

"What?" queried the others, in excited chorus.

"War! My country! Oh, my country! Fort Sumter has fallen after a terrific bombardment of thirty-six hours." And he proceeded to read aloud the account of the engagement, the others listening in almost breathless silence.

"And they have dared to fire upon the flag! The emblem of our nationality, the symbol of Revolutionary glory—to tear it down and trample it in the dust!" cried Mr. Travilla, pushing back his chair in unwonted excitement. "Shameful, shameful!"

Tears were rolling down Elsie's cheeks, and Rose's eyes were full.

"Let us adjourn to the library and learn together all these papers and letters can tell us," said Mr. Dinsmore. rising. "'Twill be better so; we shall need the support of each other's sympathy."

He led the way and the rest followed.

The papers were examined first, by the gentlemen, now the one and now the other reading an article aloud, the excitement and distress of all increasing with each item of intelligence in regard to public affairs. Rose and Elsie opened their letters, and now and then, in the short pauses of the reading, cast a hasty glance at their contents.

Elsie's were from her Aunt Adelaide, Walter, and Enna; Rose's from her mother, Richard, May, and Sophie.

The last seemed written in a state of distraction.

"Rose, Rose, I think I shall go crazy! My husband and his brothers have enlisted in the Confederate army. They, Harry especially, are furious at the North and full of fight; and I know my brothers at home will enlist on the other side, and what if they should meet and kill each other! Oh, dear! Oh, dear! My heart is like to break!

"And what is it all about? I can't see that anybody's oppressed, but when I tell Harry so, he just laughs and says, 'No, we're not going to wait till they have time to rivet our chains.' 'But,' I say, 'I've had neither sight nor sound of chains, wait at least till you hear their clank.' Then he laughs again, but says soothingly, 'Never mind, little wife, don't distress yourself. The North won't fight, or if they do try it, will soon give it up.' But I know they won't give up: they wouldn't be Americans if they did.

"Arthur and Walter Dinsmore were here yesterday, and Arthur is worse than Harry a great deal—actually told me he wouldn't hesitate to shoot down any or all of my brothers, if he met them in Federal uniform. Walter is almost silent on the subject, and has not yet enlisted. Arthur taunted him with being for the Union, and said if he was quite sure of it he'd shoot him, or help hang him to the nearest tree.

"Oh, Rose! Pray, pray that this dreadful war may be averted!"

Rose felt almost stunned with horror as she read, but her tears fell fast as she hurriedly perused the contents of the other three, learning from them that Richard, Harold, and Fred had already enlisted, and Edward would do the same should the war continue long.

"My heart is torn in two!" she cried, looking piteously up in her husband's face, with the tears streaming down her own.

"What is it, my darling?" he asked, coming to her and taking her cold hands in his.

"Oh my country! My country! My brothers, too—and yours! They are pitted against each other—have enlisted in the opposing armies. Oh, Horace, Horace! What ever shall we do?"

"God reigns, dearest; let that comfort you and all of us," he said, in moved tones. "It is dreadful, dreadful! Brothers, friends, neighbors, with hearts full of hatred and ready to imbrue their hands in each other's blood; and for what? That a few ambitious, selfish, unscrupulous men may retain and increase their power—for this they are ready to shed the blood of tens of thousands of their own countrymen, and bring utter ruin upon our beautiful, sunny South."

"Oh, papa, surely not!" cried Elsie. "These papers say the war cannot last more than three months."

"They forget that it will be American against American. If it is over in three years, 'twill be shorter than I expect."

Elsie was weeping, scarcely less distressed than Rose.

"We will, at least, hope for better things, little wife," her husband said, drawing her to him with caressing motion. "What do your letters say?"

"They are full of the war. It is the all-absorbing theme with them, as with us. Aunt Adelaide's is very sad. Her heart clings to the South, as ours do; yet, like us, she has a strong love for the old Union.

"And she's very fond of her husband, who, she says, is very strong for the Government. And then, besides her distress at the thought that he will enlist, her heart is torn with anguish because her brothers and his are in the opposing armies.

"Oh, Edward! Isn't it terrible? Civil war in our dear land! So many whom we love on both sides!"

There was a moment of sorrowful silence. Then her

father asked, "What does Enna say?"

"She is very bitter, papa: speaks with great contempt of the North; exults over the fall of Fort Sumter and the seizure of United States property; glories in the war-spirit of Dick and Arthur, and sneers at poor Walter because he is silent and sad, and declines, for the present at least, to take any part in the strife. Grandpa, she says, and his mother, too, are almost ready to turn him out of the house; for they are as hot secessionists as can be found anywhere.

"I have a letter from Walter too, papa. He writes in a very melancholy strain; hints mildly at the treatment he receives at home; says he can't bear the idea of fighting against the old flag, and still less the old friends he has at the North, and wishes he was with us or anywhere out of the country, that he might escape being forced to take part in the quarrel."

"Poor fellow!" sighed Mr. Dinsmore. "Ah, I have a letter here from my father that I have not yet opened."

He took it from the table as he spoke. His face darkened as he read—the frown and stern expression reminding Elsie of some of the scenes in her early days—but he handed the missive to Rose, remarking, in a calm, quiet tone, "My father expects me to be as strong a secessionist as himself."

"But you're for the Union, papa, are you not?" asked Horace. "You'd never fire upon the Stars and Stripes—the dear old flag that protects us here?"

"No, my son. I love the dear South, which has always been my home, better far than any other of the sections; yet I love the whole better than the part."

"So do I!" exclaimed Rose warmly. "And if Pennsylvania, my own native State, should rebel against the general government, I'd say, 'Put her down with a strong hand,' and just so with any State or section, Eastern, Northern, Middle or Western. I've always been taught that my country is the Union, and I think that teaching has been general through the North."

"It is what my mother taught me, and what I have

taught my children," said Mr. Dinsmore; "not to love the South or my native State less, but the Union more. I was very young when I lost my mother, but that, and some other of her teachings, I have never forgotten."

"There is, I believe, a strong love for the old Union throughout the whole South," remarked Mr. Travilla. "There would be no rebellion among the masses there, but for the deception practiced upon them by their leaders and politicians; and it is they who have been whirling the States out of the Union, scarce allowing the people a voice in the matter."

"I don't wonder at the indignation of the North over the insult to the flag," said Elsie, "nor the furor for it that is sweeping over the land."

"I'd like to be there to help fling it to the breeze," cried Horace excitedly, "and to see how gay the streets must be with it flying everywhere. Yes, and I'd like to help fight. Papa, am I not old enough? Mayn't I go?"

"No, foolish boy, you are much too young, and not fourteen. And suppose you were old enough, would you wish to fight your uncles? Kill one of them, perhaps? Uncle Walter, for instance?"

"Oh papa, no, no, no! I wouldn't for the world hurt one hair of dear Uncle Wal's head—no, not if he were the hottest kind of secessionist."

"Kill Uncle Wal! Why Horace, how could you ever think of such a thing?" exclaimed Rosebud. "And mamma and sister Elsie, why are you both crying so?"

All the afternoon the elders of the family remained together, talking over the news. They could scarce think or speak of anything else: very grave and sad all of them, the ladies now and then dropping a tear or two, while each paper was carefully scanned again and again, lest some item on the all-absorbing subject might have been overlooked, and every letter that had any bearing upon it read and re-read till its contents had been fully digested.

May's gave a graphic account of the excitement in Philadelphia, the recruiting and drilling of troops, the making of flags, the constant, universal singing of patriotic songs, etc., then closed with the story of the sorrowful parting with the dear brothers who might never return from the battle-field.

It had been a bright, warm day, but at evening the sea breeze came in cool and fresh; thin clouds were scudding across the sky, hiding the stars and giving but a faint and fitful view of the young moon that hung, a bright crescent, amid their murky folds.

Mr. Dinsmore was pacing slowly to and fro upon an open colonnade overlooking the bay. He walked with bent head and folded arms, as one in painful thought.

A slight girlish figure came gliding towards him from the open doorway. "Papa, dear, dear papa," murmured a voice tremulous with emotion, "you are very sad tonight. Would that your daughter could comfort you!"

He paused in his walk, took her in his arms and folded her close to his heart.

"Thank you, darling. Yes, I am sad, as we all are. Would that I could comfort you, and keep all sorrow from your life. Nay, that is not a right wish, for 'whom the Lord loveth he chasteneth, and scourgeth every son whom He receiveth.' 'As many as I love I rebuke and chasten.'"

"Yes, papa, those words make me more than willing to bear trials. But oh, how dreadful, how dreadful, to know that our countrymen are already engaged in spilling each other's blood!"

"Yes, that is harrowing enough, but that it should be also our near and dear relations! Elsie, I am thinking of my young brothers: they are not Christians, nor is my poor old father. How can they bear the trials just at hand? How unfit they are to meet death, especially in the sudden, awful form in which it is like to meet those who seek the battle-field. Daughter, you must help me pray for them, pleading the promise, 'If two of you shall agree.'"

"I will, papa; and oh, I do feel deeply for them. Poor Walter and poor, poor, grandpa. I think he loves you best of all his sons, papa, but it would be very terrible to him to have the others killed or maimed."

"Yes, it would indeed. Arthur is his mother's idol, and I daresay she now almost regrets that he has so entirely recovered from his lameness as to be fit for the army."

He drew her to a seat. "The babies are in bed, I suppose?"

"Yes, papa, I left my darlings sleeping sweetly. I am trying to train them to regular habits and early hours, as you did me."

"That is right."

"Papa, it is sweet to be a mother! To have my little Elsie in my laps, as I had but a few moments since, and feel the claps of her arms about my neck, or the tiny hands patting and stroking my face, the sweet baby lips showering kisses all over it, while she coos and rejoices over me; 'Mamma, mamma, my mamma! Elsie's dear mamma! Elsie's own sweet, pretty mamma.' Ah, though our hearts ache for the dear land of our birth, we still have many blessings left."

"We have indeed."

Mr. Travilla, Rose, and Horace now joined them, and the last-named besieged his father with questions about the war and its causes, all of which were patiently answered to the best of Mr. Dinsmore's ability, Mr. Travilla now and then being appealed to for further information, or his opinion, while the ladies listened and occasionally put in a remark or a query.

From that day the mails from America were looked for with redoubled anxiety and eagerness, though the war news was always painful, whichever side had gained a victory or suffered defeat.

At first, paper and letters had been received from both North and South, giving them the advantage of hearing the report from each side, but soon the blockade shut off nearly all intercourse with the South, a mail from thence reaching them only occasionally, by means of some Confederate or foreign craft eluding the vigilance of the besieging squadron.

Early in June there came a letter from Miss

Stanhope, addressed to Elsie. Like all received from America now, it dwelt almost exclusively upon matters connected with the fearful struggle just fairly begun between the sections. The old lady's heart seemed full of love for the South, yet she was strongly for the Union, and she said should be so if any other section or State rebelled.

Landsdale was full of excitement, flags flying everywhere. They had one streaming across from the top of the house, and another from a tree in the garden.

Harry had enlisted in response to the first call of troops, and was now away, fighting in Virginia; while she, praying night and day for his safety, was, with most of the ladies of the town, busy as a bee knitting stockings and making shirts for the men in the field, and preparing lint, bandages, and little dainties for the sick and wounded.

CHAPTER TWENTY-SECOND

Calm me, my God, and keep me calm
While these hot breezes blow;
Be like the night-dew's cooling balm
Upon earth's fevered brow.

—H. BONAR

Fear not; I will help thee.

—ISAIAH 13:13

"DEAR OLD AUNTIE! To think how hard at work for her country she is, while I sit idle here, " sighed Elsie, closing the letter after reading it aloud to the assembled family. "Mamma, papa, Edward, is there nothing we can do?"

"We can do just what they are doing," replied Rose with energy. "I wonder I had not thought of it before. Shirts, stockings, lint, bandages, we can prepare them all, and send with them such fruits and delicacies as will carry from this far-off place. What say you, gentlemen?"

"I think you can," was the simultaneous reply; Mr. Travilla adding, "And we can help with the lint, and by running the sewing machines. I'd be glad to add to the comfort of the poor fellows on both sides."

"And money is needed by their aid societies," added Mr. Dinsmore.

"And I can send that!" Elsie exclaimed, joyously.

"Yes, we all can," said her father.

Several busy weeks followed, and a large box was

packed and sent off.

"If that arrives safely we will send another," they said, for news had reached them that such supplies were sorely needed.

"What! At it again, little wife?" queried Mr. Travilla, entering Elsie's boudoir the next morning, to find her delicate fingers busy with knitting-needles and coarse blue yarn.

"Yes, sir," she said, smiling up at him, "it seems a slight relief to my anxiety about my country, to be doing something, if it is only this."

"Ah! Then I'll take lessons, if you, or Aunt Chloe there will teach me," he returned, laughingly drawing up a chair and taking a seat by her side. "Mammy, can you supply another set of needles, and more yarn?"

"Yes, massa," and laying down the stocking she was at work upon, away she went in search of them.

"Papa, see! So pitty!" cried a little voice, and "wee Elsie" was at his knee, with a diamond necklace in her hand.

"Yes," he said, gently taking it from her, "but rather too valuable a plaything for my little pet. How did she get hold of it, dearest?" he asked, turning to his wife.

"Mamma, say Elsie may. Please, papa, let Elsie have it," pleaded the little one with quivering lip and fast-filling eyes.

"I gave her leave to look over the contents of my jewel box. She is a very careful little body, and mammy and I are both on the watch," answered mamma. "It is a great treat to her; and she takes up only one article at a time, examines it till satisfied, then lays it back exactly as she found it. So please, papa, may she go on?"

"Yes, if mamma gave permission it is all right, darling," he said, caressing the child and returning the necklace.

"Tank oo, papa, mamma. Elsie be very tareful mamma's pitty sings," she cried with a gleeful laugh, holding up her rosebud mouth for a kiss, first to one, then the other.

"Let papa see where you put it, precious," he said,

following her as she tripped across the room and seated herself on a cushion in front of the box.

"Dere, papa, dus where Elsie dot it," she said, laying it carefully back in its proper place. "See, so many, many pitty sings in mamma's box."

"Yes," he said, passing his eye thoughtfully from one to another of the brilliant collection of rings, brooches, chains, bracelets, and necklaces sparkling with gems—diamonds, rubies, amethysts, pearls, emeralds, and other precious stones. "Little wife, your jewels alone are worth what to very many would be a handsome fortune."

"Yes, Edward, and it is not really a pity to have so much locked up in them?"

"No, it is a good investment, especially as things are at present."

"I could do very well without them; should never have bought them for myself. They are almost all your gifts and papa's, or his purchases."

Aunt Chloe had returned with the needles and yarn, and now Elsie began giving the lesson in knitting, both she and her pupil making very merry over it.

Rose and Mr. Dinsmore presently joined them, and the latter, not to be outdone by his son-in-law, invited his wife to teach him.

Horace was at his lessons, but Rosebud, or Rosie as she had gradually come to be called, soon followed her parents. She was a bright, merry, little girl of six, very different from what her sister had been at that age; full of fun and frolicsome as a kitten, very fond of her father, liking to climb upon his knee to be petted and caressed, but clinging still more to her sweet, gentle mamma.

Mr. Travilla and she were the best of friends; she was devotedly attached to her sister, and considered it "very nice and funny," that she was aunt to wee Elsie and baby Eddie.

"Oh," she cried, the moment she came into the room, "what is wee Elsie doing? Mamma, may I, too?"

"May you what?" asked Rose.

"Why, what is the child doing? Playing with your jewels, Elsie?" asked Mr. Dinsmore in a tone of surprise, noticing for the first time what was the employment of his little granddaughter.

"Yes, papa; but she is very careful, and I am watching her."

"I should not allow it, if she were my child. No, Rosie, you may not; you are not a careful little girl."

Rosie was beginning to pout, but catching the stern look in her father's eye, quickly gave it up, her face clearing as if by magic.

"Papa," Elsie asked in a low tone, "do you wish me to take away those costly playthings from my little girl?"

"My dear daughter," he said, smiling tenderly upon her, "I have neither the right nor the wish to interfere with you and your children, especially when your husband approves of your management. I only fear you may suffer loss. How easy a valuable ring may slip through the little fingers and roll away into some crevice where it would never be found."

"I'm afraid it is rather hazardous," she acknowledged. "Mammy, sit close to Elsie and keep careful watch, lest she should drop something."

"I begin to think there's truth in the old saw, 'It's hard to teach a dog new tricks,'" remarked Mr. Travilla, with a comically rueful face. "I've a mind to give it up. What do you say, Dinsmore?"

"That you wouldn't make a good soldier, if you are so easily conquered, Travilla."

"Oh, fighting's another thing, but I'll preserve as long as you do, unless I find I'm wearying my teacher."

"Perhaps you would learn faster with a better teacher," said Elsie. "I am sure the fault is not in the scholar, because I know he's bright and talented."

"Ah! Then I shall try harder than ever, to save your reputation. But take a recess now, for here comes my boy, reaching out his arms to papa. bring him here, Dinah. Papa's own boy, he looks beautiful and as bright as the day."

"Mamma thinks he's a very handsome mixture of

papa and grandpa," Elsie said, leaning over to caress the babe, now crowing in his father's arms.

"I'm afraid he inherits too much of grandpa's temper," remarked Mr. Dinsmore, but with a glance of loving pride bestowed upon the beautiful babe.

"I, for one, have no objection, provided he learns to control it as well," said Mr. Travilla. "He will make the finer character."

Little Elsie had grown weary of her play.

"Put box way now, mammy," she said, getting up from her cushion. "Wee Elsie don't want any more. Mamma take; Elsie so tired."

The baby voice sounded weak and languid, and tottering to her mother's side, she almost fell into her lap.

"Oh, my baby! My precious darling, what is it?" cried Elsie, catching her up in her arms. "Papa! Edward! She is dying!"

For the face had suddenly lost all its color; the eyes were rolled upward, the tiny fists tightly clenched, and the little limbs had grown stiff and rigid on the mother's lap.

Mr. Travilla hastily set down the babe, and turned to look at his little girl, his face full of alarm and distress.

Mr. Dinsmore sprang to his daughter's side, and meeting her look of agony, said soothingly, "No, dearest, it is a spasm. She will soon be over it."

"Yes; don't be so terrified, dear child," said Rose, dropping her work and hurrying to Elsie's assistance. "They are not unusual with children; I have seen both May and Daisy have them. Quick, Aunt Chloe! A cloth dipped in spirits of turpentine, to lay over the stomach and bowels, and another to put between her shoulders. It is the best thing we can do till we get a doctor here. But, ah, see! It is already passing away."

That was true: the muscles were beginning to relax, and in another moment the eyes resumed their natural appearance the hands were no longer clenched, and a low plaintive, "Mamma," came from the little lips.

"Mamma is here, darling," Elsie said, amid her fast-dropping tears, covering the little wan face with kisses, as she held it to her bosom.

"Thank God! She is still ours!" exclaimed the father, almost under his breath; then, a little louder, "Elsie, dear wife, I shall go at once for Dr. Channing, an English physician who has been highly recommended to me."

"Do, dear husband, and urge him to come at once," she answered, in a tone full of anxiety.

He left the room, returning with the physician within half an hour, to find the little girl asleep on her mother's breast.

"Ah, I hope she is not going to be very ill," said the doctor, taking gentle hold of her tiny wrist. "She seems easy now, and her papa tells me the spasm was of very short duration."

She woke, apparently free from suffering, allowed her papa to take her, that mamma's weary arms might rest, and in the course of the afternoon even got down from his knee, and played about the room for a little while, but languidly, and was soon quite willing to be nursed again, "papa, grandpa, and Mamma Rose," as she lovingly called her young and fair step-grandmother, taking turns in trying to relieve and amuse her.

She was a most affectionate, unselfish little creature, and though longing to lay again her weary little head on mamma's breast, and feel the enfolding of mamma's dear arms, gave up without a murmur, when told that poor mamma was "tired of holding so big a girl for so long," and quietly contented herself with the attention of the others.

As the early evening hour which was the children's bed-time drew near, Elsie took her little girl again on her lap.

"Mamma, pease talk to Elsie," pleaded the sweet baby voice, while the curly head fell languidly upon her shoulder, and a tiny hand, hot and dry with fever, softly patted her cheek.

"What about, darling?"

"'Bout Jesus, mamma. Do he love little chillens? Do he love wee Elsie?"

The gentle voice that answered was full of tears. "Yes,

darling, mamma and papa, and dear grandpa too, love you more than tongue can tell, but Jesus loves you better still."

"Mamma, may Elsie go dere?"

"Where, my precious one?"

"To Jesus, mamma. Elsie want to go see Jesus."

A sharp pang shot through the young mother's heart, while the hot tears chased each other down her cheeks. One fell on the child's face.

"What! Mamma ky? Mamma don't want Elsie to go see Jesus? Den Elsie will stay wis mamma and papa. Don't ky, Elsie's mamma;" and feebly the little hand tried to wipe away her mother's tears.

With a silent prayer for help to control her emotion, Elsie cleared her voice, and began in low, sweet tones the old, old story of Jesus and his love, his birth, his life, his death.

"Mamma, Elsie do love Jesus!" were the earnest words that followed the close of the narrative. "Say prayer now, and go bed. Elsie feel sick. Mamma, stay wis Elsie?"

"Yes, my precious one, mamma will stay close beside her darling as long as she wants her. You may say your little prayer kneeling in mamma's lap; and then she will sing you to sleep."

"Jesus like Elsie do dat way?"

"Yes, darling, when she's sick."

Mamma's arms encircled and upheld the little form, the chubby hands were meekly folded, and the soft cheek rested against hers, while the few words of prayer faltered on the baby tongue.

Then, the posture changed to a more restful one, the sweet voice, still full of tears, and often trembling with emotion, sang the little one to sleep.

Laying her gently in her crib, Elsie knelt beside it, sending up a petition with strong crying and tears, not that the young life might be spared, unless the will of God were so, but that she might be enabled to say, with all her heart, "Thy will be done."

Ere she had finished, her husband knelt beside her asking the same for her and himself.

They rose up together, and folded to his heart, she wept out her sorrow upon his breast.

"You are a very weary, little wife," he said tenderly, passing his hand caressingly over her hair and pressing his lips again and again to the heated brow.

"It is rest to lay my head here," she whispered.

"But you must not stand," and sitting down he drew her to the sofa, still keeping his arm about her waist. "Bear up, dear wife," he said, "we will hope our precious darling is not very ill."

She told him of the child's words, and the sad foreboding that had entered her own heart.

"While there is life there is hope, dearest," he said, with assumed cheerfulness. "Let us not borrow trouble. Does he not say to us, as to the disciples of old, 'It is I, be not afraid'?"

"Yes; and she is his, only lent to us for a season, and we dare not rebel should he see fit to recall his own," she answered, amid her tears. "Oh, Edward, I am so glad we indulged her this morning in her wish to play with my jewels!"

"Yes; she is the most precious of them all," he said with emotion.

Aunt Chloe, drawing near, respectfully suggested that it might be well to separate the children, in case the little girl's illness should prove to be contagious.

"That is a wise thought, mammy," said Elsie. "Is it not, Edward?"

"Yes, wife. Shall we take our little daughter to our own bedroom, and leave Eddie in possession of the nursery?"

"Yes, I will never leave her while she is ill."

Weeks of anxious solicitude, of tenderest, most careful nursing, followed, for the little one was very ill, and for some time grew worse hour by hour. For days there was little hope that her life would be spared, and a solemn silence reigned through the house; even the romping, fun-loving Horace and Rosie, awe-struck into stillness and often shedding tears—Horace in private, fearing to be considered unmanly, but Rosie openly and without any desire of concealment—at the thought that the darling of the house was about to pass away from earth.

Rose was filled with grief, the father, and grandfather were almost heart-broken. But the mother! That first night she had scarcely closed an eye, but continually her heart was going up in earnest supplications for grace and strength to meet this sore trial with patience, calmness, and submission.

And surely the prayer was heard and answered. Day and night she was with her suffering little one, watching beside its crib, or holding it in her arms, soothing it with tender words of mother love, or singing, in low sweet tones, of Jesus and the happy land.

Plenty of excellent nurses were at hand, more than willing to relieve her of her charge, but she would relinquish it to no one, except when compelled to take a little rest that her strength might not utterly fail her. Even then she refused to leave the room, but lay where the first plaintive cry, "Mamma," would rouse her and bring her instantly to her darling's side.

At times the big tears might be seen coursing down her cheek, as she gazed mournfully upon the baby face so changed from what it was; but voice and manner were quiet and composed.

Her husband was almost constantly at her side, sharing the care, the grief and anxiety, and the nursing, so far as she would let him. Rose, too, and Mr. Dinsmore, were there every hour of the day, and often in the night, scarcely less anxious and grief-stricken than the parents, and Mr. Dinsmore especially, trembling for the life and health of the mother as well as the child.

At length came a day when all knew and felt that wee Elsie was at the very brink of the grave, and the little thread of life might snap asunder at any moment.

She lay on her pillow on her mother's lap, the limbs

shrunken to half their former size, the face, but lately so beautiful with the bloom of health, grown wan and thin, with parched lips and half-closed, dreamy eyes.

Mr. Travilla sat close beside them, with cup and spoon in hand, now and then moistening the dry lips. Chloe, who had stationed herself a little behind her mistress to be within call, was dropping great tears on the soldier's stocking in her hand.

Mr. Dinsmore came softly in and stood by the little group, his features working with emotion. "My darling," he murmured, "my precious daughter, may God comfort and sustain you."

"He does, papa," she answered in low, calm tones, as she raised her head and lifted her mournful eyes to his face. "His consolations are not small in the trying hour."

"You can give her up?" he asked, in a choking voice, looking with anguish upon the wasted features of his almost idolized grandchild.

"Yes, papa—if he sees fit to take her. 'Twere but selfishness to want to keep her here. So safe, so happy will she be in Jesus' arms."

Mr. Travilla's frame shook with emotion, and Mr. Dinsmore was not less agitated, but the mother was still calm and resigned.

No sound had come from these little lips for hours, but now there was a faintly murmured "Mamma!"

"Yes, darling, mamma is here," Elsie answered, softly pressing a kiss on the white brow. "What shall mamma do for her baby?"

"Jesus loves wee Elsie?" and the dreamy eyes unclosed and looked up into the sweet pale face bent so lovingly over her. "Elsie so glad. Mamma sing 'Happy Land.'"

The young mother's heart was like to burst, but with a silent prayer for strength, she controlled herself and sang low and sweetly, and even as she sang a change came over the child, and it fell into a deep, calm, natural sleep that lasted for hours. All the time on the mother's lap, her eyes scarce moving from the dear little face;

her breath almost suspended, lest that life-giving slumber should be broken.

In vain husband and father in turn entreated to be allowed to relieve her.

"No, oh no!" she whispered. "I cannot have her disturbed; it might cost her life."

This was the turning point in the disease, and from that time the little one began to amend. But very weak and frail, she was still in need of weeks of continued tender, careful nursing.

"Mamma's lap" was the place preferred above all others, but patient and unselfish, she yielded without a murmur when invited to the arms of papa, grandpa, Rose, or nurse, and told that "dear mamma was tired and needed rest."

Elsie was indeed much reduced in health and strength; but love, joy, and thankfulness helped her to recuperate rapidly.

CHAPTER TWENTY-THIRD

What fates impose, that men must needs abide,
It boots not to resist both wind and tide.

—SHAKESPEARE'S HENRY VI

FROM THE TIME of Mr. Lincoln's election Walter Dinsmore's home had been made very uncomfortable to him; after the fall of Sumter it was well-nigh unendurable.

Never were two brothers more entirely unlike than he and Arthur—the latter, selfish, proud, haughty, self-willed, passionate, and reckless of consequences to himself or others, the former sweet-tempered, amiable, and affectionate, but lacking in firmness and self-reliance.

Poor fellow! His heart was divided. On the one side were home, parents, friends, and neighbors, native State and section; on the other, pride in the great, powerful Union he had hitherto called his country; love for the old flag as the emblem of its greatness and symbol of Revolutionary glory; and—perhaps more potent than all—the wishes and entreaties of a Northern girl who had won his heart and promised him her hand.

One April morning Walter, who had overslept himself, having been up late the night before, was roused from his slumbers by a loud hurrah coming from the veranda below. He recognized his father's voice, Arthur's, and that of one of the latter's particular friends, a hot secessionist residing in the adjacent city.

There seemed a great tumult in the house, running to and fro, loud laughter, repeated hurrahs and voices—

among which his mother's and Enna's were easily distinguished—talking in high, excited chorus.

"So Fort Sumter has fallen, and war is fairly inaugurated," he sighed to himself, as he rose and began to dress. "It can mean nothing else."

"Glorious news, Wal!" cried Arthur, catching sight of him as he descended the stairs. "Fort Sumter has fallen and Charleston is jubilant. Here, listen while I read the dispatch."

Walter heard it in grave silence, and at the close merely inquired how the news had come so early.

"Johnson brought it; has gone on now to Ashlands with it; says the city's in a perfect furor of delight. But you, it seems, care nothing about it," Arthur concluded with a malignant sneer.

"Not a word of rejoicing over this glorious victory"— cried Enna angrily.

"Of seven thousand over seventy-five?"

"If I were papa, I'd turn you out of the house," she exclaimed still more hotly.

"Walter, I have no patience with you," said his father. "To think that son of mine should turn against his own country!" he added, with a groan.

"No, father, I could never do that," Walter answered with emotion.

"It looks very much like it—the utter indifference with which you receive this glorious news!" cried Mrs. Dinsmore with flashing eyes. "I'm positively ashamed of you."

"No, mother, not with indifference—far from it, for it inaugurates a war that will drench the land with blood."

"Nonsense! The North will never fight. A race of shop-keepers fighting for sentiment, poh! But come to breakfast, there's the bell."

"Better," says Solomon, "is a dinner of herbs where love is, than a stalled ox and hatred therewith." The luxurious breakfast at Roselands was partaken of with very little enjoyment that morning; by Walter especially, who had to bear contempt and ridicule; threats also: he was called a Yankee, coward, poltroon, traitor, and threatened with disinheritance and denouncement unless he would declare himself for the Confederacy and enlist in its army.

The meal was but half over when he rose with flashing eyes, pale face, and quivering lips. "I am neither a traitor nor a coward," he said between his clenched teeth, "as perhaps time may prove to sorrow of a father and mother, sister and brother, who can so use one who ill deserves such treatment at their hands." And turning, he stalked proudly from the room.

Enna was beginning a sneering remark, but her father stopped her.

"Hush! We have been too hard on the lad. He was always slower than Art about making up his mind, and I've no doubt will turn out all right in the end."

Soon after breakfast the father and mother had a private talk on the subject, and agreed to try coaxing and entreaties.

"Wal always had a warm heart," remarked Mr. Dinsmore finally, "and I daresay can be reached more readily through that."

"Yes, he was your favorite always, while you have been very hard upon poor Arthur's youthful follies. But you see now which is the more worthy of the two."

Mr. Dinsmore shook his head. "Not yet, wife. 'Tisn't always the braggart that turns out bravest in time of trial."

"Yes, we shall see," she answered, with a slight toss of her haughty head. "I trust no son of mine will prove himself so cowardly as to run away from his country in her time of need, on whatever pretext."

And having winged this shaft, perceiving with pleasure that her husband winced slightly under it, she sailed from the room, ascending the stairway, and presently paused before the door of Walter's dressing-room. It was slightly ajar, and pushing it gently open she entered without knocking.

He stood leaning against the mantel, his tall erect figure, the perfection of manly grace, his eyes fixed thoughtfully upon the carpet, and his fine, open, expressive countenance full of noble sadness.

There was something of motherly pride in the glance that met his as he looked up at the sound of Mrs. Dinsmore's step. Starting forward, he gallantly handed her to a seat, then stood respectfully waiting for what she had to say.

"Walter, my dear boy," she began; "your father and I think we were all a trifle hard on you this morning."

He colored slightly but made no remark, and she went on. "Of course we can't believe it possible that a son of ours will ever show himself a coward, but it is very trying to us, very mortifying, to have you holding back in this way till all our neighbors and friends begin to hint that you are disloyal to your native State, and look scornful and contemptuous at the very mention of your name."

Walter took a turn or two across the room, and coming back to her side, "Mother," said he, "you know it is my nature to be slow in deciding any matter of importance, and this is the weightiest one that ever I had to consider. Men much older and wiser than I are finding it a knotty question to which their loyalty is due, State or General Government; where allegiance to the one ends, and fealty to the other begins."

"There is no question in my mind," she interrupted, angrily. "Of course your allegiance is due to your State, so don't let me hear any more about that. Your father and brother never hesitated for a moment, and it would become you to be more ready to be guided by them."

"Mother," he said, with a pained look, "you forget that I am no longer a boy, and you would be the first to despise a man who could not form an opinion of his own. All I ask is time to decide this question and—another."

"Pray what may that be? Whether you will break with Miss Aller, I presume," she retorted, sneeringly.

"No mother," he answered with dignity. "There is no question in my regard to that. Mary and I are pledged to each other, and nothing but death can part us."

"And"—fiercely—"you would marry her, though she is ready to cheer on the men who are coming to invade our homes and involve us in the horrors of a servile insurrection!"

"I think it is hardly an hour since I heard you say the North would not fight, and since we have shown our determination in capturing Sumter, the next news would be that we were to be allowed to go in peace. You may be right. I hope you are—but the fellows I know in the North are as full of pluck as ourselves, and I fear there is a long, fierce, bloody struggle before us." He stood before her with folded arms and grave, earnest face, his eyes meeting hers unflinchingly. "And ere I rush into it I want to know that I am ready for death and for judgment."

"No need to hesitate on that account," she said, with a contemptuous smile. "You've always been a remarkably upright young man, and I'm sure are safe enough. Besides, I haven't a doubt that those who die in defense of their country go straight to heaven."

He shook his head. "I have been studying the Bible a good deal of late, and I know that that would never save my soul."

"This is some of Horace's and Elsie's work; I wish they would attend to their own affairs and let you and others alone." And she rose and swept angrily from the room.

Walter did not appear at dinner, nor was he seen again for several days; but as such absences were not infrequent—he having undertaken a sort of general oversight of both the Oaks and Ion—this excited no alarm.

The first day in fact was spent at Ion; the next he rode over to the Oaks. Mrs. Murray always made him very comfortable and was delighted to have the opportunity, for the place was lonely for her in the absence of the family. She was on the veranda as he rode up that morning attended by his servant.

"Ah, Mr. Walter," she cried, "but I'm glad to see you! You're a sight for sair een, sir. I hope ye've come to stay a bit."

He had given the reins to his servant and dismounted. "Yes," he said, shaking hands with her, "for two or three days, Mrs. Murray."

"That's gude news, sir. Will ye come in and take a bite or sup o' something?"

"Thank you, not now. I'll just sit here for a moment. The air is delightful this morning."

`"So it is, sir. And do ye bring only news frae our friends in Naples?"

"No; I have heard nothing since I saw you last."

"But what's this, Mr. Walter, that I hear the servants saying aboot a fight wi' the United States troops?"

"Fort Sumter has fallen, Mrs. Murray. There's an account of the whole affair," he added, taking a newspaper from his pocket and handing it to her.

She received it eagerly, and with a hearty thanks.

"I am going out into the grounds," he said, and walked away, leaving her to its perusal.

He strolled down a green alley, inspected it, the lawns, the avenue, the flower and vegetable gardens, to see that all were in order; held a few minutes' conversation with the head gardener, making some suggestions and bestowing deserved praise of his faithful performance of his duties; then wandering on, at length seated himself in Elsie's bower, and took from his breast-pocket—where he had constantly carried it of late—a small morocco-bound, gilt-edged volume.

He sat there a long time, reading and pondering with grave, anxious face, it may be asking for heavenly guidance too, for his eyes were now and then uplifted and his lips moved.

The next day and the next he spent at the Oaks, passing most of his time in solitude, either in the least frequented parts of the grounds, or the lonely and deserted rooms of the mansion.

Walter had always been a favorite with Mrs. Murray. She had a sort of motherly affection for him, and watching him furtively, felt sure that he had some heavy mental trouble. She waited and watched silently, hoping that he would confide in her and let her sympathize, if she could do nothing more.

On the evening of the third day he came in from the grounds with a brightened countenance, his little book in his hand. She was on the veranda looking out for him to ask if he was ready for his tea. He met her with a smile.

"Is it gude news, Mr. Walter?" she asked, thinking of the distracted state of the country.

"Yes, Mrs. Murray, I think you will call it so. I have been searching here," and he held up the little volume, "for the pearl of great price, and I have found it."

"Dear bairn, I thank God for ye! " she exclaimed with emotion. "It's gude news indeed! "

"I cannot think how I've been so blind," he went on in earnest tones. "It seems so simple and easy—just to believe in Jesus Christ, receive his offered pardon, his righteousness put upon me, the cleansing of his blood shed for the remission of sins, and trust my all to him for time and eternity. Now I am ready to meet death on the battle-field, if so it must be."

"But, O Mr. Walter, I hope you'll be spared that, and live to be a good soldier of Christ these many years."

They were startled by the furious galloping of a horse coming up the drive, and the next moment Arthur drew rein before the door.

"Walter; so you're here, as I thought! I've come for you. Lincoln has called seventy-five thousand troops to defend the capital, but we all know what that means—an invasion of the South. The North's a unit now, and so is the South. Davis has called for volunteers, and the war-cry is resounding all over the land. We're raising a company: I'm appointed captain, and you lieutenant. Come; if you hesitate now—you'll repent it: father says he'll disown you forever."

Arthur's utterance was fierce and rapid, but now he was compelled to pause for a breath, and Walter answered with excitement in his tones also.

"Of course if it has come to that, I will not hesitate to defend my native soil, my home, my parents."

"All right; come on then; we leave tonight."

Walter's horse was ordered at once, and in a few moments the brothers were galloping away side by side.

Mrs. Murray looked after them with a sigh.

"Ah me! The poor laddies! Will they die on the battle-field? Ah, wae's me, but war's an awfu' thing! "

At Roselands all was bustle and excitement, every-one eager, as it seemed, to hasten the departure of the young men.

But when everything was ready and the final adieus must be spoken, the mother embraced them with tears and sobs, and even Enna's voice faltered and her eyes grew moist.

Mounting, they rode rapidly down the avenue, each followed by his own servant—and out at the great gate. Walter wheeled his horse. "One last look at the old home, Art," he said. "We may never see it again."

"Always sentimental, Wal," laughed Arthur, some-what scornfully, "but have your way." And he, too, wheeled about for a last farewell look.

The moon had just risen, and by her silvery light the lordly mansion—with its clustering vines, the gardens, the lawn, the shrubbery, and the grand old trees—was distinctly visible. Never had the place looked more love-ly. The evening breeze brought to their nostrils the deli-cious sent of roses in full bloom, and a nightingale poured forth a song of ravishing sweetness from a thick-et hard by.

Somehow her song seemed to go to Walter's very heart and a sad foreboding oppressed him as they gazed and listened for several moments, then turned their horses' heads and galloped down the road.

CHAPTER TWENTY-FOURTH

Is't death to fall for Freedom's right?
He's dead alone who lacks her light.

—CAMPBELL

WEE ELSIE WAS CONVALESCING rapidly, and the hearts so wrung with anguish at sight of her sufferings and the fear of losing her, relieved from that, were again filled with the intense anxiety for their country, which for a short space had been half forgotten in the severity of the trial apparently so close at hand.

Mails from America came irregularly; now and then letters and papers from Philadelphia, New York, and other parts of the North; very seldom anything from the South.

What was going on in their homes? What were dear relatives and friends doing and enduring? were questions they were often asking of themselves or each other—questions answered by a sigh only, or a shake of the head. The suspense was hard to bear; but who of all Americans, at home or abroad, who loved their native land, were not suffering at this time from anxiety and suspense?

"A vessel came in last night, which I hope has a mail for us," remarked Mr. Dinsmore as they sat down to the breakfast table one morning early in November.

"I have sent Uncle Joe to find out, and bring it, if there."

"Ah, if it should bring the glorious news that this dreadful war is over, and all our dear ones safe! " sighed Rose.

"Ah, no hope of that," returned her husband. "I think all are well-nigh convinced now that it will last for years: the enlistments now, you remember, are for three years or the war."

Uncle Joe's errand was not done very speedily, and on his return he found the family collected in the drawing-room.

"Good luck dis time, massa," he said, addressing Mr. Dinsmore, as he handed him the mail bag. "Lots ob papahs an' lettahs."

Eagerly the others gathered about the head of the household. Rose and Elsie, pale and trembling with excitement and apprehension, Mr. Travilla, grave and quiet, yet inwardly impatient of a moment's delay.

It was just the same with Mr. Dinsmore. In a trice he had unlocked the bag and emptied its contents—magazines, papers, letters—upon a table.

Rose's eye fell upon a letter, deeply edged with black, which bore her name and address in May's handwriting. She snatched it up with a sharp cry, and sank, half-fainting, into a chair.

Her husband and Elsie were instantly at her side. "Dear wife, my love, my darling! This is terrible; but the Lord will sustain you."

"Mamma, dearest mamma; oh that I could comfort you! "

Mr. Travilla brought a glass of water.

"Thank you; I am better now. I can bear it," she murmured faintly, laying her head on her husband's shoulder. "Open—read—tell me."

Elsie, in compliance with the sign from her father, opened the envelope and handed him the letter.

Glancing over it, he read in low, moved tones.

"Rose, Rose, how shall I tell it? Freddie is dead, and Ritchie sorely wounded—both in that dreadful, dreadful battle of Ball's Bluff—both shot while trying to swim the river. Freddie killed instantly by a bullet in his brain, but Ritchie swam to shore, dragging Fred's body with him, then fainted from fatigue, pain, and loss of blood.

"Mamma is heart-broken—indeed we all are—and papa seems to have suddenly grown many years older. Oh, we don't know how to bear it! And yet we are proud of our brave boys. Edward went on at once, when the sad news reached us; brought Ritchie home to be nursed, and—and Freddie's body to be buried. Oh! What a heart-breaking scene it was when they arrived!

"Harold, poor Harold, couldn't come home. They wouldn't give him a furlough even for a day. Edward went, the day after the funeral, and enlisted, and Ritchie will go back as soon as his wounds heal. He says that while our men stood crowded together on the river-bank, below the bluff, where they could neither fight nor retreat, and the enemy were pouring their shot into them from the heights, Fred came to him, and grasping his hand said, `Dear Dick, it's not likely either of us will come out of this alive, but if you do and I don't, tell mother and the rest not to grieve, for I know in whom I have believed.' Remember, dear Rose, this sweet message is for you as well as for us.

"Your loving sister,
 "May Allison."

Rose, who had been climbing about her husband's neck and hiding her face on his shoulder, vainly striving to suppress her sobs during the reading, now burst into a fit of hysterical weeping.

"Oh Freddie, Freddie, my little brother! My darling brother, how can I bear to think I shall never, never see you again in this world! Oh Horace, he was always so bright and sweet, the very sunshine of the house."

"Yes, dearest, but remember his dying message. Think of his perfect happiness now. He is free from all sin and sorrow, done with the weary marchings and fightings, the hunger and thirst, cold and heat and fatigue of war, no longer in danger from shot or bursting shell, or of lying wounded and suffering on the battle-field, or languishing in hospital or prison."

"Yes," she sighed, "I should rather mourn for poor

wounded Ritchie, for Harold and Edward, still exposed to the horrors of war. Oh, when will it end? This dreadful, dreadful war! "

All were weeping, for all had known and loved the bright, frank, noble-hearted, genial young man.

But Rose presently became more composed, and Mr. Travilla proceeded with the distribution of the remaining letters.

"From Adelaide, doubtless, and I presume containing the same sad news," Mr. Dinsmore said, breaking the seal of another black-edged epistle, directed to him.

"Yes, and more," he added, with a groan, as he ran his eye down the page. "Dick Percival was killed in a skirmish last May, and Enna is a widow. Poor fellow, I fear he was ill prepared to go."

Mr. Travilla had taken up a newspaper. "Here is an account of that Ball's Bluff affair, which seems to have been very badly managed on the part of the Federals. Shall I read it aloud? "

"Oh, yes, yes, if you please," sobbed Rose. "Let us know all."

"Badly managed, indeed," was Mr. Dinsmore's comment at the conclusion. "It looks very like the work of treason."

"And my two dear brothers were part of the dreadful sacrifice," moaned Rose.

"But oh, how brave, noble, and unselfish they, and many others, showed themselves in that awful hour!" said Elsie amid her sobs and tears. "Dear mamma, doesn't that comfort you a little?"

"Yes, dear child. Freddie's sweet message still more. Oh, I need not mourn for him! "

CHAPTER TWENTY-FIFTH

Liberty! Freedom! tyranny is dead!
—Run hence, proclaim, cry it about the streets.

—SHAKESPEARE'S JULIUS CAESAR

THE WINTER OF 1861-62 wore wearily away—the Great Republic still convulsed with all the horrors of the civil war—and the opening spring witnessed no abatement of the fearful strife.

During all these months nothing unusual had occurred in the family of our friends at Naples, but one lovely morning in April a sweet floweret blossomed among them, bringing joy and gladness to all hearts.

"Our little violet," Elsie said, smiling up at the happy face of her husband, as he bent over her and the babe. "She has come to us just as her namesakes in America are lifting their pretty heads among the grass."

"Thank you, darling," he answered, softly touching his lips to her cheek. "Yes, we will give her my mother's name, and may she inherit her lovely disposition also."

"I should be so glad, dear mother's was as lovely a character as I ever knew."

"Our responsibilities are growing, love: three precious little ones now to train up for usefulness here and glory hereafter."

"Yes," she said, with grave yet happy face, "and who is sufficient for these things?"

"Our sufficiency is of God!"

"And he has promised wisdom to those who ask it.

What a comfort. I should like to show this pretty one to Walter. Where is he now, poor fellow?"

Ah, though she knew it not, he was then lying cold in death upon the bloody field of Shiloh.

There had been news now and then from their Northern friends and relatives. Richard Allison had recovered from his wound, and was again in the field. Edward was with the army also, Harold, too, and Philip Ross.

Lucy was, like many others who had strong ties in both sections and their armies, well-nigh distracted with grief and fear.

From their relatives in the South the last news received had been that of the death of Dick Percival, nor did any further news reach there until the next November. Then they heard that Enna had been married again to another Confederate officer, about a year after her first husband's death, that Walter had fallen at Shiloh, that Arthur was killed in the battle of Iuka, and that his mother, hearing of it just as she was convalescing from an attack of fever, had a relapse and died a few days after.

Great was the grief of all for Walter. Mr. Dinsmore mourned very much for his father also, left thus almost alone in his declining years. No particulars were given in regard to the deaths of the two young men.

"Oh," cried Elsie, as she wept over Walter's loss, "what would I not give to know that he was ready for death! But surely we may rejoice in the hope that he was, since we have offered so much united prayer for him."

"Yes," returned her father, "for `If two of you shall agree on earth, as touching anything that they shall ask, it shall be done for them of my Father which is in heaven,' and God's promises are all `yea and amen in Christ Jesus.'"

"Papa," said Horace, "how can it be that good Christian men are fighting and killing each other?"

"It is a very strange thing, my son; yet undoubtedly true that there are many true Christians on both sides. They do not see alike, and each is defending what he believes a righteous cause."

"Listen all," said Mrs. Dinsmore, who was reading a letter from Daisy, her youngest sister.

"Richard is ill in the hospital at Washington, and May has gone on to nurse him. Dr. King of Lansdale, Ohio, is there acting as volunteer surgeon, and has Lottie with him. She will be company for our May. Don't worry about Ritchie. May writes that he is getting better fast."

Rose smiled as she read the last sentence.

"What is it mamma?" asked Elsie.

"Nothing much; only I was thinking how greatly Ritchie seemed to admire Miss King at the time of the wedding."

"Well, if he loses his heart I hope he will get another in exchange."

"Why, Sister Elsie, how could Uncle Ritchie lose his heart? Did they shoot a hole so it might drop out?" queried Rosebud in wide-eyed wonder. "I hope the doctors will sew up the place quick 'fore it does fall out," she added, with a look of deep concern. "Poor, dear Uncle Wal is killed," she sobbed, "and Uncle Art too, and I don't want all my uncles to die or to be killed."

"We will ask God to take care of them, dear daughter," said Rose, caressing the little weeper, "and we know that he is able to do it."

One day in the following January—1863—the gentlemen went into the city for a few hours, leaving their wives and children at home. They returned with faces full of excitement.

"What news?" queried both ladies in a breath.

"Lincoln has issued an Emancipation Proclamation freeing all the blacks."

There was a momentary pause, then Rose said, "If it puts an end to this dreadful war, I shall not be sorry."

"Nor I," said Elsie.

"Perhaps you don't reflect that it takes a good deal out of our pockets," remarked her father. "Several hundred thousand from yours."

"Yes, papa, I know, but we will not be very poor. I

alone have enough left to keep us all com.
were only sure it would add to the happiness o.
people, I should rejoice over it. But am sorely t
to know what has, or will become of them. It is n
than two years now, since we have heard a word fro.
Viamede."

"It is very likely we shall find nothing but ruins on all
our plantations—Viamede, the Oaks, Ion, and
Roselands," remarked Mr. Dinsmore, pacing to and fro
with an anxious and disturbed countenance.

"Let us hope for the best," Mr. Travilla responded
cheerfully. "The land will still be there, perhaps the
houses too. The negroes will work for wages, and gradually we may be able to restore our homes to what they
were."

"And if the war stops now, we shall probably find
them still in pretty good condition," said Elsie.

"No," her father said, "the war is not at an end, or
likely to be for a long time to come, but we will wait in
patience and hope, daughter, and not grieve over losses
that perhaps may bring great happiness to others."

"Are we poor now, papa?" asked Horace anxiously.

"No son. Your sister is still very wealthy, and we all
have comfortable incomes."

"It did me good to see Uncle Joe's delight over the
news," Mr. Travilla smilingly remarked to his wife.

"Ah, you told him then?" she returned, with a keen
interest and pleasure.

"Yes, and it threw him into a transport of joy. 'Ki!
Massa,' he said, 'neber tink to heyah sich news as dat!
Neber spects dis chile lib to see freedom come,' then
sobering down, 'but, massa, we's been prayin' for it. We's
been crying to the good Lord like the chillen ob Israel
when dey's in de house ob bondage; tousands an' tousands ob us cry day an' night, an' de Lord heyah, an' now
de answer hab come. Bress de Lord! Bress his holy name
foreber an' eber.'

"'And what will you do with your liberty, Uncle Joe?'
I asked; then he looked half frightened. 'Massa, you

.. t gwine to send us off? We lub you an' Miss Elsie an' de chillen, an' we's gettin' mos' too ole to start out new for ourselves."

"Well, dear, I hope you assured him that he had nothing to fear on that score."

"Certainly. I told him they were free to go or stay as they liked, and as long as they were with, or near us, we would see that they were made comfortable. Then he repeated, with great earnestness, that he loved us all, and could never forget what you had done in restoring him to his wife, and making them both so comfortable and happy."

"Yes, I think they have been happy with us, and probably it was the bitter remembrance of the sufferings of his earlier life that made freedom seem so precious a boon to him."

Going into the nursery half an hour later, Elsie was grieved and surprised to find Chloe sitting by the crib of the sleeping babe, crying and sobbing as if her very heart would break, her head bowed upon her knee, and the sobs half-smothered, lest they should disturb the child.

"Why, mammy dear, what is the matter?" she asked, going to her and laying a hand tenderly on her shoulder.

Chloe slid to her knees, and taking the soft white hand in both of hers, covered it with kisses and tears, while her whole frame shook with her bitter weeping.

"Mammy, dear mammy, what is it?" Elsie asked in real alarm, quite forgetting for the moment the news of the morning, which indeed she could never have expected to cause such distress.

"Dis chile don't want no freedom," sobbed the poor old creature at length, "she lubs to b'long to her darlin' young missis. Uncle Joe he sing an' jump an' praise de Lord, 'cause freedom, come, but your ole mammy don't want no freedom. She can't go for to leave you, Miss Elsie, her bressed darlin' chile dat she been done take care ob ever since she born."

"Mammy dear, you shall never leave me except of your own free will," Elsie answered, in tender soothing tones. "Come, get up, and don't cry any more. Why, it would come as near breaking my heart as yours, if we had to part. What could I or my babies ever do without our old mammy to look after our comfort!"

"Bress your heart, honey, you'se allus good an' kind to your ole mammy," Chloe said, checking her sobs and wiping away her tears, as she slowly rose to her feet. "De Lord bress you an' keep you. Now let your mammy gib you one good hug, like when you little chile."

"And many times since," said Elsie, smiling sweetly into the tear-swollen eyes of her faithful old nurse, and not only submitting to, but returning the embrace.

CHAPTER TWENTY-SIXTH

And faint not, heart of man! though years wane slow!
There have been those that from the deepest caves,
And cells of night and fastnesses below
The stormy dashing of the ocean waves,
Down, farther down than gold lies hid, have nurs'd
A quenchless hope, and watch'd their time and burst
On the bright day like wakeners from the grave.

—MRS. HEMANS

NOON OF THE SULTRY JULY DAY, 1864: the scorching sun looks down upon a pine forest; in its midst a cleared space some thirty acres in extent, surrounded by a log stockade ten feet high, the timbers set three feet deep into the ground; a star fort, with one gun at each corner of the square enclosure; on top of the stockade sentinel boxes placed twenty feet apart, reached by steps from the outside; in each of these a vigilant guard with loaded musket, constantly on the watch for the slightest pretext for shooting down some one or more of the prisoners, of whom there are from twenty-five thousand to thirty thousand.

All along the inner side of the wall, six feet from it, stretches a dead line; and any poor fellow thoughtlessly or accidentally laying a hand upon it, or allowing any part of his body to reach under or over it, will be instantly shot.

A green, slimy, sluggish stream, bringing with it all

the filth of the sewers of Andersonville, a village three miles distant, flows directly across the enclosure from east to west. Formerly, the only water fit to drink came from a spring beyond the eastern wall, which flowing under it, into the enclosure, emptied itself into the other stream, a few feet within the dead line.

It did not suffice to satisfy the thirst of the thousands who must drink or die, and the little corner where its waters could be reached was always crowded, men pressing upon each other till often one or another would be pushed against the dead line, shot by the guard, and the body left lying till the next morning; even if it had fallen into the water beyond the line, polluting the scant supply left for the living. But the cry of these perishing ones had gone up into the ears of the merciful Father of us all, and of late a spring of clear water bubbles up in their midst.

But powder and shot, famine, exposure (for the prisoners have no shelter, except as they burrow in the earth), and malaria from the sluggish, filthy streams, and the marshy ground on either side of it, are doing a fearful work: every morning a wagon drawn by four mules is driven in, and the corpses—scattered here and there to the number of from eighty-five to a hundred—gathered up, tossed into it like sticks of wood, taken away and thrown promiscuously into a hole dug for the purpose, and earth shoveled over them.

There are corpses lying about now; there are men, slowly breathing out their last life, with no dying bed, no pillow save the hard ground, no mother, wife, sister, daughter near, to weep over, or to comfort them as they enter the dark valley.

Others there are, wasted and worn till scarce more than living skeletons, creeping about on hands and feet, lying or sitting in every attitude of despair and suffering; a dull, hopeless misery in their sunken eyes, a pathetic patience fit to touch a heart of stone; while others still have grown frantic with that terrible pain, the hunger gnawing at their very vitals, and go staggering about, wildly raving in their helpless agony.

And on them all the scorching sun beats pitilessly down. Hard, cruel fate! Scorched with the heat, with the cool shelter of the pine forests on every side; perishing with hunger in a land of plenty.

In one corner, but a yard or so within the dead line, a group of officers in the Federal uniform—evidently men of culture and refinement, spite of their hatless and shoeless condition, ragged, soiled raiment, unkempt hair, and unshaven faces—sit on the ground, like their comrades in misfortune, sweltering in the sun.

"When will this end?" sighs one. "I'd sooner die a hundred deaths on the battle-field."

"Ah, who wouldn't?" exclaims another. "To starve, roast, and freeze by turns for one's country, requires more patriotism by far than to march up the cannon's mouth, or charge up hill under a galling fire of musketry."

"True indeed, Jones," returns a fair-haired, blue-eyed young man, with face so gaunt and haggard with famine that his own mother would scarcely have recognized him, and distinguished from the rest by a ball and chain attached to wrist and ankle; " and yet we bear it for her sake and for Freedom's. Who of us regrets that we did not stay at home in inglorious ease, and leave our grand old ship of state to founder and go to pieces amid the rocks of secession?"

"None of us, Allison! No, no! The Union forever!" returned several voices in chorus.

"Hark!"—as the sharp crack of a rifle was heard, and a prisoner who, half crazed with suffering, had, in staggering about, approached too near the fatal line and laid a hand upon it, fell dead—"another patriot soul has gone to its account, and another rebel earned a thirty days' furlough."

The dark eyes of the speaker flashed with indignation.

"Poor fellows, they don't know that it is to preserve their liberties we fight, starve, and die; to save them from the despotism their ambitious and unscrupulous leaders desire to establish over them," remarked Harold

Allison. "How grossly the masses of the Southern people have been deceived by a few hot-headed politicians, bent upon obtaining power for themselves at whatever cost."

"True," returned the other, dryly, "but it's just a little difficult to keep these things in mind under present circumstances. By the way, Allison, have you a sister who married a Mr. Horace Dinsmore?"

"Yes, do you know Rose?" asked Harold, in some surprise.

"I was once a guest at the Oaks for a fortnight or so, at the time of the marriage of Miss Elsie, Mr. Dinsmore's daughter, to a Mr. Travilla."

Harold's face grew a shade paler, but his tones were calm and quiet. "Indeed! And may I ask your name?"

"Harry Duncan, at your service," returned the other, with a bow and smile. "I met your three brothers there, also your sister, Mrs. Carrington and Miss May Allison."

The color deepened slightly on Harry's cheek as he pronounced the last name. The pretty face, graceful form, charming manners, and sprightly conversation of the young lady were still fresh in his memory. Having enjoyed the hospitalities of Andersonville for but a few days, he was in better condition, as to health and clothing, than the rest of the group, who had been there for months.

"Harry Duncan!" exclaimed Harold, offering his hand, which the other took in a cordial grasp and shook heartily. "Yes, I know; I have heard of you and your aunt, Miss Stanhope. I feel as if I'd found a brother."

"Thank you. Suppose we consider ourselves such; a brother is what I've been hankering after ever since I can remember."

"Agreed," said Harold. "Perhaps," he added, with a melancholy smile, "we may find the fiction turned to fact some day, if you and one of my single sisters should happen to take a fancy to each other; that is, if we live to get out of this and to see home again." His tone at the last was very desponding.

"Cheer up," said Duncan, in a low, sympathizing tone. "I think we can find a way to escape; men have done so even from the Bastille—a far more difficult task, I should say."

"What's your idea?"

"To dig our way out, working at night, and covering up the traces of our work by day."

"Yes, it's the only way possible, so far as I can see," said Harold. "I have already escaped twice in that way, but only to be retaken, and this is what I gained," shaking his chain, and pointing to the heavy ball attached. "Yet, if I were rid of this, and possessed of a little more strength, I'd make a third attempt."

"I think I could rid you of that little attachment," returned Duncan; "and the tunnel once ready, help you in the race for liberty."

The others of the group exchanging significant nods and glances.

"I think we may let Duncan into our secret," said Jones. "We're digging a well—have gone down six feet. Three feet below the surface is soapstone, so soft we can cut it with our jack-knives. We mean to work our way out tonight. Will you join us?"

"With all my heart."

"Suppose we are caught in the attempt," said one.

"We can't be in much worse condition than now," observed another; "starving in this pestiferous atmosphere filled with malaria from that swamp, and the effluvia from half-decayed corpses; men dying every day, almost every hour, from famine, disease, or violence."

"No," said Harry, "we may bring upon ourselves what Allison is enduring, or instant death; but I for one would prefer the latter to the slow torture of starvation."

"If we are ready," said Harold, in low, solemn tones. "It is appointed to men once to die, and after that the judgment."

"And what should you say was the needful preparation?" queried another, half mocking. "'Repent ye and believe the gospel.' 'Let the wicked forsake his way and the unrighteous man his thoughts, and let him return unto the Lord and He will have mercy upon him; and to our God, for He will abundantly pardon.' 'Believe on the Lord Jesus Christ and thou shalt be saved.'"

Silence fell on the little group. Duncan's eyes wandered over the field, over the thousands of brave men herded together there like cattle, with none of the comforts, few of the necessaries of life—over the living, the dying, the dead—taking in the whole aggregate of suffering with one sweeping glance. His eyes filled; his whole soul was moved with compassion, while he half forgot that he himself was one of them.

How much were the consolations of God needed here! How few, comparatively, possessed them. But some there were who did, and were trying to impart them to others. Should he stay and share in this good work? Perhaps he ought; he almost thought so for a moment, but he remembered his country's need. He had enlisted for the war; he must return to active service, if he could.

Then his eyes fell upon Harold. Here was a noble life to be saved; a life that would inevitably be lost to friends, relatives, country, by but a few weeks' longer sojourn in this horrible place. Duncan's determination was taken: with the help of God the morning light should find them both free and far on their way towards the Union lines.

"We'll try it, comrades, tonight," he said aloud.

"So we will," they answered with determination.

A man came staggering towards them, gesticulating wildly and swearing horrible oaths.

"He is crazed with hunger, poor fellow," remarked Harold.

Duncan was gazing steadily at the man who had now sunk panting upon the ground, exhausted by his own violence. Evidently he had once possessed more than an ordinary share of physical beauty, but vice and evil passions had set their stamp upon his features, and famine had done its ghastly work: he was but a wreck of his former self.

"Where have I seen that face?" murmured Harry, unconsciously thinking aloud.

"In the rogues' gallery, perhaps. Tom Jackson is his name, or one of his names, for he has several aliases, I'm told." remarked someone standing near.

"Yes, he's the very man!" exclaimed Harry. "I have studied his photograph and recognize him fully, in spite of famine's ravages. The wretch! He deserves all he suffers: and yet I pity him."

"What! The would-be assassin of Viamede?" and Harold started to his feet, the hot blood dyeing his thin cheeks.

"The same. You feel like lynching him on the spot; and no wonder. But refrain; they would bid you, and he is already suffering a worse fate than any you could mete out to him."

"God forgive me!" groaned Harold, dropping down again and hiding his face in his hands, "I believe there was murder in my heart."

"The story? What was it?" asked Jones. "Tell it, Duncan; anything to help us to a moment's forgetfulness."

The others joined in the request, and Duncan gave full particulars of the several attempts Jackson had made upon the lives of Mr. Travilla and Elsie.

Allison never once lifted his face during the recital, but the rest listened with keen interest.

"The fellow richly deserves lynching." was the unanimous verdict, "But, as you say, is already suffering a far worse fate."

"And yet no worse than that of thousands of innocent men," remarked Jones bitterly. "Where's the justice of it?"

"Do you expect even-handed justice here?" inquired another.

"Perhaps he may be no worse in the sight of God, than some of the rest of us," said Harold, in low, grave tones "We do not know what evil influences may have surrounded him from his very birth, or whether, exposed to the same, we would have turned out any better."

"I'm perishing with thirst," said Jones, "and must try pushing through that crowd about the spring."

He wandered off and the group scattered, leaving Harold and Duncan alone together.

The two had a long talk: of home, common friends and acquaintance; of the war, what future movements were likely to be made, and how the contest would end; neither doubting the final triumph of the government.

"And that triumph can't be very far off either," concluded Harry. "I think the struggle will be over before this time next year, and I hope you and I may have a hand in the winding up."

"Perhaps you may," Allison rejoined a little sadly, "but I, I fear, have struck my last blow for my native land."

"You are not strong now, but good nursing may do wonders for you," answered Harry cheerily. "Once within the Union lines, and you will feel like another man."

"Ah, but how to get me there? That's the tug of war," said Harold, but with a smile and in tones more hopeful than his words. "Duncan, you are a Christian?"

"Yes, Allison; Jesus is the Captain of my salvation, in whom I trust, and in whose service I desire to live and die."

"Then are we brothers indeed!" and with the words their right hands joined in a more cordial grasp than before.

The sun was nearing the western horizon when at length Harold was left alone. He bowed his head upon his knees in thought and prayer, remaining thus for many minutes, striving for a spirit of forgiveness and compassion towards the coward wretch who would have slain one dearer to him than life.

At last, as the shadows of evening were gathering over the place, he lifted a pale, patient face; and rising, made his way slowly and with difficulty towards the spot where Jackson lay prostrate on the ground, groaning and crying like a child.

Sitting down beside the miserable creature, he spoke to him in gentle, soothing tones. "You have been here a long time?"

"The longest year that ever I lived! But it won't last much longer;" and he uttered a fearful oath.

"Are you expecting to be exchanged?"

"Exchanged! No. What do those fellows at Washington care about our lives? They'll delay and delay till we're all starved to death, like hundreds and thousands before us;" and again concluded with a volley of oaths and curses, bestowed indiscriminately upon the President and Congress, Jeff Davis, Wirtz, and the guard.

Harold was shocked at his profanity. "Man," said he solemnly, "do you know that you are on the brink of the grave? And must soon appear at the bar of him whose holy name you are taking in vain?"

"Curse you!" he cried, lifting his head for a moment, then dropping it again on the ground. "Take your cant to some other market, I don't believe in a God, or heaven or hell, and the sooner I die the better, for I'll be out of my misery."

"No; that is a fatal delusion, and unless you turn and repent, and believe on the Lord Jesus Christ, death can only plunge you into deeper misery. You have only a little while! Oh, I beseech you, don't cast away your last chance to secure pardon, peace and eternal life!"

"You're 'casting your pearls before swine,'" returned the man, sneeringly. "Not to say that I'm a hog exactly, but I've not a bit more of a soul than if I was. Your name's Allison, isn't it?"

"It is."

"D'ye know anybody named Dinsmore? Or Travilla?"

"Yes; and I know who you are, Jackson, and of your crimes against them. In the sight of God you are a murderer."

"You tell me to repent. I've repented many a time that I didn't take better aim and blow his brains out—yes, and hers too. I hoped I had, till I saw the account in the papers."

Harold's teeth and hands were tightly clenched, in an

almost superhuman effort to keep himself quiet; and the man went on without interruption.

"He'd nearly made a finish of me, but I was smart enough to escape them, bloodhounds and all. I got over the border into Texas; had a pretty good time there for awhile—after I recovered from that awful blood-letting—but when succession began, I slipped off and came North. You think I'm all bad, but I had a kind of love for the old flag, and went right into the army.

"Besides, I thought it might give me a chance to put a bullet through some o' those that had thwarted my plans, and would have had me lynched, if they could."

Harold rose and went away, thinking that verily he had been casting his pearls before swine.

Jackson had, indeed, thrown away his last chance, rejected the last offer of salvation, for ere morning, life had fled. Starved to death and gone into eternity without God and without hope! His bitterest foe could not have desired for him a more terrible fate.

There was no moon that night, and the evening was cloudy, making a favorable condition of affairs for the prisoners contemplating an escape. As soon as the darkness was dense enough to conceal their movements from the guard, the work of the tunneling began.

It was a tedious business, as they had none of the proper tools and only one or two could work at a time at the digging and cutting away of the stone; but they relieved each other frequently at that, while those on the outside carried away in their coats or whatever came to hand, the earth and fragments of stone dislodged, and spread them over the marshy ground near the creek.

Duncan, returning from on of these trips, spoke in an undertone to Harold Allison, who with a rude file made of a broken knife-blade, was patiently endeavoring to free himself from his shackles.

"Jackson is dead. I half stumbled over a corpse in the dark, when a man close by—the same one that told us this afternoon who the fellow was; I recognized the voice—said, 'He's just breathed his last, poor wretch!

Died with a curse on his lips.' 'Who is he?' I asked; and he answered, 'Tom Jackson was one of his names.' "

"Gone!" said Harold. "And with all his sins upon his head."

"Yes; it's awful! Here, let me work that for awhile. You're very tired."

The proffered assistance was thankfully accepted, and another half-hour of vigorous effort set Harold's limbs free. He stretched them out, with a low exclamation of gratitude and relief.

At the same instant a whisper came to their ears.

"The work's done at last. Jones is out. Parsons close at his heels. Cox behind him. Will you go next?"

"Thanks, no; I will be the last," said Duncan, "and take charge of Allison here, who is too weak to travel far alone."

"Then I'm off," returned the voice. "Don't lose a minute in following me."

"Now, Allison," whispered Harry, "summon all your strength and courage, old fellow."

"Duncan, you are a true and noble friend! God reward you. Let me be last."

"No, in with you man! Not an instant to spare;" and with kindly force he half lifted his friend into the well, and guided him to the mouth of the tunnel.

Allison crept through it as fast as his feeble strength would permit, Duncan close behind him.

They emerged in safety, as the others had done before them; at once scattering in different directions.

These two moved on together, for several minutes, plunging deeper and deeper into the woods, but presently paused to take a breath and consider their bearings.

"Oh, the air of liberty is sweet!" exclaimed Duncan, in low, exultant tones. "But we mustn't delay here."

"No; we are far from safe yet," panted Allison, "but—'prayer and provender hinder no man's journey.' Duncan, let us spend one moment in silent prayer for success in reaching the Union lines."

They did so, kneeling on the ground, then rose and pressed forward with confidence. God, whose servants they were and whose help they had asked, would guide them in the right direction.

"What a providence!" exclaimed Duncan, grasping Harold's arm, as they came out upon an opening in the wood. "See!" and he pointed upward "The clouds have been broken away a little, and there shines the North star. We can steer by that."

"Thank God! And, so far, we have been traveling in the right direction."

"Amen! And we must press on with all speed, for daylight will soon be upon us, and with it, in all probability, our escape will be discovered and pursuit begun."

No more breath could be spared for talk, and they pushed on in silence, now scrambling through a thicket of underbrush, tearing their clothes and not seldom lacerating their flesh also; now leaping over a fallen tree, anon climbing a hill, and again fording or swimming a stream.

At length Harold, sinking down upon a log, said, "I am utterly exhausted! Can go no farther. Go on, and leave me to follow as I can after a little rest."

"Not a step without you, Allison," returned Duncan, determinedly. "Rest a bit, and then try it again with the help of my arm. Courage, old fellow, we must have put at least six or eight miles between us and our late quarters. Ah, ha! Yonder are some blackberry bushes, well laden with ripe fruit. Sit or lie still while I gather our breakfast."

Hastily snatching a handful of oak leaves, and forming a rude basket by pinning them together with thorns, he quickly made his way to the bushes, a few yards distant, while Harold stretched himself upon the log and closed his weary eyes.

He thought he had hardly done so when Duncan touched his arm.

"Sorry to wake you, Allison, but time is precious; and, like the beggars, we must eat and run."

The basket was heaped high with large, delicious berries, which greatly refreshed our travelers.

"Now, then, are you equal to another effort?" asked Duncan, as the last one disappeared, and he thrust the leaves into his pocket, adding, "We mustn't leave these to tell tales to our pursuers."

"Yes, I dare not linger here," returned Allison, rising but totteringly.

Duncan threw an arm about him, and again they pressed forward, toiling on for another half-hour; when Allison again gave out, and sinking upon the ground, begged his friend to leave him and secure his own safety.

"Never!" cried Duncan. "Never! There would be more, many more, to mourn your loss than mine. Who would shed a tear for me but Aunt Wealthy? Dear old soul, it would be hard for her, I know; but she'd soon follow me."

"Yes, you are her all; but there's a large family of us, and I could easily be spared."

Duncan shook his head. "Was your brother who fell at Ball's Bluff easily spared? But hark! What was that?" He bent his ear to the ground. "The distant bay of hounds! We must push on!" he cried, starting up in haste.

"Bloodhounds on our track? Horrible!" exclaimed Harold, also starting to his feet, weakness and fatigue forgotten for the moment, in the terror inspired by that thought.

Duncan again gave him the support of his arm, and for the next half-hour they pressed on quite rapidly; yet their pursuers were gaining on them, for the bay of the hounds, though still distant, could now be distinctly heard, and Allison's strength again gave way.

"I—can—go no father, Duncan," he said, pantingly; "let me climb up on a tall oak and conceal myself among the branches, while you hurry on."

"No, no, they would discover you directly, and it would be surrender or die. Ah, see! There's a little log cabin behind those bushes, and who knows but we may find help there. Courage, and hope, my boy," and almost carrying Harold, Duncan hurried to the door of the hut.

Pushing it open, and seeing an old negro inside, "Cato, Caesar—"

"Uncle Scip, sah," grinned the negro.

"Well, no matter for the name. Will you help us? We're Federal soldiers just escaped from Andersonville, and they're after us with bloodhounds. Can you yell us anything that will put the savage brutes off the scent?"

"Sah?"

"Something that will stop the hounds from following us—quick, quick! If you know anything."

The negro sprang up, reached a bottle from a shelf and handing it to Harry, said, "Turpentine, sah; rub um on your feet, gen'lemen, an' de hounds won't follah you no moah. But please, sahs, go a little ways off into the woods fo' you use um, so de rebs not tink dis chile gib um to ye."

Harry clutched the bottle, throwing down a ten-dollar bill (all the money he had about him) at Uncle Scip's feet, and dragging Harold some hundred yards farther into the depths of the wood, seated him on a log, applied the turpentine plentifully to his feet, and then to his own.

All this time the baying of the hounds came nearer and nearer, till it seemed that the next moment would bring them into sight.

"Up!" cried Harry, flinging away the empty bottle. "One more tug for life and liberty, or we are lost!"

Harold did not speak, but hope and fear once more inspiring him with temporary strength, he rose and hurried on by the side of his friend. Coming presently to a cleared space, they almost flew across it, and gained the shelter of the woods beyond. The cry of the hounds was no longer heard.

"They've lost the scent, sure enough," said Duncan, exultingly; "a little farther and I think we may venture to rest awhile, concealing ourselves in some thicket. Indeed 'twill now be safer to hide by day, and continue our journey by night."

They did so, spending that and the next day in hiding, living upon roots and berries, and the next two nights in traveling in the supposed direction of the nearest Union camp, coming upon the pickets about sunrise of the third day. They were of Captain Duncan's own regiment, and he was immediately recognized with a delighted, "Hurrah!"

"Hurrah for the Union and the old flag!" returned Harry, waving a green branch above his head, in lieu of the military cap he had been robbed of by his captors.

CHAPTER TWENTY-SEVENTH

In peace, love tunes the shepherd's reed;
In war, he mounts the warrior's steed;
In halls, in gay attire is seen;
In hamlets, dances on the green;
Love rules the court, the camp, the grove,
And men below and saints above;
For love is heaven, and heaven is love.

—SCOTT

"ESCAPED PRISONERS from Andersonville, eh?" queried the guard gathering about them.

"Yes; and more than half-starved; especially my friend here, Captain Allison of the—"

But the sentence was left unfinished, for at that instant Harold reeled, and would have fallen but for the strong arm of another officer quickly outstretched to save him.

They made a litter and carried him into camp, where restoratives were immediately applied.

He soon recovered from his faintness, but was found to be totally unfit for duty, and sent to the hospital at Washington, where he was placed in a bed adjoining that of his brother Richard, and allowed to share with him in the attentions of Dr. King, Miss Lottie, and his own sister May.

How they all wept over him—reduced almost to a skeleton, so wan, so weak, so aged, in those few short months.

He recognized his brother and sister with a faint smile, a murmured word or two, then sank into a state of semi-stupor, from which he roused only when spoken to, relapsing into it again immediately.

Slowly, very slowly, medical skill and tender, careful nursing told upon his exhausted frame till at length he seemed to awake to new life, began to notice what was going on about him, was able to take part in a cheerful chat now and then, and became eager for the news from home and of the progress of the war.

Months had passed away. In the meantime Richard had returned to camp, and Harry Duncan, wounded in a late battle, now occupied his deserted bed in the hospital.

Harry was suffering, but in excellent spirits.

"Cheer up, Allison," he said; "you and I will never go back to Andersonville, the war won't last much longer, and we may consider the Union saved. Ah! This is a vast improvement upon Andersonville fare," he added gaily, as Lottie and May appeared before them, each bearing a tray with a delicious little lunch upon it. "Miss Lottie, I'm almost tempted to say it pays to be ill or wounded, that one may be tended by fair ladies' hands."

"Ah, that speech should have come from Mr. Allison, for May is fair and her hands are white, while mine are brown," she answered demurely, as she set her tray within his reach, May doing the same for Harold.

"None the less beautiful, Miss King," returned Duncan gallantly. "Many a whiter is not half so shapely or so useful. Now reward me for that pretty compliment by coaxing your father to get me well as fast as possible, that I may have a share in the taking of the Richmond."

"That would be a waste of breath, as he's doing all he can already, but I'll do my part with coddling, write all your letters for you—business, friendship, love—and do anything else desired, if in my power."

"You're very good," he said, with a furtive glance at May, who seemed to see or hear nothing but her brother, who was asking about the last news from home; "very good indeed, Miss King, especially as regards the love letters. I presume it would not be necessary for me even to be at the trouble of dictating them?"

"Oh, no, certainly not!"

"Joking aside, I shall be greatly obliged if you will write to Aunt Wealthy today for me."

"With pleasure; especially as I can tell her your wound is not a dangerous one; and you will not lose a limb. But do tell me. What did you poor fellows get to eat at Andersonville?"

"Well, one week's daily ration consisted of one pint of corn-meal ground up cob and all together, four ounces of mule meat, generally spoiled and emitting anything but an appetizing odor; but then we were not troubled with want of—the best of sauce for our meals."

"Hunger?"

"Yes; we'd plenty of that always. In addition to the corn-meal and meat, we had a half pint of peas full of bugs."

"Oh! You poor creatures! I hope it was a little better the alternate week."

"Just the same, except, in lieu of the corn-meal, we had three square inches of corn bread."

"Is it jest; or earnest?" asked Lottie, appealing to Harold.

"Dead earnest, Miss King; and for medicine we had sumac and white-oak bark."

"No matter what ailed you?"

"Oh, yes; that made no difference."

To Harry's impatience the winter wore slowly away while he was confined within the hospital walls; yet the daily, almost hourly sight of May Allison's sweet face, and the sound of her musical voice, went far to reconcile him to this life of inactivity and "inglorious ease," as he termed it in his moments of restless longing to be again in the field.

By the last of March this ardent desire was granted, and he hurried away in fine spirits, leaving May pale and tearful, but with a ring on her finger that had not been there before.

"Ah," said Lottie, pointing to it with a merry twinkle in her eye, and passing her arm about May's waist as she spoke, "I shall be very generous, and not tease as you did when somebody else treated me exactly so."

"It is good of you," whispered May, laying her wet cheek on her friend's shoulder; "and I'm ever so glad you're to be my sister."

"And won't Aunt Wealthy rejoice over you as over a mine of gold!"

Poor Harold, sitting pale and weak upon the side of his cot, longing to be with his friend, sharing his labors and perils, yet feeling that the springs of life were broken within him, was lifting up a silent prayer for strength to endure to the end.

A familiar step drew near, and Dr. King laid his hand on the young man's shoulder.

"Cheer up, my dear boy," he said, "we are trying to get you leave to go home for thirty days, and the war will be over before the time expires; so that you will not have to come back."

"Home!" and Harold's eye brightened for a moment. "Yes, I should like to die at home, with mother and father, brothers and sisters about me."

"But you are not going to die just yet," returned the doctor, with assumed gaiety; "and home and mother will do wonders for you."

"Dr. King," and the blue eyes looked up calmly and steadily into the physician's face, "please tell me exactly what you think of my case. Is there any hope of recovery?"

"You may improve very much. I think you will when you get home; and though there is little hope of the entire recovery of your former health and strength, you may live for years."

"But it is likely I shall not live another year? Do not be afraid to say so: I should rather welcome the news. Am I not right?"

"Yes; I—I think you are nearing home, my dear boy;

the land where the inhabitant shall not say, 'I am sick.' "

There was genuine feeling in the doctor's tone.

A moment's silence, and Harold said, "Thank you. It is what I have suspected for some time; and it causes me to regret, save for the sake of those who love me and will grieve over my early death."

"But don't forget that there is still a possibility of recuperation. While there's life there's hope."

"True! And I will let them hope on as long as they can."

The doctor passed on to another patient, and Harold was again left to the companionship of his own thoughts. But not for long; they were presently broken in upon by the appearance of May with a very bright face.

"See!" she cried joyously, holding up a package. "Letters from home, and Naples too. Rose writes to mamma, and she has enclosed the letter for our benefit."

"Then let us enjoy it together. Sit here and read it to me; will you? My eyes are rather weak, you know, and I see the ink is pale."

"But mamma's note to you?"

"Can wait its turn. I always like to keep the best till the last."

Harold hardly acknowledged to himself that he was very eager to hear news from Elsie—even more than to read the loving words from his mother's pen.

"Very well, then. There seems to be no secret," said May, glancing over the contents. And seating herself by his side she began.

After speaking of some other matters, Rose went on: "But I have kept my greatest piece till now. Our family is growing; we have another grandson who arrived about two weeks ago, Harold Allison Travilla by name.

"Elsie is doing finely; the sleepy little newcomer is greatly admired and loved by old and young; we make as great a to-do over him as though he were the first instead of the fourth grandchild. My husband and I are growing quite patriarchal.

"Elsie is the loveliest and the best of mothers, perfectly devoted to her children; so patient and so tender, so loving and gentle, and yet so firm. Mr. Travilla and she are of one mind in regard to their training, requiring as prompt and cheerful obedience as Horace always has, yet exceedingly indulgent wherever indulgence can do no harm. One does not often see so well-trained and yet so merry and happy a family of little folks.

"Tell our Harold—my poor dear brother—that we hope his name-child will be an honor to him."

"Are you not pleased?" asked May, pausing to look up at him.

"Yes," he answered, with a quiet, rather melancholy smile. "They are very kind to remember me so. I hope they will soon bring the little fellow to see me. Ah, I knew Elsie would make just such a lovely mother."

"Nothing about the time of their return," observed May, as she finished reading. "But they will hardly linger long after the close of the war."

May had left the room, and Harold lay languid and weak upon his cot. A Confederate officer, occupying the next, addressed him, rousing him out of the reverie into which he had fallen.

"Excuse me, sir, but I could not help hearing some parts of the letter read aloud by the lady—your sister, I believe—"

"Yes. Of course you could not help hearing, and there is no harm done," Harold answered with a friendly tone and smile. "So no need for apologies."

"But there is something else. Did you know anything of a Lieutenant Walter Dinsmore, belonging to our side, who fell in the battle of Shiloh?"

"Yes; knew and loved him!" exclaimed Harold, raising himself on his elbow, and turning a keenly interested, questioning gaze upon the stranger.

"Then it is, it must be the same family," said the latter, half to himself, half to Harold.

"Same as what, sir?"

"That letter I could not help hearing was dated Naples, signed Rose Dinsmore, and talked of Elsie, Mr.

Travilla, and their children. Now Lieutenant Dinsmore told me he had a brother residing temporarily in Naples, and also a niece, a Mrs. Elsie Travilla; and before going into the fight he intrusted to me a small package directed to her, with the request that if he fell, I would have it forwarded to her when an opportunity offered. Will you, sir, take charge of it, and see that it reaches the lady's hands?"

"With pleasure. How glad she will be to get it, for she loved Walter dearly."

"They were near of an age?"

"Yes; the uncle a trifle younger than the niece."

"Dinsmore and I were together almost constantly during the last six months of his life, and became very intimate. My haversack, Smith, if you please," addressing a nurse.

It was brought, opened, and a small package taken from it and given to Harold.

He gazed upon it with sad thoughtfulness for a moment. Then, bestowing it safely in his breast-pocket, "Thank you very much," he said. "I will deliver it with my own hand, if she returns from Europe as soon as we expect."

CHAPTER TWENTY-EIGHTH

She led me first to God;
Her words and prayers were my young spirit's dew.

—JOHN PIERPONT

ELMGROVE, THE COUNTRY-SEAT of the elder Mr. Allison, had never looked lovelier than on a beautiful June morning in the year of 1865.

The place had been greatly improved since Elsie's first sight of it, while it was still Rose's girlhood's home where Mr. Dinsmore and his little daughter were so hospitably entertained for many weeks.

There was now a second dwelling-house on the estate, but a few hundred yards distant from the first, owned by Edward Allison, and occupied by himself, wife, and children, of whom there were several.

Our friends from Naples had arrived the night before. The Dinsmores were domiciled at the paternal mansion, the Travillas with Edward and Adelaide.

The sun was not yet an hour high as Elsie stood at the open window of her dressing-room, looking out over the beautiful grounds to the brook beyond, on whose grassy banks, years ago, she and Harold and Sophie had spent so many happy hours. How vividly those scenes of her childhood rose up before her!

"Dear Harold!" she murmured, with a slight sigh. "How kind he always was to me."

She could not think of him without pain, remembering their last interview and his present suffering. She had not seen him yet, but had learned from others that those months at Andersonville had injured his health so seriously that it was not likely ever to be restored.

"What happy children we were in those days," her thoughts ran on, "and I am even happier now, my treasures have so increased with the rolling years. But they! What bitter trials they are enduring; though not less deserving of prosperity than I, who am but a miserable sinner. But it is whom the Lord loveth he chasteneth."

At that moment the sound of hurrying feet, entering the room, and glad young voices crying, "Good-morning, dear mamma!" broke in upon the current of her thoughts.

"Good-morning, my darlings," she said, turning from the window to embrace them. "All well and bright! Ah, how good our heavenly Father is to us!"

"Yes, mamma, it is like my text," said wee Elsie. "We have each a short one this morning. Mine is, 'God is love.'"

Mamma had sat down and taken Violet on her lap, while Elsie and Eddie stood one on each side.

Three lovelier children fond mother never looked upon. Elsie, now seven years old, was her mother's miniature. Eddie, a bright manly boy of five, had Mr. Dinsmore's dark eyes and hair, firm mouth and chin; but the rest of his features, and the expression of countenance, were those of his own father. Violet resembled both her mother and the grandmother whose name she bore. She was a blonde, with exquisitely fair complexion, large deep blue eyes, heavily fringed with curling lashes several shades darker than the ringlets of pale gold that adorned the pretty head.

"True beautiful words," the mother said, in reply to her little daughter. "'God is love!' Never forget it, my darlings; never forget to thank him for his love and goodness to you; never fear to trust his love and care. Can you tell me, dear, of some of his good gifts to you?"

"Our dear, kind mamma and papa," answered Eddie quickly, leaning affectionately against her, his dark eyes lifted to her face, full of almost passionate affection.

"Mammy too," added Violet.

"And dear, dear grandpa and grandma, and oh, so many more," said Elsie.

Rose was called grandma now, by her own request.

"Yes, dear grandpa and grandma, and so many more," echoed the other two.

"But Jesus the best gift of all, mamma," continued little Elsie.

"Yes, my precious ones," returned the mother, in moved tones, "Jesus the best of all, for he loves you better than even papa and mamma do, and though they should be far away, he is ever near, ready and able to help you. Now, Eddie, what is your verse?"

"A little prayer, mamma, 'Lord help me.'"

"A prayer that I hope will always be in my children's hearts when trouble comes, or they are tempted to any sin. The dear Saviour loves to have you cry to him for help, and he will give it."

"Now Vi's tex', mamma," lisped the little one on her knee. "'Jesus wept.'"

"Why did Jesus weep, little daughter?"

"'Cause he so tired? So sick? Naughty mans so cross to him?"

"No, dear; it was not for any sorrow or trouble of his own that Jesus shed those tears. Can you tell us why it was, Elsie?"

"Yes, mamma. He was sorry for poor Martha and Mary, 'cause their brother Lazarus was dead."

"Yes and for all the dreadful sufferings and sorrows that sin has brought into the world. We are not told that Jesus wept for his own trials and pains, but he wept for others. We must feel for others, and do what we can to make them happy. Now we will kneel down and ask the dear Saviour to help us to do this."

The prayer was very short and simple, so that even Baby Vi could understand every word.

There was a moment's quiet after they had risen from their knees; then the children went to the window to look out upon the grounds, which they had hardly seen last night.

"Mamma!" said Elsie. "I see a brook away over yonder, and there are big trees there, and nice green grass. Mamma, is that where you and Aunt Sophie and Uncle Harold used to play when you were a little girl?"

"Yes, daughter."

"Oh, mamma, please tell us again about the time when you waded in the brook, and thought you'd lost your rings, and dear grandpa was so kind and didn't scold or punish you at all."

"Yes, mamma, do tell it."

"Please mamma, do," joined in the other little voices, and mamma kindly complied.

That story finished, it was, "Now, mamma, please tell another. Please tell about the time when you wanted to go with the school children to pick strawberries, and grandpa said 'No.'"

"Ah, I was rather a naughty little girl that time, and cried because I couldn't have my own way," answered the mother musingly, with a dreamy look in her eyes and a tender smile playing about her lips as she almost seemed to hear again the loved tones of her father's voice, and to feel the clasp of his arm as he drew her to his knee and laid her head against his breast, asking, "Which was my little daughter doubting, this afternoon—papa's wisdom, or his love?"

But her own little Elsie's arm had stolen about her neck, the cherry lips were pressed again and again to her cheek, and the sweet child voice repelled the charge with indignation.

"Mamma, you couldn't help the tears coming when you were so disappointed; and that was all. You didn't say one naughty word. And grandpa says you were the best little girl he ever saw."

"And papa says just the same," added a pleasant, manly voice from the door, as Mr. Travilla came in, closing it after him.

Then the three young voices joined in a glad chorus,

"Papa! Papa! Good-morning, dear papa."

"Good-morning, papa's dear pets," he said, putting his arm round all three at once, as they clustered about him, and returning with interest their affectionate caresses.

"And so you have already been teasing poor mamma for stories?"

"Did we tease and trouble you, mamma?" asked Elsie, a little remorsefully, going back to her mother's side.

"No darling; it always gives me pleasure to gratify my dear children. And, papa, they have been very good."

"I am glad to hear it."

"Mamma and papa, may we go down and play by the brook after breakfast?" asked Elsie.

"And wade in the water like mamma did when she was a little girl?" added Eddie.

"Yes, with Uncle Joe and Aunt Chloe to take care of you, if mamma is willing," answered their father.

Mamma said yes, too, and made the little hearts quite happy.

They returned to the window, and presently sent up a joyous shout. "Grandpa, our dear grandpa, is coming!"

"Shall I go down and bring him up here, mamma?" asked Elsie.

"No, dear, we will go down to grandpa, and not trouble him to come up. Besides, Aunt Adelaide wants to see him as well as we."

"Yes, mamma's plan is the best," said Mr. Travilla, giving Elsie one hand and Eddie the other, while his wife led the way with little Violet.

They found Mr. Dinsmore in the lower hall, with Adelaide weeping almost hysterically in his arms.

"You are the only brother I have left," she sobbed. "Poor, poor dear Walter and Arthur! Oh, that dreadful, dreadful war!"

He caressed and soothed her with tender words. "Dear sister, I will do all I can to make up their loss to you. And our father is left us; your husband spared, too.

And let us not forget that almighty Friend, that Elder Brother on the throne, who will never leave or forsake the feeblest one who trusts in him."

"Oh, yes, I know, I know! He has been very good to me; but I must weep for the dear ones gone—"

"And he will not chide you—he who wept with Martha and Marry over their dead brother."

The children were awed into silence and stillness by the scene; but as Adelaide withdrew herself from her brother's arms, while he and her husband grasped each other by the hand in a cordial greeting, little Elsie drew near her, and taking gently hold of her hand, dropped upon it a kiss and a sympathizing tear.

"Darling!" said Adelaide, stooping to fold the child in her arms; then looking up at her niece, "What a wonderful likeness, Elsie! I can hardly believe it is not yourself, restored to us as you were at her age."

The morning greetings were soon exchanged, and Adelaide led the way to her pleasant sitting-room.

"What is the latest news from home, Adelaide?" asked Mr. Dinsmore, with evident anxiety. "I have not heard a word for months past."

"I had a long letter from Lora yesterday;" she answered, "the first since the close of the war. Her eldest son, Ned, and Enna's second husband, were killed in the battle of Bentonville, last March. Lora's husband has lost an arm, one of his brothers a leg. The others are all killed, and the family utterly ruined."

"The Carringtons—father and sons—have all fallen. Sophie is here, with her orphan children; her mother-in-law, with her own daughter, Lucy Ross. Philip has escaped unhurt. They will all be here next week to attend May's wedding.

"Papa, Louise—you know that she too has lost her husband—and Enna are all at the Oaks, for Roselands is a ruin, Ion not very much better, Lora says."

"And the Oaks has escaped?"

"Yes, almost entirely; not being visible from the road. Papa sends a message to you. He is too heart-broken to write. He knows he is welcome in your house. He is longing to see you, now his only son—" Adelaide's voice faltered, and it was a moment ere she could go on—"but he would have you stay away till September, not risking a return during the hottest season, and, if you wish, he will attend to the plantation, hiring blacks to work it."

"My poor, poor old father!" Mr. Dinsmore exclaimed, with emotion. "Welcome in my house? If I had but a dollar, I would share it with him."

"He shall never want a home, while any of us live!" sprang simultaneously from the lips of Mr. Allison and Mr. Travilla.

Adelaide and Elsie were too much moved to speak, but each gave her husband a look of grateful affection.

"Thank you both," Mr. Dinsmore said. "Adelaide, I shall write my father today. Does Lora say that he is well?"

Mrs. Allison could hardly speak for tears, as she answered, "He is not ill, but sadly aged by grief and care. But you shall read the letter for yourself. Stay to breakfast with us—there's the bell—and I'll give it to you afterwards."

"Thanks, but I fear they may wait breakfast for me at the other house."

"No; I will send them word at once that we have kept you."

There was an effort after cheerfulness as they gathered about the plentiful board, but too many sad thoughts and memories had been called up in the hearts of the elders of the party, and only the children were really gay.

Edward Allison was pale and thin, his health having suffered from the hardships incident to his army life.

Elsie remarked it, in a tone of grief and concern, but he answered with a smile, "I have escaped so much better than many others, that I have more reason for thankfulness than complaint. I am hearty and robust compared to poor Harold."

A look of deep sadness stole over his face as he thus

named his younger brother.

Elsie understood it when, an hour later, the elder Mr. Allison entered the parlor, where she and Adelaide were chatting together, with Harold leaning in his arm.

They both shook hands with her, the old gentleman saying, "My dear, I am rejoiced to have you among us again;" Harold silently, but with a sad, wistful, yearning look out of his large bright eyes, that filled hers with tears.

His father and Adelaide helped him to an easy chair, and as he sank back pantingly upon its cushions, Elsie—completely overcome at sight of feeble, wasted frame, and wan, sunken features—stole quickly from the room.

"Oh, Aunt Adie," she sobbed; "he's dying!"

"Yes," Adelaide answered, with the tears coursing down her own cheeks, "we all know it now—all but father and mother, who will not give up hope. Poor May! Hers will be but a sad wedding. She would have put it off, but he begged her not, saying he wanted to be present and to greet Duncan as his brother—Duncan, to whom he owed so much. But for him, you know, Harold would have perished at Andersonville—where, indeed, he got his death."

"No, I have heard very little about it."

"Then Harold will tell you the story of their escape. Oh, Rose dear," turning quickly, as Mrs. Dinsmore and Mrs. Carrington entered, "how kind! I was coming to see you directly, but it was so good of you not to wait."

Elsie was saying, "Good-morning, mamma," when her eye fell upon the other figures. Could it be Sophie with that thin, pale face and large, sad eyes? Sophie arrayed in widow's weeds. All the pretty golden curls hidden beneath the widow's cap? It was indeed, and the next instant the two were weeping in each other's arms.

"You poor, poor dear girl! God comfort you!" Elsie whispered.

"He does, he has helped me to live for my children, my poor fatherless little ones," Sophie said, amid her choking sobs.

"We must go back to father and Harold," Adelaide said presently. "They are in the parlor, where we left them very unceremoniously."

"And Harold, I know, is longing for a chat with Elsie," Sophie said.

They found the gentlemen patiently awaiting their return. Elsie seated herself near Harold, who, somewhat recovered from his fatigue, was now able to take part in the conversation.

"You were shocked by my changed appearance?" he said, in an undertone, as their eyes met and hers filled again. "Don't mind it, I was never before so happy as now; my peace is like a river—calm, deep, and ever increasing as it nears the ocean of eternity. I'm going home!" And his smile was both bright and sweet.

"Oh, would you not live—for your mother's sake? And to work for your Master?"

"Gladly, if it were his will; but I hear him saying to me, 'Come up hither'; and it is a joyful summons."

"Harold, when—" her voice faltered, but with an effort she completed her sentence—"when did this begin?"

"At Andersonville. I was in perfect health when I entered the army," he answered quickly, divining the fear that prompted the question. "But bad air, foul water, wretched and insufficient food, rapidly and completely undermined my constitution. Yet it is sweet to die for one's country! I do not grudge the price I pay to secure her liberties."

Elsie's eyes sparkled through her tears. "True patriotism still lives!" she said. "Harold, I am proud of you and your brothers. Of dear Walter, too; for his heart was right, however mistaken his head may have been."

"Walter? Oh, yes, and I—"

But the sentence was interrupted by the entrance of his mother and sisters, May and Daisy, Mr. Dinsmore, and his son and daughter. Fresh greetings, of course, had to be exchanged all round, and were scarcely finished when Mr. Travilla came in with his three children.

Elsie called them to her, and presented them to Harold with all a mother's fond pride in her darlings.

"I have taught them to call you Uncle Harold. Do you object?"

"Object? Far from it; I am proud to claim them as my nephew and nieces."

He gazed with tender admiration upon each dear little face. Then, drawing the eldest to him and putting an arm about her, said, "She is just what you must have been at her age, Elsie, a little younger than when you first came to Elmgrove. And she bears your name?"

"Yes; her papa and mine would hear of no other for her."

"I like to have mamma's name," said the child, in a pretty, modest way, looking up into his face. "Grandpa and papa call mamma Elsie, and me wee Elsie and little Elsie, and sometimes daughter. Grandpa calls mamma daughter too, but papa calls her wife. Mamma, has Uncle Harold seen baby?"

"My namesake! Ah, I should like to see him."

"There is mammy on the porch now, with him in her arms," cried the child.

"Go, and tell her to bring him here, daughter," Elsie said; and the little girl hastened to obey.

It was a very fine babe, and Harold looked at it with interest.

"I am proud of my name-child," he said, turning to the mother with a gratified smile. "You and Mr. Travilla were very kind to remember me."

The latter, who had been engaged in the exchange of salutations with the others, hearing his name, now came up and took the hand of the invalid in his. He was much moved by the sad alteration in the young man, who, when last seen by him, was in high health and spirits—the full flush of early manhood's prime.

Taking a seat by his side, he inquired with kindly interest how he was, who was his physician, and if there had been any improvement in the case of late.

"Thank you, no; rather the reverse," Harold said, in

answer to the last inquiry. "I am weaker than when I left the hospital."

"Ah, that is discouraging. Still, we will hope the disease may yet take a favorable turn."

"That is what my parents say," he answered, with a grave, sweet smile; "and though I have little hope, I know that nothing is too hard for the Lord, and am more than willing to leave it in his hands."

"Uncle Harold," said Elsie, coming to the side of his chair and looking up into his face with eyes full of tender sympathy, "I'm so, so sorry for you. I'll ask Jesus to please make you well, or else take you soon to the happy land where you'll never have any more pain."

"Thank you, darling," he said, bending down to kiss the sweet lips. "I know the dear Saviour will listen to your prayer."

"You used to play with mamma when you were a little boy like me; didn't you, Uncle Harold?" queried Eddie, coming up close on the other side.

"Not quite so small, my man," Harold answered, laying his hand gently on the child's head. "Your mamma was about the size of your Aunt Rosie, yonder, and I some three or four years older."

"We've been down to the brook where you played together—you and mamma and Aunt Sophie," said Elsie. "Papa took us, and I think it's a lovely place to play."

"Sophie and I have talked over those dear old times more than once, of late," Harold remarked, turning to Mrs. Travilla. "It does not seem so very long ago, and yet—how many changes! How we are changed! Well, Rosie, what is it?" For she was standing by his chair, waiting with eager face till he should be ready to attend to her.

"Uncle Harold, do you feel able to tell us the story about your being a prisoner, and how you got free, and back to the Union army?" she asked, with persuasive look and tone. "Papa and mamma, and all of us that haven't heard it, would like so much to hear it, if it won't tire you to talk so long."

"It is not a long story, and as my lungs are sound, I do not think it will fatigue me, if you will all come near enough to hear me in my ordinary tone of voice."

They drew around him, protesting against his making the effort, unless fully equal to it, as another time would do quite as well.

"Thank you all," he said; "but I feel able for the task, and shall enjoy gratifying my nieces and nephews, as well as the older people."

He then proceeded with his narrative; all listening with deep interest.

Among other incidents connected with his prison life, he told of his interview with Jackson, and the poor wretch's death that same night.

Elsie shuddered and turned pale, yet breathed a sigh of relief as she laid her hand in that of her husband, and turned a loving, grateful look upon her father, to meet his eyes fixed upon her with an expression of deep thankfulness, mingled with the sadness and awe inspired by the news of the miscreant's terrible end.

Harold spent the day at his brother's, and availed himself an opportunity, which offered that afternoon, to have a little private talk with Elsie, in which he delivered Walter's packet, telling her how it came into his hands.

"Dear, dear Walter," she said, weeping, "I have so wanted to know the particulars of his death, and am so thankful to hear that he was a Christian."

"His friend told me he was instantly killed, so was spared much suffering."

"I am thankful for that. I will open this now; you will like to see the contents."

They were a letter from Walter to her, and two photographs—both excellent and striking likeness; one of her in her bridal robes, the other of himself in his military dress.

The first Elsie threw carelessly aside, as of little worth; the other she held long in her hands; gazing intently upon it, again and again wiping away the fast-falling tears.

"It is his own noble, handsome face," she murmured. "Oh, to think I shall not see it again in this world! How good of him to have it taken for me!" and again she gazed and wept.

Turning to her companion she was startled by the expression of mingled love and anguish in his eyes, which were intently fixed upon the other photograph, he having taken it up as she threw it aside.

"Oh Harold!" she moaned, in low, agitated tones.

He sighed deeply, but his brow cleared, and a look of peace and resignation stole over his face as he turned his eyes on her.

"I think there is no sin in the love I bear you now, Elsie," he said. "I rejoice in your happiness and am willing to see you in the possession of another—more than willing, since I must soon pass away. But it was not always so. My love and grief were hard to conquer, and this—bringing you before me just as you were that night that gave you to another and made my love a sin— brought back for a moment the anguish that wrung my heart at the sight."

"You were there, then?"

"Yes; just for a few moments. I found I must look upon the scene, though it broke my heart. I arrived at the last minute, stood in the shadow of the doorway during the ceremony, saw you look up towards me at its conclusion, then turned and fled from the house, fearful of being recognized and forced to betray my secret which I felt I could not hide.

"But don't weep for me, dear friend, my sorrow and disappointment proved blessings in disguise, for through them I was brought to a saving knowledge of him

" 'whom my soul desires above;
All earthly joy or earthly love.' "

"And oh, Harold, how infinitely more is his love worth than mine!"

But her eye fell upon Walter's letter lying forgotten in her lap. She took it up, glanced over it, then read it more carefully, pausing often to wipe away the blinding tears. As she finished, Mr. Travilla came in.

"Here is a letter from Walter, Edward," she said, in tremulous tones, as she handed it to him.

"Then the report of his death was untrue?" he exclaimed inquiringly, a glad look coming into his face.

"Only too true," she answered, with a fresh burst of tears; and Harold briefly explained.

"Shall I read it aloud, wife?" Mr. Travilla asked.

"If Harold cares to hear. There is no secret."

"I should like it greatly," Harold said. And Mr. Travilla read it to him, while Elsie moved away to the farther side of the room, her heart filled with a strange mixture of emotions, in which grief was uppermost.

The letter was filled chiefly with an account of the writer's religious experience. Since his last visit to the Oaks he had been constantly rejoicing in the love of Christ, and now, expecting, as he did, to fall in the coming battle, death had no terrors for him. And he owed this, he said, in great measure to the influence of his brother Horace and Elsie, especially to the beautiful consistency of her Christian life through all the years he had known her.

Through all her grief and sadness, what joy and thankfulness stirred in her breast at that thought. Very humble and unworthy she felt, but oh, what gladness to learn that her Master had thus honored her as an instrument in his hands.

The door opened softly, and her three little ones came quietly in and gathered about her. They had been taught thoughtfulness for others: Uncle Harold was ill, and they would not disturb him.

Leaning confidingly on her lap, lifting loving, trustful eyes to her face, "Mamma," they said, low and softly, "we have had our supper. Will you come with us now?"

"Yes, dear, presently."

"Mamma," whispered little Elsie, with a wistful, tender gaze into the soft sweet eyes still swimming in tears, "dear mamma, something has made you sorry. What can

I do to comfort you?"

"Love me, darling, and be good. You are mamma's precious little comforter. See dears," and she held the photograph so that all could have a view, "it is dear Uncle Walter in his soldier dress." A big tear rolled down her cheek.

"Mamma," Elsie said quickly, "how good he looks! And he is so happy where Jesus is."

"Yes, daughter, we need shed no tears for him."

"Dear Uncle Walter," "Poor Uncle Walter!" the other two were saying.

"There, papa has finished reading. Go now and bid good-night to him and Uncle Harold," their mother said; and they hastened to obey.

They climbed their father's knees and hung about his neck with the most confiding affection, while he caressed them over and over again, Harold looking on with glistening eyes.

"Now some dood fun, papa: toss Vi up in oo arms," said the little one, expecting the usual game of romps.

"Not tonight, pet; some other time. Another sweet kiss for papa, and now one for Uncle Harold."

"After four years of camp, prison, and hospital life, it is a very pleasant change to be among the children," Harold said, as the door closed upon Elsie and her little flock.

"I feared their noise and perpetual motion might disturb you," Mr. Travilla answered.

"Not at all. Yours are not boisterous, and their pretty ways are very winning."

Aunt Chloe and Dinah were in waiting, and soon had the three small figures robed each in its white night-dress.

Then mamma—seated upon a sofa with little Violet on her lap, the other two, one on each side—was quite at their disposal for the next half hour or so, ready to listen or to talk, her sweet sympathy and tender love encouraging them to open all their young hearts to her, telling her of any little joy or sorrow, trouble, vexation, or perplexity.

"Well, darlings, have you remembered your verses and our little talk about them this morning?" the mother asked. "Elsie may speak first, because she is the eldest."

"Mamma, I have thought of them many times," answered the sweet child voice. "We had a nice, nice walk with papa this morning, and the little birds, the brook, and the trees, and the pretty flowers and the beautiful blue sky all seemed to say to me, 'God is love.' Then mamma, once I was tempted to be naughty, and I said in my heart, 'Lord, help me,' and Jesus heard me."

"What was it, dear?"

"We had a little tea party, mamma, with our cousins, out under the trees, and there was pie and very rich cake—"

"And 'serves," put in Eddie.

"Yes, mamma, and preserves too, and they looked so good, and I wanted some, but I remembered that you and papa don't let us eat those things because they would make us sick. So I said, 'Lord, help me,' and then I felt so glad and happy, thinking how Jesus loves me."

"My darling! He does, indeed," the mother said, with a gentle kiss.

"And Eddie was good, and said, 'No, thank you; mamma and papa don't let us eat 'serves and pie.'"

"Mamma's dear boy," and her hand passed softly over the curly head resting on her shoulder.

"Mamma, I love you. I love you so much," he said, hugging her tight; "and dear papa, too, and Jesus. Mamma, I wanted to be naughty once today when one o' zese cousins took away my own new whip that papa buyed for me; but I remembered I mustn't be selfish and cross, and I said my little prayer jus' in my heart, mamma—and Jesus did help me to be good."

"Yes, my dear son, and he will always help you when you ask him. And now, what has Vi to tell mamma?"

"Vi naughty girl one time, mamma: ky 'cause she didn't want mammy wash face and brush curls. Vi solly now;" and the golden head dropped upon mamma's breast.

"Mamma's dear baby must try and be patient. Mamma is sure she will, and Jesus will help her if she asks him, and forgive her, if she is sorry for being naughty," the mother said, with a tender caress. "Now let us sing, 'Jesus loves me.'"

The child voices blended very sweetly with the mother's as they sang in concert. Then she told them a Bible story, heard each little prayer, saw them laid in their beds, gave each a tender good-night kiss, and left them to their rest.

Passing into her dressing-room, she found her husband there, pacing thoughtfully to and fro. At sight of her a smile irradiated his whole countenance, while his arms opened wide to receive her.

"My dear, dear husband!" she said, laying her head on his shoulder, while he folded her to his heart. "How bravely you bear trials; how patient and cheerful you always are under all circumstances."

"Not more so than my little wife. We have heard much saddening news-today, love, but most of it such as to make us weep for our friends and neighbors rather than for ourselves."

"That is true; our losses are slightly, very slightly, compared with those of multitudes of others, and yet it must sadden your heart to know that your dear old home is in ruins."

"Yes, wife, it does; but I were an ungrateful wretch to murmur and repine, had I lost everything but you and our four treasures in yonder room. But you are all spared to me, and I am by no means penniless yet."

"Very far from it, my own noble husband," she answered, with a look of proud, loving admiration. "For all I have is yours as much as mine."

"Thanks, dearest. I am not too proud to accept your assistance, and we will build up the old home and make it lovelier than ever, for ourselves and for our children. What a pleasant work it will be to make it as nearly as possible an earthly paradise for them."

"Yes," she said, smiling brightly, "the cloud has a silver lining."

"As all our clouds have, dearest."

"Yes; for 'we know that all things work together for good to them that love God!' But oh, Edward, what an awful end was Jackson's. I shudder to think of it! And yet—oh, I fear it is not right—but I cannot help feeling it a relief to know that he is dead. Even in Europe, I could not divest myself of the fear that he might turn up unexpectedly, and attempt the lives of my dear ones."

"It is a relief to me also, and not wrong, I think, to feel it so; for we do not rejoice in his destruction, but would have saved him, if we could. Has not the news of Walter comforted you in some measure?"

"Yes, oh yes; the dear, dear fellow! You have not seen this," she added, taking the photograph from her pocket.

"No; it is a striking likeness, and you will value it highly."

"Indeed I shall. Ah, how strange it will be to go home and not find him there."

CHAPTER TWENTY-NINTH

O war!—what, what art thou?
At once the proof and scourge of man's fallen state.

—HANNAH MORE

RICHARD ALLISON had gone to Lansdale for his bride a fortnight ago. They were now taking their bridal trip and expected to reach Elmgrove a day or two before the wedding of May and Harry Duncan. The latter would bring Aunt Wealthy with him, and leave her for a short visit among her friends.

Sophie's mother and sister-in-law, Mrs. Carrington, and Lucy Ross, came earlier, arriving only two days after our party from Europe.

There was great pleasure, yet mingled with profound sadness, in the meeting of these old and dear friends. Lucy and her mother were in deep mourning, and in Mrs. Carrington's countenance Christian resignation blended with heart-breaking sorrow. Grief and anxiety had done the work of a score of years, silvering her hair and ploughing deep furrows in the face that five years ago was still fresh and fair.

Mr. Travilla had taken wife and children for a morning drive, and on their return, Adelaide, meeting them at the door, said to her niece, "They have come, they are in Mrs. Carrington's dressing-room, and she begs that you will go and meet her there. She always loved you so dearly, and I know is longing for your sympathy."

Elsie, waiting only to lay aside hat and gloves, hastened to grant the request of the gentle lady for whom she cherished almost a daughter's affection.

She found her alone. They met silently, clasping each other in a long, tearful embrace, Mrs. Carrington's sobs for many minutes the only sound that broke the stillness of the room.

"I have lost all," she said at length, as they released each other and sat down side by side upon a sofa. "All: husband, sons, home—"

Sobs choked her utterance, and Lucy coming hastily in at the open door of the adjoining room, dropped on her knees by her mother's side, and taking one thin, pale hand in hers, said tearfully, "Not all, dear mamma; you have me, and Phil, and the children."

"Me too, mother dear, and your Harry's children," added Sophie, who had followed her sister, and now knelt with her.

"Yes, yes, dear daughters, I was wrong: I have lost much, but have many blessings still left, your love not the least; and my grandchildren are scarcely less dear than my own. Lucy, dear, here is Elsie."

"Yes, our own dear, darling, Elsie, scarcely changed at all!" Lucy cried, springing up to greet her friend with a warm embrace.

A long talk followed, Mrs. Carrington and Sophie giving their experiences of the war and its results, to which the others listened with deep interest.

"Thank God it is over at last!" concluded the elder lady. "And oh, may he, in his great goodness and mercy, spare us a repetition of it. Oh, the untold horrors of civil war—strife among brethren who should know nothing but love for each other—none can imagine but those who have passed through them! There was fault on both sides, as there always is when people quarrel. And what has been gained? Immense loss of property, and far more precious lives, an exchange of ease and luxury for a hard struggle with poverty."

"But it is over, dear mother, and the North will help the South to recuperate," said Lucy. "Phil says so, and

I've heard it from others too. Just as soon as the struggle ended, people were saying, 'Now they have given up, the Union is safe, and we're sorry for them and will do all we can to help them, for they are our own people.'"

"Yes, I have been most agreeably surprised at the kind feeling here," her mother answered. "Nobody has had a hard word to say of us, so far as I have been able to learn, and I have seen nothing like exultation over a fallen foe, but on the contrary there seems a desire to lend us a helping hand and set us on our feet again."

"Indeed, mother, I assure you that it is so," said Sophie.

"And all through the war," added Lucy, "there was but little hard feeling towards the people of the South; 'deceived and betrayed by their leaders, they are more to be pitied than blamed,' was the opinion commonly expressed by those who stood by the government."

"And papa says there will be no confiscation of property," Sophie said, "unless it may be merely that of the leaders, and that he will help us to restore Ashlands to what it was. So you will have your own home again, mother."

"How generous! I can never repay the obligation," Mrs. Carrington said, in a choking voice.

"But you need not feel overburdened by it, dear mother. It is for Herbert, you know, his own grandson."

"And mine! Ah, this news fills me with joy and gratitude."

"Yes, I feel papa's kindness very much," Sophie said, "and hope my son will never give him cause to regret it."

Elsie rose. "I hear my baby crying, and I know that he wants his mother. Dear Mrs. Carrington, you are looking very weary; and it is more than an hour yet to dinner-time; will you not lie down and rest?"

"Yes, and afterwards you must show me your children. I want to see them."

"Thank you; I shall do so with much pleasure," the young mother answered smilingly, as she hastened from the room; for Baby Harold's cries were growing importunate.

This was the regular hour for Eddie and Vi to take a nap, and Elsie found them laying quietly in their little bed, while the screaming baby stoutly resisted the united efforts of his elder sister and Aunt Chloe to pacify and amuse him.

"Give him to me, mammy," she said, seating herself by the open window; "it is his mother he wants."

Little Elsie, ever concerned for her mother's happiness, studied the dear face intently for a moment, and seeing the traces of tears, drew near and, putting an arm about her neck, "Mamma," she said tenderly, "dear mamma, what troubles you? May I know about it?"

Mrs. Travilla explained briefly, telling of Mrs. Carrington's trials, and of those of other old friends and neighbors in the South.

"Mamma," said the child, with eyes filled to overflowing, "I am very sorry for them all, and for you. Mamma, it is like Jesus to shed tears for other people's troubles, but, mamma, I think it is too much. There are so many, it makes you sorry all the time, and I can't bear it."

The mother's only answer was a silent caress, and the child went on: "I hope nobody else will come with such sad stories to make you cry. Is there anybody else to do it, mamma?"

"I think not, dear. There are only Aunt Wealthy, who has not lost any near friend lately, and—Why there she is now! The dear old soul!" she broke off joyously, for at that instant a carriage, which she had been watching coming up the drive, drew up before the door, and a young gentleman and a little old lady alighted.

Aunt Chloe took the babe, and Elsie hastened down to meet her aunt, her little daughter following.

To the child's great relief it was an altogether joyous greeting this time. Both Miss Stanhope, and her escort, Harry Duncan, were looking very happy, which caused her to regard them with much satisfaction, and the kisses asked of her were given very readily.

"Were you expecting us today, Mrs. Allison?" Harry

asked, turning to Adelaide.

"Yes; I received your telegram."

"Business hurried us off two days sooner than we expected," said Miss Stanhope. "I would have written, but was so very busy with papers and painterers doing the house all up new; and putting down new curtains, and tacking up new carpets, till, Elsie, the old place would hardly know you."

The old lady's heart was evidently full to overflowing, with happiness at the prospect of seeing May installed as future mistress in the pretty cottage at Lansdale.

Yet there was no lack of sympathy in the sorrows or joys of others. She wept with them all over their losses past and prospective, for she, too, saw that Harold must soon pass away from earth, and while rejoicing with him, when she learned how gladly he would obey the summons, her heart yet bled for those to whom he was so dear.

Richard and his bride arrived in due season. The latter had lost no near relative by the war, and—to wee Elsie's delight—the meeting between "Aunt Lottie and mamma" seemed one of unalloyed pleasure.

Unlike those of her older sisters, May's was a private wedding—none but the family and a few near relatives and connections being present. Though deeply attached to Harry, and trusting him fully, much of sadness was unavoidably mingled with her happiness as she prepared for her bridal. It could not be otherwise, as she thought of Fred in his soldier grave, Harold soon to follow, and Sophie—whose had been the last wedding in the paternal home, and so gay and joyous a one—now in her widow's weeds and well-nigh broken-hearted.

"Mine will not be a gay bridal," May had said, in arranging her plans. "And I will just wear my traveling suit."

But Harold objected. "No, no, May. I want to see you dressed as Rose and Sophie were—in white, with veil and orange blossoms. Why shouldn't your beauty be set off to the best advantage as well as theirs, even though only the eyes of those who love you will look upon it?"

And so it was, for Harold's wishes were sacred now.

They were married in the morning; and after a sumptuous breakfast the bridal attire was exchanged for the traveling suit, and the new-made husband and wife set out upon their wedding trip. It was very sad for poor May to leave, not only childhood's home, parents, and brothers and sisters whose lease of life seemed as likely to be long as her own, but to part from the dying one to whom she was most tenderly attached.

But Harry promised to bring her back, and she was to be immediately summoned, in case of any marked unfavorable change in the invalid.

Then, too, Harold was so serenely happy in the prospect before him, and talked so constantly of it as only going home a little while before the rest, and of how at length all would be reunited in that better land, to spend together an eternity of bliss, that it had robbed death of half its gloom and terror.

It was Harold's earnest desire that all his dear ones should be as gay and happy as though he were in health. He would not willingly cast a shadow over the pathway of any of them, for a day, especially the newly married, whose honeymoon, he said, ought to be a very bright spot for them to look back upon in all after years.

So Lottie felt it right to let her heart swell with gladness in the new love that crowned her life, and the time passed cheerfully and pleasantly to the guests at Elmgrove.

Mrs. Ross and her mother, and Miss Stanhope, remained for a fortnight after the wedding. All were made to feel themselves quite at home in both houses. The two families were much like one, and usually spent their evenings together, in delightful social intercourse—Harold in their midst on his couch, or reclining in an easy chair, an interested listener to the talk and occasionally joining in it.

One evening when they were thus gathered about him, Mrs. Carrington, looking compassionately upon the pale, patient face, remarked, "You suffer a great deal, Captain Allison?"

"Yes, a good deal," he answered cheerfully, "but not more than I can easily endure, remembering that it is 'whom the Lord loveth He chasteneth.'"

"You take a very Christian view of it. But do your sufferings arouse no bitterness of feeling towards the South?"

"Oh, no!" he answered, earnestly, "Why should they? The people of the South were not responsible for what was done at Andersonville; perhaps the Confederate government was so only in measure; and Wirtz was a foreigner. Besides, there was a great deal endured by rebel prisoners in some of our Northern prisons. Father," turning to the elder Mr. Allison, "please tell Mrs. Carrington about your visit to Elmira."

The others had been chatting among themselves, but all paused to listen as Mr. Allison began his narrative.

"We learned that a young relative of my wife was confined there, and ill. I went at once to see what could be done for him, and finding the prison in charge of a gentleman who was under much obligation to me, gained admittance without much difficulty. It was a wretched place, and the prisoners were but poorly fed; which was far more inexcusable here than at the South, where food was scarce in their own army and among the people."

"I know that to have been the case," said Mrs. Carrington. "The farmers were not allowed to make use of their grain for their families, till a certain proportion had been taken for the army; and there were families among us who did not taste meat for a year."

"Yes; the war has been hard for us, but far harder upon them. I found our young friend in a very weak state. I succeeded in getting permission to remove him to more comfortable quarters, and did so, but he lived scarcely two days after."

"How very sad," remarked Elsie, with emotion. "Oh, what a terrible thing is war!"

"Especially civil war," said the elder Mrs. Allison; "strife among brethren; its fruits are bitter, heart-rending."

"And being all one people there was equal bravery, talent, and determination on both sides, which made the struggle a very desperate one," said Harold.

"And the military tic-tacs were the same," added Aunt Wealthy. "And then speaking the same language, and looking so much alike, foes were sometimes mistaken for friends, and versa-vice."

"A brother-in-law of Louise's was confined in Fort Delaware for some months," said Adelaide, addressing her brother, "and wrote to me for some article of clothing he needed badly, adding, 'If you could send me something to eat, it would be most thankfully received.' I sent twice, but neither package ever reached him."

"Too bad! Too bad!" said Mr. Dinsmore. "Yet very likely it was through no fault of the government."

"No; I am satisfied that individuals—selfish, unscrupulous men of whom there were far too many on both sides, were the real culprits, and that the government intended every prisoner should be made as comfortable as circumstances would permit," said Mr. Allison. "But there are men who made large fortunes by swindling the government and robbing our brave soldiers; men unworthy of the name! Who would sell their own souls for gold!"

"You are right, sir!" said Mr. Travilla. "One who could take advantage of the necessities of his own country, to enrich himself by robbing her, is not worthy to be called a man."

"And I esteem an officer who could rob the soldiers very little better," said Daisy. "Again and again canned fruits and other niceties, sent by ladies for the comfort of the sick and wounded men, were appropriated by officers who did not need them, and knew they were not given to them."

"And the conclusion of the whole matter," said Harold, with his placid, patient smile, "is that there were on both sides men who, loving and seeking their own interest above country, personal honor, or anything else, would bring disgrace upon any cause. No, Mrs.

Carrington, I have no bitter feeling towards the South. My heart aches for her people in their bereavements, their losses, and all the difficulties of reconstruction and adapting themselves to the new order of things which is the result of the war."

Elsie had several times expressed to her husband and father a deep anxiety to hear from Viamede, and had written to both Mr. Mason and Spriggs, inquiring about the people and the condition of the estate, yet with but slight hope of reply, as all communication with the place had been cut off for years, and it was more than likely that one or both had been driven, or drifted away from his post during the progress of the war.

She was therefore greatly pleased when, on entering the parlor one morning on her return from a drive, she found Mr. Mason there waiting for an interview.

"You are not direct from Viamede!" she asked, when they had exchanged a cordial greeting.

"No, Mrs. Travilla," he answered. "I stayed as long as I could, but not being willing to go into the army, was finally compelled to leave. That was more than two years ago. But I received a letter from Spriggs only yesterday, written from the estate. He was in the Confederate service; and when the struggle was over, went back to Viamede.

"He says it was not visited by either army, and has suffered only from neglect. The old house-servants are still there—Aunt Phillis, Aunt Sally, and the rest; many of the field hands, too, occupying their old quarters, but looking ragged and forlorn enough.

"They are willing to work for wages, and Spriggs begs of me to find out where you are, and tell you that, if you wish it and will furnish the means, he will hire them, and do the best he can to restore the place and make it profitable to you.

"I saw your name in the list of arrivals by late steamer, and with some little painstaking, at length learned where you were."

"I am very glad to have you come, Mr. Mason, and I

am inclined to think well of Mr. Spriggs' position," Elsie answered. "But I must consult my—Ah, here they are!" as her husband and father entered the room together.

The matter was under discussion for the next half-hour, when it was decided to accept Mr. Spriggs' proposal, for the present at least.

Elsie then said to Mr. Mason that she hoped he was not engaged, as she would be glad to have him return to Viamede and resume his former duties there.

He colored and laughed, as he answered, "I am engaged, Mrs. Travilla, though not in the sense you mean, and shall be glad to comply with your wish, if you do not object to my taking a wife with me."

"Not at all," she answered, smiling. "The Bible says, 'it is not good for man to be alone,' and I hope you will be all the happier and more useful in the Master's service for having a better-half with you. A suite of rooms shall be placed at your service and your wants attended to as formerly."

Mr. Mason returned warm thanks for her kindness, and took his departure, evidently well-pleased with the result of his call.

CHAPTER THIRTIETH

War, war, war!
Misery, murder, and crime;
Crime, murder, and woe.

THE TRAVILLAS ACCOMPANIED Miss Stanhope on her return to Lansdale, and were there to assist at the reception of Harry and his bride. After that, a few weeks were spent by them with Mr. and Mrs. Ross.

They then returned to Elmgrove, where, detained, partly by business matters, partly by Harold's condition and his earnest wish to have them all near him to the last, they lingered until September.

Harold "went home," early in that month, dying as calmly and quietly as "fades a summer cloud away," or "sinks the gale when storms are o'er."

He was buried with military honors, and the friends returned to the house, sorely to miss, indeed, the wasted form, and wan, yet patient, cheerful face, and the loved voice, ever ready with words of consolation and hope; but while weeping over their own present bereavement, rejoicing in his joy and the assurance of a blessed reunion in a better land, when they, too, should be able to say, "I have fought a good fight, I have finished my course. I have kept the faith."

It was a melancholy satisfaction to Rose that she had been with him almost constantly during the last three months of his life; her husband had not hurried her. But now both they, and Mr. Travilla and Elsie, felt that the time had come when they should hasten their return to their own homes.

They set out the next week, not a gay party, but filled with a subdued, quiet cheerfulness. Some of their dear ones, but lately journeying with them towards the Celestial City, had reached the gates and entered in; but they were following after, and would overtake them at length; and, though the way might be at times rough and stony to their weary feet, the path compassed by foes both wily and strong, yet there was with them One mightier than all the hosts of hell, and who had promised never to leave nor forsake. "In all these things they should be more than conquerors, through him that loved them."

After entering Virginia, they saw all along the route the sad ravages of the war, and their hearts sent up earnest petitions that those waste places might speedily be restored, and their dear native land never again be visited with that fearful scourge.

The scenes grew more saddening as they neared their journey's end, and could recognize, in the ruined houses and plantations, the wrecks of the former happy homes of friends and neighbors.

They all went directly to the Oaks, where the Travillas were to find a home until Ion could be made again comfortably habitable. It was late in the afternoon of a cloudy, showery day that they found themselves actually rolling quietly along the broad winding drive that led through the grounds to the noble mansion they had left more than five years before.

Even here there were sad signs of neglect: the grounds had forgotten their former neat and trim appearance, and the house needed paint and some slight repairs. But this was all, and they felt it a cause for thankfulness that things were no worse.

A group of relatives and retainers were gathered in the veranda to greet them: an aged, white-haired man the central figure, around him three ladies in deep mourning, a one-armed gentleman, and a crowd of children of both sexes and all ages, from the babe in arms to the youth of sixteen, while in the rear could be seen Mrs. Murray's portly figure, and strong, sensible Scotch face, beaming with pleasure, relieved by a background of dusky faces, lighted up with joy and expectation.

Mr. Dinsmore alighted first, gave his hand to his wife, and leaving young Horace to attend to Rosebud, hastened to meet his father.

The old man tottered forward and fell upon his neck, weeping bitterly. "My son, my son, my only one now. I have lost all—everything—wife, sons, home; all swept away, nothing left to my old age but you."

"Yes, that's it always," sneered a sharp voice near at hand. "Daughters count for nothing; grandchildren are equally valuable. Sons, houses, and lands are the only possessions worth having!"

"Enna, how can you!" exclaimed Mrs. Howard.

But neither father nor brother seemed to hear, or heed the unkind, unfilial remark. The old man was sobbing on his son's shoulder: he soothing him as tenderly as ever he had soothed wife or daughter.

"My home is yours as long as you choose to make it so, my dear father; and Roselands shall be restored, and your old age crowned with the love and reverence of children and children's children."

Hastily recovering himself, the old gentleman released his son, gave an affectionate greeting to Rose, and catching sight of young Horace, now a handsome youth of nineteen, embraced him, exclaiming, "Ah, yes, here is another son for me! One of whom I may well be proud. Rosie, too, grown to a great girl! Glad to see you, dear." But the first carriage had moved on; the second had come up and discharged its living freight, and Mr. Travilla, with Vi in his arms, Elsie leading her eldest daughter and son, had stepped upon the veranda, followed by Dinah with the babe.

"Dear grandpa," Mrs. Travilla said, in tender, tremulous tones, dropping her children's hands to put her arms about his neck, as he turned from Rosebud to her, "my poor, dear grandpa, we will all try to comfort you, and make your old age bright and happy. See, here are your great-grandchildren ready to rise up and call you blessed."

"God bless you, child!" he said, in quivering tones, embracing her with more affection than ever before. "And this," laying his hand on wee Elsie's head, "is yourself as you were at the same age."

"I'm very sorry for you, dear old grandpa. Mamma has told me all about it," the little girl softly whispered, putting her small arms about his neck as he stooped to give her a kiss.

"Me too," Eddie put in, offering his hand and lips.

"That's right; good boy; good children. How are you, Travilla? You've come back to find ruin and desolation where you left beauty and prosperity," and the aged voice shook with emotion.

Mr. Travilla had a kindly, hearty hand-shake, and gently sympathizing words for him, then presented Vi and Baby Harold.

Meanwhile the greetings were being exchanged by the others. Lora met her brother, and both Rose and Elsie, with the warm affection of earlier days, mingled with grief for the losses and sorrows that had befallen since they parted.

Mr. Howard, too, was cordial in his greeting, but Louise and Enna met them with coldness and disdain, albeit they were pensioners upon Horace's bounty, self-invited guests in his house.

Louise gave the tips of her fingers to each, in sullen silence, while Enna drew back from the offered hands, muttering, "A set of Yankees come to spy out the nakedness of the land. Don't give a hand to them, children."

"As you like," Mr. Dinsmore answered indifferently, stepping past her to speak to Mrs. Murray and the servants. "You know I will do a brother's part by my widowed sisters all the same."

"For shame, Enna!" said Lora. "You are here in Horace's house, and neither he nor the others ever took part against us."

"I don't care, it was nearly as bad to stay away and give no help," muttered the offender, giving Elsie a look of scorn and aversion.

"Be quiet, will, you, Madam Johnson," said her old father. "It would be no more than right if Horace should turn you out of the house. Elsie," seeing tears coursing the cheeks of the latter, "don't distress yourself, child. She's not worth minding."

"That is quite true, little wife," said Mr. Travilla; "and though you have felt for her sorrows, do not let her unkindness wound you."

Elsie wiped away her tears, but only waiting to speak to Mrs. Murray and the servants, retired immediately to the privacy of her own apartments, Mr. Travilla accompanying her with their children and attendants.

Wearied with her journey, and already saddened by the desolations of the country over which they had passed, this cold, and even insulting reception from the aunts—over whose bereavements she had wept in tender sympathy—cut her to the quick.

"Oh, Edward, how can they behave so to papa and mamma in their own house!" she said, sitting down upon a sofa in her boudoir and laying aside her hat, while her eyes again overflowed; "dear papa and mamma, who are always so kind!"

"And you, too, dearest," he said, placing himself by her side and putting an arm about her. "It is shameful conduct, but do not allow it to trouble you."

"I will try not to mind it, but let me cry; I shall get over it the sooner. I never thought to feel so uncomfortable in my father's house. Ah, if Ion were only ready for us!" she sighed.

"I am glad that your home must be with me for the present, daughter, if you can only enjoy it," said her father, who, still ever watchful over her happiness, had followed to soothe and comfort her. "It grieves me that your feelings should be so wounded," he added, seating himself on the other side, and taking her hand in his.

"Thank you, dear papa. It is for you and mamma,

even more than myself, that I feel hurt."

"Then never mind it, dearest. Enna has already cooly told me that she and Louise have settled themselves in the west wing, with their children and servants, where they purpose to maintain a separate establishment, having no desire to associate with any of us—though I, of course, am to supply their table at my own expense, as well as whatever else is needed," he added, with a slight laugh of mingled amusement and vexation.

"Considering it a great privilege to be permitted to do so, I presume," Mr. Travilla remarked, a little sarcastically.

"Of course. For cool impudence Enna certainly exceeds every other person of my acquaintance."

"You must let us share the privilege."

"Thanks; but we will talk of that at another time. I know you and Elsie have dreaded the bad influence of Enna's spoiled children upon yours; and I, too, have feared it for them, and for Rosebud. But there is to be no communication between theirs and ours—Louise's one set, and Enna's two, keeping to their own side of the building grounds, and ours not intruding upon them. Enna had it all arranged, and simply made the announcement to me, probably with little idea of the relief she was affording."

"It is a great relief," said Elsie. "Aunt Lora's are better trained, and will not—"

"They do not remain with us; Pinegrove is still habitable, and they are here only for today to welcome us home."

Elsie's face lightened up with pleasure. "And we shall have our own dear home to ourselves, after all! Ah, how foolish I have been to so borrow trouble."

"I have shared the folly," her father said, smiling. "But let us be wiser for the future. They have already retired to their own quarters, and you will see no more of them for the present. My father remains with us."

Mrs. Howard was deeply mortified by the conduct of her sisters, but tried to excuse them to those whom they were treating with such rudeness and ingratitude.

"Louise and Enna are very bitter," she said, talking with Rose and Elsie in the drawing-room after tea, "but they have suffered much in the loss of their husbands and our brothers, to say nothing of property. Sherman's soldiers were very lawless—some of them, I mean; and they were not all Americans—and inflicted much injury. Enna was very rude and exasperating to the party who visited Roselands, and was roughly handled in consequence—robbed of her watch and all her jewelry and money.

"They treated our poor old father with great indignity also; dragged him down the steps of the veranda, took his watch, rifled his pockets, plundered the house, then set it on fire and burned it to the ground."

Her listeners wept as she went on to describe more minutely the scenes of violence at Roselands, Ashlands, Pinegrove, and other plantations and towns in the vicinity; among them the residences of the pastor and his venerable elder, whose visits were so comforting to Mrs. Travilla in her last sickness.

"They were Union men," Lora said, in conclusion, "spending their time and strength in self-denying efforts for the spiritual good of both whites and blacks, and had suffered much at the hands of the Confederates; yet were stripped of everything by Sherman's troops, threatened with instant death, and finally left to starve, actually being without food for several days."

"Dreadful!" exclaimed Rose. "I could not have believed any of our officers would allow such things. But war is very cruel, and gives opportunity to wicked, cruel men, on both sides to indulge their evil propensities and passions. Thank God, it is over at last; and oh, may he, in his great goodness and mercy, spare us a renewal of it."

"I say amen to that!" responded Mrs. Howard earnestly. "My poor Ned! My brothers! My crippled husband! Oh, I sometimes think my heart will break!"

It was some minutes ere she could speak again, for weeping, and the others wept with her.

But resuming. "We were visited by both armies," she

said, "and one did about as much mischief as the other, and between them there is but little left. They did not burn us out at Pinegrove, but stripped us very bare."

"Aunt Lora, dear Aunt Lora!" Elsie sobbed, embracing her with much tenderness. "We cannot restore the loved ones, but your damages shall be repaired."

"Ah, it will take a lifetime; we have no means left."

"You shall borrow of me without interest. With the exception of the failure of income from Viamede, I have lost nothing by the war but the negroes. My husband's losses are somewhat heavier. But our united income is still very large, so that I believe I can help you all, and I shall delight to do it, even should it involve the sale of most of my jewels."

"Dear child, you are very very kind," Lora said, deeply moved, "and it may be that Edward, proud as he is, will accept some assistance from you."

The next morning Mr. Dinsmore and Rose, Mr. Travilla and Elsie, mounted their horses directly after breakfast, and set out to view for themselves the desolations of Roselands and Ion, preparatory to considering what could be done to restore them to their former beauty.

Roselands lying nearest, received their attention first, but so greatly were the well-remembered landmarks changed, that on arriving, they could scarce believe themselves there.

Not one of the noble old trees, that had bordered the avenue and shaded the lawn, was left standing. Many lay prostrate upon the ground, while others had been used for fuel. Of the house naught remained but a few feet of stone wall, some charred, blackened beams, and a heap of ashes. The gardens were a desert, the lawn was changed to a muddy field by the tramping of many feet, and furrowed with deep ruts where the artillery had passed and repassed. Fences, hedge-rows, shrubbery— all had disappeared; and the fields, once cultivated with great care, were overgrown with weeds and nettles.

"We have lost our way! This cannot be the place!"

cried Rose, as they reined in their horses on the precise spot where Arthur and Walter had taken their farewell look at home.

"Alas, alas, it is no other!" Mr. Travilla replied, in moved tones.

The hearts of Mr. Dinsmore and Elsie were too full for speech, and hot tears were coursing down the cheeks of the latter.

Mr. Dinsmore pressed forward, and the others followed, slowly picking their way through the ruins, grief swelling in their hearts at every step. Determined to know the worst, they made the circuit of the house and of the whole estate.

"Can it ever be restored?" Elsie asked at length, amid her tears.

"The house may be rebuilt in a few months, and fields and gardens cleared of weeds, and made to resume something of the old look," Mr. Dinsmore answered; "but the trees were the growth of years, and this generation will not see their places filled with their like."

They pursued their way to Ion in almost unbroken silence. Here the fields presented the same appearance of neglect; lawn and gardens were a wild, but scarcely a tree had fallen, and though the house had been pillaged, furniture destroyed, windows broken, and floors torn up, a few rooms were still habitable; and here they found several of the house-servants, who hailed their coming with demonstrations of delight.

They had lived on the products of the orchard and grapery, and by cultivating a small patch of ground and keeping a few fowls.

Elsie assumed an air of cheerfulness, for her husband's sake; rejoiced that the trees had been spared, that the family burial-place had escaped desecration, and talked gaily of the pleasure of repairing damages, and making improvements till Ion should not have a rival for beauty the country round.

Her efforts were appreciated, and met full halfway by her loving spouse.

The four, taking possession of the rustic seat on the top of a little knoll, where the huge branches of a giant oak protected them from the sun, took a lengthened survey of the house and grounds, and held a consultation in regard to ways and means.

Returning to the Oaks, the gentlemen went to the library, where old Mr. Dinsmore was sitting alone, and reported to him the result of the morning conference. Roselands was to be rebuilt as fast as men and materials could be procured, Elsie furnishing the means—a very large sum of money, of which he was to have the use, free of interest, for a long term of years, or during his natural life.

Mr. Horace Dinsmore knew his father would never take it as a gift, and indeed, it cost him a hard struggle to bring his pride down to the acceptance of it as offered. But he consented at last, and as the other two retired, begged that Elsie would come to him for a moment.

She came in so quietly that he was not aware of her presence. He sat in the corner of a sofa, his white head bowed upon his knees, and his aged frame shaking with sobs.

Kneeling at his side, she put her arms about him, whispering, "Grandpa, my poor, dear grandpa, be comforted, for we all love and honor you."

"Child! Child! I have not deserved this at your hands," he sobbed. "I turned from you when you came to my house, a little, desolate motherless one, claiming my affection."

"But that was many years ago, dear grandpa, and we will 'let the dead past bury it dead.' You will not deny me the great pleasure of helping to repair the desolations of war in the dear home of my childhood? You will take it as help sent by him whose steward I am?"

He clasped her close, and his kisses and tears were warm upon her cheek, as he murmured, in low, broken tones, "God bless you, child! I can refuse you nothing. You shall do as you will."

At last, Elsie had won her way to her stern grandfather's heart; and henceforth she was dear to him as ever one of his children had been.

It is a sweet October morning in the year 1867. Ion, restored to more than its pristine loveliness, lies basking in the beams of the newly risen sun; a tender mist, gray in the distance, rose-colored and golden where the rays of light strike it more directly, enveloping the landscape; the trees decked in holiday attire—green, russet, orange, and scarlet.

The children are romping with each other and their nurses, in the avenue, with the exception of wee Elsie, now a fair, gentle girl of nine, who occupies a rustic seat a little apart from the rest. She has a Bible in her hand, and the sweet young face is bent earnestly, lovingly, over the holy book.

On the veranda stands the mother, watching her darlings with eyes that grow misty with glad tears, while her heart sends up its joyous thanksgiving to him who had been the Guide of her youth and the stay and staff of maturer years.

A step approaches, and her husband's arm encircles her waist, while, as she turns her head, his kindly gray eyes gaze into the depths of her soft hazel ones, with a love stronger than life—or than death.

"Do you know, little wife, what day this is?"

She answered with a bright, glad smile; then her head dropped upon his shoulder.

"Yes, my husband. Ten years ago today I committed my happiness to your keeping, and never for one moment have I regretted the step."

"Bless you, darling, for the word! How great are the mercies of God to me! Yonder is our first-born. I see you as you were when first I met and coveted you; and here you stand by my side, the true wife who has been for ten years the joy and light of my heart and home. Wife, I love you better today than ever before, and if it be the will of God, may we yet have five times ten years to live together in love and harmony."

"We shall!" she answered earnestly. "Eternity is ours, and death itself can part us but for a little while."

The End